SPI
EGE
L&G
RAU

EXILES

EXILES

A NOVEL

Cary Groner

SPIEGEL & GRAU

NEW YORK

2011

Exiles is a work of fiction. Names, characters, places, and incidents are the products of the author's imagination or are used fictitiously. Any resemblance to actual events, locales, or persons, living or dead, is entirely coincidental.

Published in the United States by Spiegel & Grau, an imprint of The Random House Publishing Group, a division of Random House, Inc., New York.

SPIEGEL & GRAU and Design is a registered trademark of Random House, Inc.

Grateful acknowledgment is made to Alfred Music Publishing Co., Inc., for permission to reprint an excerpt from "Cherokee Louise," words and music by Joni Mitchell, copyright © 1991 by Crazy Crow Music. All rights administered by Sony/ATV Music Publishing, 8 Music Square West, Nashville, TN 37203. All rights reserved. Used by permission of Alfred Music Publishing Co., Inc.

Library of Congress Cataloging-in-Publication Data
Groner, Cary.
Exiles: a novel / Cary Groner.
p. cm.
ISBN 978-1-4000-6978-1
eBook ISBN 978-0-679-60491-4
I. Title.
PS3607.R637E95 2011
813'.6—dc22 2010040769

Printed in the United States of America on acid-free paper

www.spiegelandgrau.com

246897531

First Edition

Book design by Caroline Cunningham

If you don't know where you are, any road will do.

—TIBETAN PROVERB

EXILES

ONE

April 2006

He sat against the earthen wall, hungry and exhausted, with his knees pulled up in front of him, as if they could somehow shield him from what was coming. The wall was cool and damp behind him. It made him ache, the cold seeping into his bones the way water freezes inside rocks and cracks them apart.

Night sounds: wind in pines, the peep and rasping of insects, subdued human voices, fires popping. From higher up the mountain came the clack and heavy rumble of a rockfall; the dirt floor quivered with its subtle seismic waves. He was alert, by now, to any sound that might promise deliverance, but the slide had probably just been set off by gravity or by one of the myriad little temblors that rattled the mountains.

He drifted in and out of sleep. Dream images seemed to appear on the hut's dark walls. He was back in California, walking with his daughter in sunlight. They passed under a tree, and leaf shadows danced across her face. She smiled at him and asked a question, but she spoke in a language he didn't understand. He tried to make out her words. She grew frustrated then, and finally strode on without him. When he tried to follow, he found that he had taken root there. He watched her walk away for what seemed hours, until she was lost, a speck on a smudged horizon.

"Peter," said a voice. He shuddered. "Try to stay awake." It was Devi. "We don't have much time."

He dreaded sleep, and he desired it more than anything. "Right," he whispered. Even more than sleep, he wanted water.

As the dream receded, he saw reflected firelight playing on the wall, and he could just make out Devi's silhouette and shadowed face. Alex, his daughter, lay curled on her side, asleep, her head in Devi's lap. Her skin was covered with grime. He and Devi had decided to wait, to awaken her as close to the end as possible.

Devi's eyes gleamed in the darkness. She sat cross-legged, her right hand on Alex's shoulder, her left on her own knee. She was strong, formidable even in stillness, her face serene. She was only a year older than Alex, but the troubles of her life had tempered her to a degree that was becoming fully evident only now, when others would have broken and she did not.

Ten or twelve people crouched or lay in the hut, people who had presumably been here far longer. There was quiet moaning, though it was impossible to tell if it came from those who slept or those who were awake, whether it was due to hunger, or cold, or thirst, or dysentery, or indeed some combination of all these, to the general deprivation and depravity of the place.

Teenagers with rifles loitered outside, smoking and laughing. The hut reeked from unwashed bodies and from the plastic five-gallon bucket in the corner that served as a latrine. During the day, a cloud of flies hovered over it, and there was, of course, no toilet paper. Everyone's clothes stank of shit. Peter had averted his eyes, a couple of hours earlier, as Alex squatted miserably over the bucket, her pants around her ankles, emptied by diarrhea until her bones seemed to grow through her gleaming, sweaty skin.

She finally crawled back—but to Devi, not to him. She would be eighteen in three weeks. Would have been eighteen, that is, if things had not gone so quickly and catastrophically wrong. Civilization's comforts had turned out to be a thin crust of ice over deep, cold waters, and it had taken only a couple of days to reduce the three of them from their comfortable life in Kathmandu to this.

Soon they would have to clump together to hold off the cold. The camp sat in a valley at twelve thousand feet, choked with rhododendrons and mist. Someone lit a kerosene lantern outside, and its yellow glare pressed into the hut, filtered into tiny specks by the tattered burlap hanging in the doorway. An avalanche of cool air gathered at the head of the valley and began to roll down, stirring the trees. Peter heard it for fifteen or twenty seconds before it finally blew into camp, flapping canvas and filling the air with dust. The lantern swayed, splashing light around drunkenly. Somewhere a piece of corrugated tin made a woofing noise and a dog barked back. The door curtain billowed in, and outside stood a short, skinny kid with a Kalashnikov half as tall as he was. He glanced in at them, looking indignant that he had to be there at all, barefoot in the night. His eyes had the contemptuous glare of most of these soldiers, kids who had been forced from their families by hunger and fear, who couldn't afford the softnesses of childhood.

After a few minutes the wind died as fast as it had started. Outside, a boom box came on, playing American heavy metal.

Peter cursed himself, remembering his conversation with the commandant. He'd been outflanked without even realizing it. Now he was trembling as much from fear as from cold. He wished he could believe in something comforting, but he was long past trying to convince himself. Anyway, when they came for them, what difference would it make? So what if you wept, begging, as he half expected to do? A couple of minutes later it would all be the same.

Someone shouted outside. Peter pulled himself further into wakefulness and looked around. Devi hadn't moved. Alex breathed softly. He'd missed a leech inside his boot, he was sure of it now, but he was too exhausted to go rooting after it. Scratching at the bites just made them bleed, anyway.

In one way, the feeling of relinquishment was a relief, as if he'd been pulling an oxcart his whole life and had just walked over a cliff into free fall. He didn't know how to reconcile this feeling with all the others—with the dread, with the regret and guilt about his daughter and Devi. His mind seemed to be fracturing into prisms, like a piece of quartz struck with a hammer. Each piece refracted the world differently, and cohesion had become impossible. Was this really new, or had he just failed to realize it until desperation and despair made it plain? There was argument inside his head, even a kind of war, as if the violence outside had finally kicked down the doors and stormed in, knocking everything askew.

He'd hold out hope until the very end, he couldn't help it. And even though he probably wouldn't pray, he wasn't above a little bargaining. If you took man to be made in God's image, this made more sense, anyway. Mercy was in short supply, but commerce was common as dirt and understood by everyone.

He formed the offer in his mind and sent it out: Kill me, then. I'm all I have to trade. But let Alex live; she's worked hard, and she's young, and she deserves to see something come of it.

As if this thought had somehow penetrated her sleeping mind, Alex stirred and murmured. "Dad?" she said.

"Here." His voice a dry rag in the wind, caught on some nail.

She crawled toward him. He met her halfway and helped her to his little section of wall. She draped herself across his lap, facing out, toward the doorway, and he stroked her hair. He'd always done this when she was a child.

She whispered, her throat parched, "Will anyone find out what happened to us?"

He knew what she meant by this; she meant her mother. He doubted anybody would ever know. He wasn't sure Cheryl would care, anyway, at least about him, but there was no reason to point this out. "It might be better if she didn't."

Alex lifted a hand, then touched her fingertips to the packed earth, as if testing its solidity. "I guess so."

She adjusted her position. Her ribs pressed on Peter's thigh, and his foot was going to sleep. He wanted her to be comfortable, so he held still; he wouldn't be needing the foot, anyway, once the sun rose.

Beneath the odors of sweat and shit, Alex smelled the way she always had. The scent was like a small, shy creature, something he'd loved since she was a baby, and that hadn't changed as she grew. She had been a beautiful child and then, as a young woman, slender and smart and athletic, her hair the color of wheat and her blue-green eyes as melancholy as a late-autumn sky. The ordeal of the past day—the long march at altitude with almost no food, the bad water, and now the diarrhea—had utterly drained her strength, though, and her mind was blurring toward a forgetting that might have been more frightening had it not also been merciful.

"I want to sleep some more," she mumbled. "I hope they won't take us too early."

He stroked her hair. What world was she inhabiting? Was she delirious? She was hot with fever. In any case, it would be cruel to remind her. "Sleep as long as you like," he said. Her breathing evened out and slowed.

She curled tighter around him as the night grew chilly. A little while later he could see that Devi was still sitting up. "Are you cold?" he asked. "Do you want to come over?"

"I'm all right," she replied. "Thanks."

He felt relieved at the final word. He didn't want her to die hating him. Another thing that didn't matter, of course, but in some way it did.

"I'm sorry," he said again, quietly.

Devi exhaled. "You did your best. You just misjudged."

He lay back against the wall, shivering. What could you do with six hours? Nothing but wait.

Off in the distance someone rang a bell, and from all around the village dogs began to howl.

TWO

September 2005

The plane turned into its final approach to Tribhuvan Airport, cutting down through a cottony sheet of cloud, as the sun dropped toward the western ridges. A moment of vertigo: the fuselage sliding in the air, the land tilted beneath them. An orange laser of sunlight penetrated the windows and burned through the cabin, briefly igniting faces as hands came up, reflexively, to shield eyes. They crossed a last, low range, the wings swung back to level, and the Kathmandu Valley spread out before them, green and brown, geometric with fields. The flaps came out and down, then the plane dropped so sharply that people gasped. Alex gripped her father's hand as if she were hanging from a cliff, her pupils dilated with fear.

"It's okay," Peter said. "Just how they do it here."

"How would you know?"

He shrugged, as nonchalantly as he could, because he didn't know. To the north, the great matriarchs of the Himalayas rolled into view, awash in alpenglow as the pink remnants of the season's monsoon clouds spurled beneath them.

"Look," he said, to distract her, and she peered nervously out. His eyes were on the mountains, hers on the earth rising rapidly to meet them.

"The stupa," she said suddenly, pointing at the dome of the temple in Boudhanath. "My God, it's huge."

| | |

They caught a cab into the city as the valley fell into evening and lights blinked on around them. A warm breeze pushed in through the open windows, carrying the scent of flowers, of human sweat and animal dung and diesel. Two- and three-story buildings, with shops below and living quarters above, pressed close to the sides of the street. Oil lanterns threw giant human shadows against medieval-looking stone walls.

"How you doing?" he asked.

"I'm glad to be on the ground," she said. "At least, I think so."

She turned back to the window, and he saw her fine nose, the elegant profile. Her hair picked up what little light there was. She leaned back, arranging her long limbs as best she could. It had been hard for her, cooped up so long.

He knew, of course, that there was more to it. She was far from convinced that she wanted to be here at all. He felt his own mix of emotions, stirrings of pleasant anticipation tempered by the apprehension that grew from experience.

The cab dodged through narrow streets full of people and dogs and cattle, bikes and motorbikes and three-wheeled contraptions—*tempos,* their cabdriver said—as well as the occasional bus. They drove on the left; Peter kept flinching at head-ons that didn't happen.

After the third or fourth time Alex looked at him and managed a tight smile. "Want to hold my hand?" she asked.

"Thanks," he said, and took it. He was gentle at first, but he gradually increased the pressure. She fought as long as she could, then she laughed and pulled her hand away.

"Now you know how it feels," he said.

"Now *you* know how it feels."

She was right. For her it was planes, for him traffic—and for both of them, too often, it was life in general. He didn't so much mind dealing with anxiety, though, because he knew that on the other side of it lay despair, and it wasn't a border he liked to cross. Fear was an easier land to inhabit, one for which reliable medications were available.

They swung through the neighborhood the driver identified as Naxal, then turned north, through a dark world of mooing and whistling, car horns and bicycle bells. They finally reached Bhatbhateni, the district where Peter had rented a house. The driver found the address and pulled in to the curb. They got out and hauled their bags from the trunk. Peter counted out a stack of rupees, unfolding them one at a time, the paper worn and slick as it passed his fingers.

"Thank you very much, sir." The driver beamed, looking a little surprised. He placed his hands together in prayer position. "Namaste."

"Namaste," said Peter. The one word he'd learned.

They hauled their bags toward the door and, when the driver was gone, Alex said, "You got took."

Peter affected indignation. "Apparently you missed the fact that he worships me."

She swung her head from side to side, a display of mournful tolerance. "Dad, Dad," she said. "Took, took, took."

The house was built of bricks but with an ornately carved wooden door and window frames. A high wall surrounded it, topped with broken glass to discourage thieves. Peter found the door unlocked, so they wrestled their stuff inside.

Alex shivered. "It's freezing," she said. Peter went hunting for a thermostat. There was a light on in a room at the back of the house. As he moved toward the room, a small figure burst through the doorway and nearly collided with him. Peter jumped back a step, startled.

"Forgive me, sir!" said the woman excitedly. "You certainly good reflexes has!"

Alex laughed.

"Who the hell are you?" Peter asked. Irritation born of surprise, he knew, a brand of annoyance that hadn't afflicted him as a younger man. He was embarrassed by it, but what was he supposed to do?

The woman looked briefly taken aback by his rudeness, but she presented her hand. "I am Sangita, *didi*," she said.

Peter took the hand a little hesitantly. "Sangita Didi?" he said. "I'm Peter, and this is Alex."

The woman's brow furrowed, as if she wasn't used to having such difficulties with basic communication. "No, *didi* is what I am, name not," she said, sounding a little annoyed herself now. She glanced at Alex as if hoping for reinforcements.

"Of course," said Peter. He had no idea what she was talking about and turned to Alex as well.

"It means big sister," Alex said. "And housekeeper, right?"

Sangita relaxed a little and smiled. "This correct—sister, housekeeper, also cook. Dr. Franz at the clinic has made this very kind arrangement for you."

"Dr. Franz?" said Peter. "At what clinic?" He'd arranged to work at the teaching hospital and hadn't dealt with anyone named Franz. "And how did you get in? You have a key?"

Sangita looked at him and squinted a little. "I think all this soon clear becoming," she said, with an evident attempt at patience. "Perhaps now best eat."

Peter and Alex looked at each other; they were both famished. "Okay," he said warily. "But could we turn on the heat?"

"Heat?" Sangita replied. She smiled and turned back toward the kitchen. "Oh, no, sorry. No heat."

"No heat of any kind?"

She waved nonchalantly, though Peter was pretty sure he detected a hint of victory in her dismissive tone. "Nepali houses not have what you call, mm, furnace," she said. "We just more clothes use."

| | |

Peter and Alex, bundled in their fleece jackets, tramped into the kitchen. There was a small table with benches, so they squeezed in next to each other to share a little warmth. Alex shoved her shoulder into his arm, and he pushed back. Sangita stirred something on a three-burner gas hot plate connected to a rubber hose running through the wall to the outside.

"So, you father-daughter?" she asked, not quite looking at them.

"Sure," said Peter. "Of course."

Sangita smiled knowingly. "Some Western men I seeing in Kathmandu, young girls with them, but daughter not. You not so old-looking, Doctor, sir. I think the girls might like."

"In this case, father-daughter," Peter said, suppressing a smile. Alex looked at him in disgust.

"Smug," she whispered. "Tell it to your bald spot."

Peter picked up his fork and casually jabbed at her with it, but she deflected it and then, with a lightning move, twisted it out of his grip. She grabbed her own so she had one in each hand and waved them menacingly. She had that predatory feline look in her eyes.

"Ooh," said Sangita, with appreciative mockery. "I watch out for you."

"I sue for peace," said Peter.

"The pacifism of the defeated," replied Alex. She handed him back his fork, tines first, so it stuck him a little.

"You like my daughter," said Sangita. "Scary-scary."

Alex turned to her, apparently brightened by this prospect. "You have a daughter?"

"Oh, sure. Husband, son, daughter. Dog, chickens."

"How old are your kids?"

"Daughter, eighteen. Son . . ." Sangita paused, her face clouded for a moment. "Twenty now, would be."

Peter and Alex looked at each other, both wondering why Sangita had trouble remembering her son's age.

She loaded the plates and brought them to the table. *"Dalbhat,"* she said, and smiled. The plates were heaped with white rice, and each had a bowl of cooked lentils on the side. She carried over several smaller dishes and taught Peter and Alex the vocabulary as she put them on the table: flatbread (called *nan*), a vegetable curry (*tarkari*), pickled mangoes (*achar,* she said), and half a stick of goat butter. Finally, she fixed a plate for herself and stood, leaning against the counter, as she spooned lentils over her rice.

"Won't you join us?" Peter asked.

Sangita fluttered her hand, looking embarrassed. "I fine," she said.

"We're not used to having a *didi,*" Alex said. "This kind of thing makes us feel guilty."

Sangita regarded them as if she were indulging a couple of crazy children, but she came to the table and sat on the opposite bench.

"It's very good," Peter said, just before he tried the buttered flatbread and gagged. Alex looked at him disapprovingly, but Sangita smiled.

"Goat butter strong," she said. "Maybe some cow butter tomorrow getting."

Peter nodded his agreement and took a drink of water. Alex was scarfing like a *T. rex,* and watching her, Sangita beamed. After a few minutes, when they'd taken the edge off their hunger and could sit back for a breath, Peter asked Sangita where she lived.

"Not far," she said. She'd already finished her plate, as she ate only about half of what they did. She got up and ran some hot water into the sink from a little on-demand propane water heater bolted to the wall. "Up road, near Italian embassy," she added.

When they were finished, Peter offered to help her with the dishes, but she flicked a dish towel at him. "You not clean house, I not treat patients," she said. "Fair okay?"

THREE

For a few groggy seconds the next morning, he couldn't remember where he was. Sun streamed through the windows, birds sang outside, and the room was so cold he could see his breath. The past few days of packing and traveling seemed vaguely hallucinatory. He ducked his head lower into his sleeping bag. The bag was dirty and torn, with duct-taped patches and tiny plumes of Polarguard geysering out here and there. The bag was three or four years older than his daughter. He'd slept in it as a young man, climbing in Yosemite and Joshua Tree and at Smith Rock; he'd slept in it in the Olympic Mountains and the Cascades and the Sierra, and in the Great Basin country and the Sonoran Desert. Over time it had taken on his smells and absorbed the smoke of innumerable campfires. Wherever he found himself, the bag had always felt like home.

At least until now. His sense of dislocation was stronger than it had ever been, so strong that even familiar things seemed alien.

He lay on a hard bed four thousand feet above sea level, in a valley surrounded by mountains that brushed outer space. His room held only the bed, a wooden chair, and a battered dresser.

The walls were covered in a chalky green wallpaper, some of which had peeled off in strips so fine they lay on the dusty floor in filaments. An empty glass stood on the dresser, though when Peter looked more closely he saw that it wasn't completely empty; a spider had spun a web inside it and waited there for insects that never came. It hung now, a desiccated husk, in its own trap.

His side hurt, so he rolled over. There, on the gray-striped mattress in front of his face, lay the traveling pouch he wore around his neck. Passport, two credit cards, medical license, medevac card, dollars and rupees. He opened the passport and studied the picture, which had been taken seven years earlier but already looked like some other person, someone enthusiastic and hopeful. The physical particulars hadn't altered much: a few fine worry lines creasing the forehead, the early warning signs of jowlish softening, dark hair shot through with gray—though in the photo it was pulled into a ponytail that had since been cut off.

The change was mainly in the eyes. There was an eagerness in the man in the photo, and Peter hadn't seen that look in the mirror for some time. It had been replaced by the steady, resigned gaze of a guy who had grown used to getting through the day on stamina instead of joy.

He missed joy, in fact, yearned for it. It troubled him, sometimes, that he found it in the company of his daughter but rarely anywhere else. He suspected that a broader distribution might be healthy. This would be easier if the rest of the world were as funny and peculiar and engaging as she was.

As if the world had a response to this thought, the door popped open and Alex stood there, encased in her own mummy bag and peering out from under the hood.

"Make room," she said crossly. Peter slid over. She hopped to his bed and fell in beside him, her teeth chattering dramatically. "You and your goddamn wall map," she said.

He watched the breath steam out of him. "You threw the fucking dart. If you wanted warm, you should have aimed at Fiji."

"I didn't aim," she said. "That was the point."

"What you mean is you didn't aim *well*."

"We're in a country with a king," she said. "An actual king, and Maoists in the mountains."

"You read your guidebook," he said testily. He sat up and rubbed his eyes. "Let's get our big butts out of this meat locker."

"Speak for your own butt."

"My butt speaks for itself," he said, and farted. She shrieked with disgust, rolled off the bed, and hopped back to her room. A few minutes later they met on the landing in their fleece, ready to explore the place in daylight.

A hallway circled the stairs and led to Alex's bedroom, which overlooked the back garden. Downstairs, to the left as they faced the front door, a capacious living room ran the length of the house. It held a rattan couch, a few chairs, and a couple of dusty glass-topped coffee tables. Alex dragged her finger along the surface of one of them, then blew the dust into the air. Evidently Sangita hadn't had a chance to get to such things yet.

On the other side of the stairs was a small dining room with a table and chairs, and behind it, the kitchen, which also had a doorway into the back of the living room—the opening Sangita had burst through the night before. You could, if you wanted, walk a complete circle around either floor. Peter figured that on long, fretful nights he might find himself doing just that.

They opened windows to bring in some warm air, then went out back. The yard was small but had a stone patio and two trees: a tall jacaranda covered with purple flowers, and a persimmon. As if they'd been cued, a small flock of bright green parakeets flew into the jacaranda and began to sing.

Peter watched them and said, "Maybe it won't be so bad."

Alex eyed the birds skeptically. She crossed her arms over herself and shivered. "I think I'm coming down with some sort of tropical fever," she said.

He put a hand on her forehead. It was cool and smooth. "More likely hypothermia."

"Well, that's *much* better."

| | |

The summer monsoon had washed Kathmandu's air of most of its smog, and now the light etched everything with the hard, crystalline clarity of a mountain morning. The streets were as full as they had been the night before, and Peter's last foggy notions of exotic paradise burned off in the brightness.

He'd decided to walk the mile to the teaching hospital, where he would be a visiting instructor and attending physician for the year. He planned to start after the weekend, but he wanted to meet his new boss, the chief of cardiology, and get a sense of the situation. On the way, he stepped around piles of garbage, cow shit, dog shit, and what was possibly human shit. People traveled on foot or by bicycle, or straddled little Honda Heroes and other motorbikes. Some rode in rickshaws with landscapes painted on the back. They led goats and water buffalo by ropes, dodging buses and bicycles, as dogs roamed free in small packs, happily investigating the garbage piles.

Peter was taller and paler than just about everyone else, but there were a few other Westerners in the throng, and he wasn't much noticed. This apparent invisibility came as a relief; he was just another "Ingie" shambling along among these small, lithe people, getting in the way of oxen and bikes. Kathmandu was bigger and more chaotic than he'd expected. But it was a pretty morning, he had a job, and he figured his daughter would eventually adjust.

Both sides of the street were fronted by small shops displaying everything from handmade copper kettles to plastic bangles to the elaborate icons of Buddhist deities called *thangkas*. Every now and then he stopped to gawk. Boys of ten or eleven carried bundles on their heads with tumplines—giant, planetoid-like bales of rags and other amalgamations twice the boys' size that probably weighed more than they did. Incense wafted out of storefronts in stringy white clouds. Peter saw a kid of about ten riding one of the ubiquitous green Chinese bicycles, with six or seven live chickens tied to it, upside down by their feet, their wings and beaks bound.

Chickens, to him, had become slabs of flesh in a package. It was a startling pleasure to remember that the real thing had claws and would take out your eye, given half a chance. It made the situation seem a little fairer.

He walked on. After Alex had thrown the dart that pierced Nepal, Peter felt the need for reassurance. He tracked down an old climbing buddy, Bruce Wang, who'd practiced medicine overseas.

Bruce thought Nepal a reasonable choice. He gave Peter the contact at the hospital and added, with good-natured condescension, that a lot of people in Kathmandu spoke passable English, and that the city would offer at least some of the amenities spoiled Americans were used to. Although central heating, Peter reflected now, was apparently not on the list.

He found the hospital and the office of Dr. Banerjee. The receptionist was in her forties, with graying hair, and shockingly thin. When Peter introduced himself she stared at him with troubled eyes.

"Peter Scanlon?" she said. "The American doctor?"

"If he's busy, I can wait," Peter answered affably.

"Dr. Scanlon, you have not received our several communications?" The receptionist pulled on her pen with both hands, as if it might stretch like taffy.

Peter regarded her quizzically, and she began to explain. A sort of nauseating fog descended on him; by the end he'd missed some of the details but had gotten the gist. First, something about the funding. Second, Banerjee having gone back to India, a family emergency possibly requiring a lengthy stay. Third, a competing doctor with different ideas that didn't include giving any of their scant money to visiting Americans. Peter thought maybe she'd actually said "vacationing" Americans, but he couldn't tell if this had been the editorial slant of the doctor or of the receptionist, or if he himself had just misunderstood.

Still, he couldn't comprehend why they hadn't reached him. "You had my number," he said. "My email was supposed to be forwarded."

The receptionist responded by consulting a piece of paper, then matter-of-factly picking up the receiver of her phone and punching in a series of numbers. She handed it to him. He was startled to hear himself at the other end, but it was his old message, not the one he thought he'd recorded just before leaving, providing his cell number. Had he forgotten to press Save, or something? He was fine with medical technology, but this mundane stuff invariably drove him nuts.

"I assumed you received the message and the email," she said, sounding angry. He wondered what *she* had to be upset about.

"What email?"

"The email!" she exclaimed. "The one explaining everything I have just told you."

For Christ's sake, he thought. He vaguely remembered the IT guy saying something about a firewall problem when they tried to forward emails from international addresses, but by then Peter's life was in an advanced state of disintegration. He was extricating himself from a busy practice and moving out of his house; he figured the firewall would be fixed, just as he'd figured the voicemail had taken his changed message, and he hadn't really paid attention.

Now he just felt heavy, his senses dulled, as if this conversation had coated him in warm lead that was gradually solidifying.

"I gave up a medical practice to come here," he said. "My daughter is missing her senior year of high school, and she isn't happy about it. Why would you assume I got your messages if you didn't hear back from me?"

The woman folded her hands in front of her, looking somewhat contrite but not overly so, as if the matter were embarrassing but resolved. "You are certainly in a problematic position," she said. "I must wish you better luck!"

He shook his head, which seemed to crack the coating of lead. If this was any indication of how the hospital functioned, it would be hell to work in anyway, but he was still pretty much screwed. He stalked down the hallway, where he noticed that half the offices were abandoned and held nothing but a desk, a chair, and a phone. He picked one, went in, closed the door, and, among the phone books in the desk drawer, found one in English.

The U.S. embassy clinic was fully staffed. Subsequent calls revealed that none of the hospitals in town had the funds to hire a cardiologist, even at the pittance they paid. One doc he spoke to directed him to CIWEC, the international clinic that catered to a mix of poor Nepalis and visiting Westerners. It wasn't far, so he left and walked over, but they were full up too. The nurse, a red-haired Australian in her thirties, suggested he check out something that sounded like Phwoof.

"I'm sorry?" Peter said, thinking she'd coughed or used some sort of Aussie slang.

She smiled. "Physicians without Frontiers. Phwoof, we call it. They've got a clinic down the hill. One of their docs pissed off home last month, so they might be worth a go."

He decided to clean up and try again after lunch.

| | |

Alex put her face in her hands. "Jesus, Dad."

He sat on the couch beside her. "Look, it's cheap enough that we can live here awhile if we want to."

"I thought you let Mom take all the money."

"*Almost* all of it."

She slumped back, fighting tears. He put a hand on her knee.

"We'll find a way to make it work," he said.

She turned to him, her eyes fierce. "*Why?*" she said. "What's so compelling about this place? The house is freezing, there's cow shit everywhere, and so far every meal consists of lentils and rice."

She stormed upstairs and slammed her door. Peter was about to go after her, but Sangita was in the kitchen, leaning quietly against the counter by the sink. He went in and apologized. "I'm sure she didn't mean it about the food," he said.

She shrugged and said, "*Ke garne?*" He'd soon be hearing a lot of this expression, which meant, basically, "What to do?"

"I know place, Western things buying," she said. "We make menu. She be okay."

"You don't know her," said Peter.

"I know someone great much like her." She turned back to the stove, humming to herself, and stirred the pot.

"So what clinic were you talking about the night we arrived?" Peter asked. "And who's Franz?"

Sangita looked at him over her shoulder and smiled.

| | |

"I heard about the little imbroglio at the teaching hospital," Franz said, shaking Peter's hand. "I had a feeling you were going to be available." He ran the Phwoof clinic Peter was already planning to visit, as it turned out.

"Apparently everyone did but me," Peter replied. "Is this a smaller town than it seems?"

Franz turned on the coffee. "It's like anywhere," he said. "You become acquainted with one or two of the right people and you can find out most of what you need to know."

"Such as where I live, apparently."

"Oh, all kinds of things," Franz said, and smiled.

Franz was a thickset Austrian in his fifties with short white hair surrounding a shiny bald pate. His English was nearly flawless. He had a bull neck and a strong jaw, his face softened only by a slight middle-aged dewlap and by his small, octagonal rimless glasses. He wore a blue canvas shirt with old, wrinkled khakis and brown Rockports. His arms and hands were thick and sinewed, but for all his obvious physical strength he seemed imbued with an air of reticence or regret. When they'd shaken hands his grip was soft, the touch tentative and probing. Peter had seen this combination before.

"Orthopedic surgeon?" he ventured.

"And you're a psychic, I guess. Not nearly enough of those in Nepal." He seemed jovial, more or less, but with an edge worth noting.

Phwoof was in a modest two-story house on a side street about a half hour's walk from Peter's place. Franz's office was painted bright yellow and had windows on three sides. Milk crates full of medical texts were stacked against the walls. The open window brought a warm breeze and the scent of flowers.

"Not a lot of American cardiologists come over here," Franz said. "Forgive me for being blunt, but any malpractice issues I should know about?"

"All my patients die," Peter said. "Eventually."

Franz chuckled. When the coffee was ready, he poured them each a cup. The men sat in the office's squeaky, tattered chairs.

"Thanks for sending Sangita," said Peter, "even though it was a little creepy to find her there."

"It's politically incorrect to say this, but you may as well know: Sangita is industrious and she doesn't steal, which sets her apart from most *didis*. She's Tibetan, even though she wears a *bindi* and pretends to be Nepali."

"Why would she pretend?"

"She'll tell you if she wants to," Franz said. It was a subtle but distinctly anti-imperialist remark, Peter thought, respectful of Sangita's privacy and informative of Peter's place in the pecking order, just in case this was required. "And by the way, don't expect subservience. She'll give you an honest day's work, but she won't kowtow."

"I'm figuring that out," Peter said. "It's a relief."

Franz nodded approvingly, sipped his coffee, and fixed Peter with an oddly penetrating gaze. "We generally get three kinds here: missionaries, misfits, and malcontents," he said. "Mind my asking which one you are?"

"Jesus, this really *is* a job interview, isn't it? Suppose I ask why there's an opening on the staff?"

Franz shrugged. "We often need doctors because I don't mind firing them," he said. "We had a Belgian in here last month who was so afraid of catching something that he'd barely touch the patients." Franz raised his hand and brought it down on the desk like a hatchet onto a block.

"Well," said Peter, "I'm definitely not a missionary."

"Good," Franz said. "Misfits and malcontents I can work with. You'll get the salary of a fry cook and an education in a variety of compelling and terrifying diseases you'd rarely cross paths with at home. What do you think?"

As much as Peter disliked being cornered, the alternative was giving up and catching a plane home. "What do you get out of it?" he asked.

"A chance to keep the place open," Franz said. Phwoof clinics, it seemed, were sponsored by a loose-knit consortium involving the WHO and a couple of international NGOs. Most of the money had lately been redirected to Darfur, Somalia, Iraq, and Afghanistan. The Nepali government had stepped in, but they would commit for only a year.

"Six months from now, if they decide they don't like us, that's it," Franz said. "I'll go back home and eat *kaisersemmel* and sausage, I guess."

"Are you sure a cardiologist is the best choice?"

"Our patients walk everywhere, eat too little, and die young of something else," he said. "But there *are* some heart problems I'm not used to seeing. You might understand something about them; if so, I'd like to know."

Peter told him what he knew: that Nepalis and Indians were four times more likely to have coronary artery disease and heart attacks than Caucasians, that half the attacks happened before age fifty and a quarter before age forty.

"Do you know why?" Franz asked.

"Something to do with how lipoprotein is processed," Peter said. "When they get prosperous they get away from traditional dietary fats, and that's when the trouble starts."

Franz rubbed his forehead. "Big Indian community where you live?"

"We wouldn't have enough engineers without them."

"I didn't know about any of what you just said, but it wouldn't look bad in a grant proposal. If we actually did something for the prosperous once in a while, it might help us."

"So what am I going to be dealing with?"

"I mainly treat TB, conjunctivitis, dysentery, miscellaneous infections, and bullet wounds," Franz said. "Tapeworms and flukes and protozoa. Occasionally there's a mountaineer with a compound fracture, thank God. It keeps my hand in."

"Bullet wounds?"

Franz regarded him, surprised. "You should read the papers, Yank," he said. "You've enlisted for service in a civil war."

Peter shifted in his seat. "I thought the whole Maoist thing was mainly out in the countryside," he said.

Franz replied simply, "It *was*."

| | |

"So we're staying," Alex said. She sounded almost relieved, but not quite.

"If you're miserable three months from now, we'll negotiate."

They walked over to the Bhat-bhateni Supermarket, which occupied five floors on a half acre of land and was surrounded on the outside by stalls selling fresh fruits and vegetables. The building also contained a hair salon, a dry cleaner, a shop with bright ground spices in wooden bins, and a dozen other stores. Alex's face lit up, taking it all in. She stopped dead in the street and was immediately nudged from behind by a goat on a leash. Its owner spoke to it, then gently led it around her.

Inside, they each took a cart. Peter picked out electric heaters for the bedrooms and a big kerosene beast for downstairs. Alex found Rice Krispies, which made her nearly ecstatic. She bought toilet paper, tampons, milk, rice milk, yogurt, Wheat Chex, and Toasties. He bought eggs, flour, chicken, steak, hamburger, lettuce, cabbage, beans, chocolate-chip cookies in a giant paper bag, charcoal and lighter fluid, and, just for good measure, a purple Frisbee.

On another floor he found sheets, pillowcases, and down comforters.

When they arrived at the checkout line, Alex eyed her father's cart. "I thought you hated to shop," she said.

"I hate to shop in America. Here, they need us."

"Oh, you're a philanthropist now."

A grin tugged at the corners of her mouth, but part of the game was giving as good as he got. He scowled. "I'm going to be glad in a few years, when you become pleasant," he said.

She patted his stomach. "If you're nice to me, you might live long enough to see it."

On the way home, crammed into a cab with their plunder, he watched her as she looked dreamily out. When they were stuck in traffic and the huge, broad face of an ox suddenly appeared at her window, she jumped, startled, and then laughed.

"Hello, ox," she said. "Are you as strong as yourself?" She giggled self-consciously at her own dumb joke, and Peter knew she'd have to find friends soon.

FOUR

"What on earth are you doing?" said a voice.

Peter turned away from the patient—a girl about Alex's age—and saw the woman staring at him.

"You must be Mina," he said. Franz had warned him about the Nepali RN who'd help him learn the ropes. Poised in the doorway, slender in a shiny, mottled blouse, with her intently focused eyes and sharp nose, she looked like a snake about to strike. Apparently her father was a retired colonel in the Royal Nepalese Army, and she'd gotten some of the genes.

"The question stands," she said.

"What on earth I'm doing is trying to get a leech out of this girl's nose without pulling her whole septum out with it," he answered, briefly grateful that his patient didn't speak English. He had a hemostat on the slimy thing, but it wouldn't budge, and he was pulling so hard the girl had begun to weep. She was his third patient, and he was already flailing, but clearly he couldn't leave a fat, thumb-sized leech in there.

Mina hissed with exasperation and went to the sink. She filled a glass with water, then brought it over and held it under the girl's nose. She stared at Peter with unsettling calm; he stepped back and tried to pay attention to the leech, but it was hard not to notice Mina's eyes. They were wide-set and such a deep brown that they were almost black. Peter felt a surge of energy pass from her to him—there was hostility, to be sure, but there was something more, something confusing. Her eyes were stunning; in fact, *she* was stunning, though it hadn't been clear at first. It was as if for just a moment, tending the girl, she let down her scaly armor and revealed an aspect of herself that was genuine and warm.

But then, as if aware of this unintended revelation, she averted her eyes. Once again she looked like an ordinary woman, and an irritated one at that. Even so, Peter couldn't completely shake the sense of a hidden life, as if she guarded herself from the world because she had something of great value to protect.

The leech let go and plopped into the glass.

"When they're engorged, they just want to get back into the pond," Mina said. "So we bring the pond to them." She set the glass on the counter. The leech sunk to the bottom, wiggling.

The girl's nose started bleeding profusely. Peter grabbed some gauze and put pressure on it.

"It'll stop in a little while," Mina said. "Where did you go to medical school, for heaven's sake?"

"I'm a cardiologist, not an ENT."

"Then presumably you've heard of heparin."

"What about it?"

"Leeches invented it; that's why she's bleeding. When you can't get any heparin and you have a patient with thrombosis, remember this and maybe he won't lose his leg."

Peter huffed. "Great," he said. "Let's also get some maggots for debriding wounds."

"I've tried them, and they work pretty well. But that's not the sort of thing they teach you at Stanford."

"How did you know I went to Stanford?"

"There's this thing called the Internet, Doctor. Check it out sometime."

"But if you knew, why did you ask?"

"It was a rhetorical question," she said. "Perhaps you've heard of those too." She picked up the glass with the leech and left.

The girl in the chair stared at him, wide-eyed. He took a couple of breaths to calm himself down and spoke gently to her. "It's okay," he said, figuring she'd get the tone even if she didn't understand the words. "You'll be out of here in a bit."

He wished he spoke Nepali so he could find out how she'd gotten a leech up her nose in the first place, but Mina had disappeared and there was no one to translate. He showed the girl how to apply the pressure, left her holding the gauze, and walked down to Franz's office.

"Any chance I could work with someone else?" he asked.

"Someone other than Mina?" said Franz, smiling. "Oh, no. She's a necessary terror. Remember the Belgian?"

"What about him?"

"She threw a book of practice guidelines at his head. A *thick* book. Said if he wouldn't read it, perhaps it could make an impression some other way."

"And how long after that did you fire him?"

"Within the week, as I recall." Franz was practically humming with pleasure at the memory of it.

"So it was him or her, and that was your choice."

"Oh, absolutely," said Franz. "Best to keep it in mind."

| | |

Peter had fled one cage, seeking freedom, and now to his chagrin he found himself in a different one in another part of the world, and a dirtier cage at that. How had everything gotten screwed up so quickly? He had come here to deliver his daughter from a nasty situation, and now she was indignant and he was lost in a maze of frustration and bafflement. She didn't appreciate anything he tried to do for her, but then everything he attempted seemed to fall apart before his eyes. He had patients to attend to here in the clinic, but mainly he felt like bolting for the door, disappearing down some street until he was as ragged as a beggar. His skin raised up in prickly welts under his shirt, as if something had infested him and begun to bite.

"*Ankhaa,*" said the boy, pointing. He was not crying at the moment, but he had tear tracks, outlined with dust, on his cheeks.

"Your eyes."

"*Ankhaa.*"

"Okay, let's have a look."

Peter forced himself to focus. The boy was about fourteen, shirtless and bony. His mother, also thin, rested a hand on his arm. She looked fifty, so Peter figured, based on what was now four days of experience, that she was in her late thirties. She wore a clean but threadbare sari, and like her son she was shoeless, with thick calluses on the bottoms of her feet. They'd walked to the clinic from one of the sprawling refugee camps that surrounded the city, shantytowns filled with villagers driven from the mountains by fighting between the RNA and the communist rebels.

Mina leaned calmly against the counter, legs crossed at the ankles, arms folded over her chest, watching and translating as needed. Her eyes retained their cool, unnerving gaze. Peter felt those eyes on him, persistent and relentlessly acute. Already he couldn't stand to be in the same room with her, for reasons far more complex and troubling than simple loathing (though loathing was certainly part of the mix). She seemed equally ill at ease.

He shone a light into the boy's eye and pulled down the lid while the boy looked up, to the left, down, to the right. The pupil dilated normally and there was no obvious inflammation, but his cornea didn't look right. Peter peeled back the upper lid, then checked the other eye. He'd read about this in med school but had never seen a case. He looked at Mina.

"Much trachoma in the camps?" he asked.

"There you go, Doctor."

The infection had scarred the undersides of the boy's eyelids. The scar tissue, in turn, pulled the lashes under so that they raked the cornea every time he blinked. The boy must have felt like he had sandpaper glued under his lids.

"Ask her how long he's been like this."

Mina spoke to the mother and then translated. "Off and on for two or three years."

"*Years?*"

"That's how things are here, I'm afraid."

"What's your luck with antibiotics?"

"They're better for a while, then they usually get it again," Mina said. "The flies spread it. How well the cornea heals depends on how strong the child is, how much he gets to eat, all the usual things. If he wants to keep his eyesight, he probably ought to have the surgery."

"Can they do it at the teaching hospital, or at Kanti?"

Mina's lips pulled into a thin smile. "This woman has no money for a hospital, Doctor."

"It's not something I'm trained to do," he said impatiently, as if she ought to know this.

"I think if you watch me two or three times, you'll have it."

Peter looked at her. The smile remained on her lips, though it had compressed just slightly in the middle and begun to look smug. "You can do it?" he asked.

"Of course."

Of course, he thought. He almost wanted her to fail, then felt ashamed for having the thought. They took the boy to the room with the tilt chair and brought in a seat for his mother. Mina and Peter scrubbed up and put on gloves, then she talked soothingly to the boy as they rolled in the stools, one on each side. Peter was surprised, again, by her sudden gentleness, but this time he deliberately avoided her eyes.

"Numb him up, will you?" she said.

"Outer lid?"

She nodded. But when the boy looked over and saw the needle

headed toward his eye, the eyeball rolled up and he passed out cold. The mother came to her feet, apparently fearing the worst, but Mina reassured her.

"Well, go ahead and do it now, while he's out," she said to Peter.

Peter gave him a small injection in each lid, then Mina broke an ammonia capsule under his nose and he came to.

"*Aama,*" he said. His mother spoke to him, and he settled down.

"Next time we see one of these, which should be in a few days, come over the top and pull the lid up so the child doesn't see the needle," Mina said, a little more patiently. "It requires a certain amount of stealth."

She pulled the right lid up, reached in with the scalpel, and made an incision the length of the lid's underside. She lifted the side with the lashes outward so it would be placed correctly, then removed the scar tissue with a few more strokes.

"Hold this with a clamp," she said.

Peter reached in and did as she asked. She wielded the scalpel with calm, steady hands. She stitched the lid closed so the lashes stayed where they should, then moved to the next eye. In all, it took less than half an hour.

Peter was impressed enough that he felt a little conciliatory in spite of himself. "You learned that at UCSF?" he asked.

"You've discovered the Internet."

"No, I just went into Franz's office and read your file."

She nearly smiled, but not quite. "At UCSF they never would have handed a scalpel to a lowly nurse," she said. "I learned it here, courtesy of a visitor from the Carter Center. A few earnest souls make the rounds doing cleft palates and eyelids, things like that. They like to refer to it as the Journey of Conscience, but I just call it the Guilt Trip."

Now Peter had to stifle a smile. "What do you send the kids home with?" he asked.

"A course of Zithromax is the best way to go, but we won't have any for another few weeks. So it's drops."

She spoke forcefully to the boy's mother, pointing to a calendar and apparently insisting that they return the following week. The woman made all manner of assenting bows and namastes, and Mina showed them to the door and waved goodbye. After she closed the door, she turned and said, "They won't be back until he's got it again."

FIVE

Peter lay on their couch as Alex fanned him with a handful of parakeet feathers she'd collected from the backyard. The fanning was intended ironically, of course, but he didn't care. His back ached and his feet hurt, and the air felt good.

He was thinking about how he might have to suck it up, admit that he'd been stupid and rash, and take her home. The prospect was humiliating; what sort of example was he setting, for Christ's sake? But what if things only got worse?

"You all caught up with your homeschooling?" he asked.

"I'm a week ahead already," she said. "You owe me a calculus test."

"Now I have a headache along with everything else."

"In fact, I've been so good I believe I'm due a reward."

"You do, do you?"

"Think of it, Dad," she said. "We could be in Rockridge tonight, for pizza at Rustica. Or we could be in Kathmandu eating *dal-bhat* again."

"Who are you torturing, me or yourself?"

She spoke to him the way a mother might soothe a distraught child. "Guess what I heard about today?"

Resistance would be futile, and he didn't really want to resist anyway, so he prepared to be assimilated. They caught one of the quiet electric *tempos* downtown, then walked over toward Thamel, the district where Western tourists hung out. The evening was warm and inviting, the streets busy. What was most striking about the Nepalis, Peter realized, was not their physical grace or their bright saris and *dauras* but their demeanor. Nobody was angry, nobody was rushed; everyone was just going about their lives and seemed reasonably considerate of one another. Male-female couples didn't often touch each other in public—a cultural thing, apparently—but women strolled comfortably arm in arm, as did some men. It was like San Francisco's Castro district, except on lithium, and with cows.

They passed a street demonstration, a few dozen people carrying signs and chanting. Soldiers in riot gear lined the street, but they stayed back and things seemed relatively calm.

"Communists?" Peter asked.

Alex squinted, trying to decipher the signs. "I think so, but there are like fifty political parties, so it's hard to tell. You used to be a commie in college, right, Dad?"

He vaguely remembered something about this, about idealism and dreams of an equitable world. The young man who'd believed those things seemed like some other person now, viewed through a fog of time. "Pampered college commies are a dime a dozen," he said. "In the real world the problem is income disparity, not ideology."

She staggered, and even her staggering was ironic. "I feel a lecture coming on," she said. "Let me just sit down and put my head between my knees."

Which made him a little indignant. "Look at this place," he said. "Everybody gets around on bikes and oxcarts while the army officers drive Mercedes and the royal family has Bentleys. You want a revolution, that's how to get one. The rest is rhetoric."

She patted his shoulder affectionately. *"Paternas pompous in-sufferabilis,"* she said. "You'd better get that blood sugar back up before you hurt yourself with some sort of Great Leap Forward."

Soon they saw more Americans and Europeans, heard English and French and German spoken, passed scruffy trekkers with duct-taped backpacks and trashed boots. There were also fresh tourists in lethal cologne and immaculate white safari clothing who seemed to lack only a mahogany walking stick and a pith helmet. Peter and Alex looked at each other.

"We're locals now," she said. "We've only been here ten days, but we can smell those twerps a mile off, huh?"

She led him down the street and came to a stop in front of a pizzeria called Fire and Ice. The smell of oily sausage and cheese filled the air. "So this was your mad plan," Peter said.

She laughed her evil-genius laugh, the "bwa-ha-ha-heee" that went up at the end into a range so high it was possibly audible only to dogs.

He could see, though, that she was tense about something. Possibly she'd laid a trap; she was good at that. He sometimes wished he loved her less—or, more precisely, he wished that loving her wasn't so complicated. The pleasure and pain of it were two sides of a banner, whipped back and forth in the wind like the prayer flags that adorned buildings here, translucent, the surfaces nearly indistinguishable. Fatherhood held at its heart a sweet, paradoxical masochism, the self-abnegation of one willing to die for another. Why else would he have come to this place?

A blind man sat on the entryway floor playing a steel-stringed sarod. He was old and emaciated, with long white hair and skin like dusty tea, his eyes whited out by cataracts. He smiled and swayed as he played, the music seeming to bounce gently off water and echo through air, all within the wooden body of the instrument. Alex bent down and put a few rupees in his cup. The old man inclined his head at the sound, never breaking his rhythm.

They went inside, where an Italian woman named Mariana greeted them and took them upstairs to the veranda overlooking the street. Peter was touched by Alex's gesture to the old man. She'd always been mercurial this way—joking and goofy one minute, then genuinely moved or sobered by something the next.

She was quiet as she sat across the table from him. In the twilight, between the trees, the city lights blinked on. Electricity was a sometimes thing here, which had made Peter appreciate it for the first time. The evening sky stretched out, leopard-spotted with high ice clouds turning pink. To the north, the mountains trembled in the warm air, their snowcapped faces blushing as the sun fell. Miles to the east rose the gleaming white dome of the great stupa.

"Sooner or later we've got to talk about this situation," Alex said.

So here it was: the ambush. He had a sudden feeling of vertigo, as if he'd missed his footing on a steep staircase and begun to tumble down. He looked around to see if anyone could overhear. All the people at the nearby tables were engrossed in their own conversations, most of which were in other languages.

"I had to get you out of there, you know that," he said quietly, hoping she'd accept this at face value and let it go.

She pursed her lips, as if she were trying to be patient. "Dad," she said, "when people want out of Berkeley they think Orinda or Walnut Creek, not Kathmandu."

"That's exactly the point."

A few weeks before they left the United States, Alex had called Peter from home. She needed just to say the name "Wayne Lee" to put him in a panic.

Wayne Lee Fordham was a big, long-haired dude with wide shoulders and large hands who rode an old yellow Ducati. He and Cheryl, Peter's wife, had been briefly involved before she met Peter.

She had sworn off him then, calling him an addiction, but unfortunately he proved her right. He'd shown up again, unannounced, when Alex was six. Cheryl disappeared, then came back five days later, hungry, strung out on meth, and with a nasty case of the clap.

Peter was incensed, and his rage only deepened over time. Cheryl surreptitiously kept herself supplied with the drug for a few weeks, and by the time he figured it out—he was preoccupied with work but also naïve, at the beginning of that dark age—she'd lost fifteen pounds and her teeth had begun to loosen and turn brown. Her skin hung on her, her eyes were huge and vividly blue and feral, her hair electrified straw.

This transformation only threw into relief how far they'd fallen. It had always been a hard relationship, with more than the usual share of acrimony, but at the beginning, at least, Cheryl had been bright and sexy and full of mischief. These qualities had drawn Peter out of his academic shell and enlivened him, at least until the mischief began to show its dark side.

When he finally realized what was happening with the meth, he cut off the money. With startling alacrity, Cheryl filed for divorce. Peter could hardly believe it when he got the papers. He told her, not very kindly, that without him she'd be dead in a matter of months. She screamed that she'd rather *be* dead than live with the dead, whatever the hell that meant.

But later she cried, she apologized, and though her sincerity had always been hard to gauge, she broke him down. He got her into rehab, and she recovered, that time, but she was never the same. There was a look in her eyes like that of a caged tiger, a slight lowering of the upper lid that appeared vigilant and lethal.

It was during this time that Alex began to show signs of real distress—her grades fell, she started nail-biting and scratching at her arms until they bled. The school counselor called them in for the ghastly, predictable conference—what on earth was going on at home? Was it possible Alex was *at risk*?

Which scared the bejesus out of them, as it was supposed to. Cheryl fanned her tiny coal of maternal instinct into a little flame, and they tried again to make it work. They cut a deal, for lack of a better word—staged a sort of happy home to shield their daughter, the way a realtor stages an empty house to make it sell. And when Wayne Lee returned, three or four years later, Cheryl sent him away. She gripped the half-open door, and Peter waited behind her as Wayne Lee stood outside on the walk, illuminated from below by their little solar lamps like some kind of black-leather Halloween monster. He glowered at Peter and muttered, then turned on his boot heel and stalked back to the bike.

Did Peter dream of fighting him? Sure. Did he have any illusions about what would happen to him if he did? None. He knew Cheryl was one of those women who considered it your male duty to go land a punch or two, for the sake of appearances, before getting the shit beat out of you. If he'd ever actually loved her, he'd have thought about it. He stayed, those years, partly because he knew it would be harder for Alex if they divorced and Cheryl went under.

A few weeks before they left for Kathmandu, though, the issue had been forced. One night Peter discerned the Ducati's distinctive rumble as Wayne Lee circled the block around their house like a shark checking the status of a bleeding fish. They both grew restless in their separate beds—Peter furious, Cheryl hearing the call of the wild. Peter didn't even so much care what she did anymore, except that it affected Alex, and when word got around, as it invariably would, he'd end up looking like a cuckold and a jerk.

The next day, Alex phoned him at the hospital the second Wayne Lee crossed the threshold—which he did, this time, with a friend in tow. Peter was in the middle of an emergency heart surgery and couldn't leave without killing his patient, so by the time he got there Alex was in her bedroom, sobbing. While Wayne Lee and Cheryl had busied themselves in the master bedroom, it turned out that the friend had come looking for Alex. She locked her door, then called the cops, but they were reluctant to get involved in what they saw as a domestic dispute instead of a home invasion, given that Cheryl had willingly let the gentlemen in, and that Alex had been frightened but not harmed. In any case, Cheryl and the two bikers had thundered off for greener pastures, after the police left, and twenty minutes before Peter finally arrived.

"It was too close a call," Peter told Alex now, seated at the table in Kathmandu. "I didn't want us in Orinda or Walnut Creek, I wanted us *gone*."

They'd stayed with Peter's sister across the bay in San Anselmo while they got their visas and their shots. Peter waited for the divorce papers to come through. Cheryl's angry gash of a signature surprised him only in that they'd actually found her—but this was another reason, his able lawyer pointed out, for offering her the house and most of the money; she had an address and a compelling reason to agree to terms.

"I guess you got your wish," Alex said, sounding somber. "We're definitely gone."

The waitress brought the pizza. It sat between them until eventually Alex picked a black olive off it and put it in her mouth.

"Mothers are supposed to put their children above everything," she said. "Isn't that the deal?"

"Most do," Peter said. He started to reach for the pizza but then thought he shouldn't be the first to take a piece, that it would seem too casual a gesture, given the subject at hand.

"Other doctors' wives get addicted to Xanax or booze, but they still take care of their kids," Alex said. "Mom just never got the class thing, did she?"

He had to smile. He wasn't completely sure she was joking, but it sounded like it. She lifted out a slice of pizza and took a bite. "It's good," she said.

Peter picked up a piece for himself. It was rich with pepperoni and oil, wonderful after all the lentils.

"You might like it here if you give it some time," he said. He could as well be saying it to himself, he knew.

There was a tree next to the veranda. A sudden gust brushed its branches, and tiny pink flowers snowed down. When she spoke again, he knew he'd relaxed too much. It was the wake-up slap he should have been ready for.

"Sometimes I wonder who you think I am," she said.

| | |

That night he sat by his window, trying to read, but he was too restless to concentrate. He heard a bird like a whip-poor-will outside, its call resembling a drop of water hitting the still surface of a lake. Somewhere a couple argued. The woman yelled, the man bellowed back, then a door slammed and there was a brief silence, followed by the startled yelp of a dog.

In some ways he had a pretty good idea who his daughter was. By the time she was eleven or twelve he'd been able to see in her face the woman she was becoming. Her eyes were lively and intelligent, and she would turn out to be more or less of a language prodigy, first mastering Latin, then becoming fluent in Spanish and French by her junior year.

When she had been thirteen, though, signs of trouble had appeared again. If she didn't get enough exercise, her nervous energy became jitters and tics. She was prone to tantrums if she didn't do well enough in school—she had issues around not being appreciated—and she was sometimes as hard on her friends as she was on herself. But she could also be incredibly generous, and routinely gave away clothes, and once even a prized bike, to classmates she thought needed them more than she did.

All this, it seemed clear, was in reaction to Cheryl, who evidently didn't care that much about school or anything else. Peter had come to understand it as Alex's way of tacitly creating an alliance with him, who cared very much. Alex and Cheryl had fought since Alex was young, over anything and everything, and by the time Alex was a teenager it didn't look like there was any way for her to improve the situation other than by finishing school and getting the hell out of town. Peter had figured that when she was safely ensconced in college he could finally end the marriage without having to worry about shared custody and the risk it posed of Alex being left alone in the company of her mother's scumbag friends. But events with Wayne Lee had overtaken him.

He would have fought for her to the death; he was good in a crisis. But he'd never felt confident about the day-to-day decisions, which had largely been left to him. The love and the protectiveness were all mixed up, and he was always trying to sort out which was which. He had to guess how much freedom to give her—how strict to be, or how permissive. Sometimes he wondered if any of it really made a difference.

When she was fifteen he realized she'd been cutting herself—though mercifully, with intervention, that phase had been brought to a quick halt. Sometimes he thought she was going to be just fine, and sometimes he lay awake half the night, considering at length all the possible ways in which she might not be fine at all.

One time he'd gone in to talk to her shrink, when the urgent issues were winding down and things seemed to be on the upswing. Edelstein was a slender, gentle fellow with salt-and-pepper hair and a prominent Adam's apple. He had posed more or less the same question.

"How well do you feel you know your daughter?" he asked, in that neutral way, and Peter just stared at him because he had no idea how to respond.

SIX

In the mornings he girded himself emotionally for the skirmishes at work. There was Mina, of course, and Franz too, since he'd taken her side. There were the two other nurses, who were clearly too cowed by Mina to risk affiliation with anyone else. And then the patients, in their abject poverty and their calm acceptance of their fates. He knew the poverty wasn't their fault and acceptance was almost certainly a virtue, but this didn't stop him from feeling frustrated with them. He felt petty and ugly for having such thoughts, and this fouled his mood even further. In any case, their only alternative would have been futile railing against the heavens, which was more in Peter's line.

Mainly, Peter felt rage against the filth of the city and the plagues that flourished in it, bacteria and viruses and protozoa and spirochetes that infected anyone they could, the living expression of the world's immense talent for creating and destroying life. These tiny bugs were just like Peter himself, of course, just like anyone or anything that had ever lived. They were programmed by their DNA to survive, and that was all they demanded of the universe—to live and pass that life along to their descendants. The viruses—the hepatitis, dengue, HIV, and the rest—weren't even alive, strictly speaking, but they displayed the same relentless and avaricious drive to reproduce, doing so using the cells of others instead of their own. It was this commonality of purpose that chilled Peter the most—the knowledge that he would be hard pressed to distinguish what he wanted from what they wanted, if they could be said to want (and he believed, for complicated reasons, that they could). Malaria was a parasite in the body of a human, and humans were a parasite on the body of the earth, all of them fighting for dominance, reproducing and dying in droves.

One morning, as Peter toiled away in this sunny mood, a spindly old fellow came in. He had a bad cough and blood in his sputum, and he smelled like sweat and goats. Mina checked his lymph nodes, which were swollen.

"Masks on," she said.

Peter donned his mask, reflecting on another paradox—that though he was frequently annoyed by patients as an abstract mob, each time he met one alone in the exam room he felt genuine fondness, even tenderness, and wanted to do his best to deliver them from whatever was ravaging their bodies. He didn't understand this dichotomy, which occurred at such a deep emotional level that it seemed to defy explanation.

He asked the man, through Mina, if he'd ever been diagnosed with TB. The old fellow rambled on at length, and when he'd finished, Mina translated.

"Eight or nine years ago," she said. "They gave him a drug, he doesn't remember what. He took it for a while, but then it ran out, so he stopped."

Peter watched her. She seemed tired, less ready for battle. He was glad; it meant he could let down his guard a little. "Anything since?"

She spoke to the man. "He says no. He says he got a little better, then in the past year it came back. He's losing weight and coughing a lot. He says he's very weak."

"And it feels like it felt before, when he had it."

"Yes."

TB was the primeval, archetypal guerrilla warrior, a terrorist whose very body was an explosive device. Endemic in the population, quick to seize advantage of weakness, deftly mutating into drug-resistant forms, impossible to eradicate, merciless and deadly. It always made Peter nervous, from fear not only of getting it himself but of giving it to Alex. The months-long antibiotic treatments were hard enough, but if you got a multi-drug-resistant strain, you were finished as a physician and very possibly dead. Cardiologists usually didn't have to deal with much in the way of infectious disease, so as promised, this place was turning out to be an education all its own. He was gaining more sympathy for the Belgian.

"We probably don't need an X ray," he said.

Mina nodded. "We're almost out of film, anyway, and it's going to be three weeks before we get any more." There was no record of what the man had been given the last time around, but she was pretty sure it would have been isoniazid.

"Alone or with other drugs?" Peter asked.

"Most likely alone."

"That might be a good thing, if there's resistance. Any way to do a sputum culture or DST?"

"Not without sending him to the hospital, which he can't afford."

"Right." You could be the best doctor on earth, but if you found yourself practicing in the Stone Age, you were going to be reduced to decoctions of roots and berries, just like everybody else. "What other TB drugs do we have?" he asked.

"Rifampicin and pyrazinamide."

"Anything second-line?"

"Not at the moment."

"Can we give him both, then?"

"If you want to," she said. She spoke to the man and told Peter that he lived in a crate in the camp over in Bhaktapur, on the other side of the river. It had taken him five hours to walk to the clinic. She thought it unlikely they'd see him again, or that anyone would take the trouble to find him. If he stopped taking the drugs, they'd just be creating one more resistant strain of the disease, contributing to a potential disaster no one wanted to contemplate.

"Ask him, if I give him a lot of medicine, will he take it all, just as we say, until it's finished six months from now? And then come back?"

She asked, and the old man nodded agreeably. Peter could tell that Mina didn't believe him. He'd already seen five cases like this, and for every one he saw there were probably twenty or thirty people out there living with the disease and making do. The clinic was always low on drugs, always digging up a supply just at the last minute, through pharma company write-offs or the WHO or whatever else they could scrape together.

After the old man left, Mina took off her mask and opened the window. She headed for the door, and as she passed Peter she met his eyes, just for a moment. He couldn't tell what the look conveyed. It unnerved him, because her sudden proximity seemed both aggressive and sensual. There was something in the lightness and ease of her movements, and in the mutual physical danger of the situations they faced, that put him on edge in ways so confusing that it spurred his desire to flee even more than the open conflict did.

| | |

Peter bought a little red Hero for getting around. He'd ridden a Kawasaki 750 when he was younger, and compared to that, the motorbike accelerated like a concrete block in mud, but *ke garne*? For Kathmandu it was enough; he didn't want to go faster than thirty-five, anyway, because he figured either he'd run into something (a dog, a person, a cow) or something would run into him (a *tempo*, an ox, a bus). He rode with a bicycle helmet and a surgical mask, because the smog was returning after the monsoon. Otherwise, with all the diesel and other soot in the air, he'd come home looking as though he'd been snorting ink. He understood now why everyone in the city had a cough.

As he rode home one day, he saw two teenage girls walking ahead of him, hand in hand. The hand-holding was common enough; what got his attention was that one of the girls looked like Alex. He pulled alongside and saw that she *was* Alex, in fact. The. other girl was even taller and wore a T-shirt and jeans.

Alex had continued to plow through her homeschooling, and given her academic proclivities, she didn't need any prodding. So even though Peter was relieved that she'd made a friend, he wasn't sure how she'd managed it. It made him realize he had no clear picture of how she'd been spending her days. She was hitting the books, but she also had a healthy desire to get out and explore the city.

In any case, acculturation was apparently under way on both sides. He pulled down his sunglasses.

"Is that you?" he asked.

She looked at the Hero and smiled. "I don't know," she said. "Is that you?" She let go of the girl's hand and made a sort of formal introductory gesture. "This is Devi. Sangita's daughter."

"Oh, right." He stuck out his hand, and they shook. Devi was a striking beauty with wide, dark eyes. As she gave his hand a strong shake, she smiled and said, "Pleased to meet you," with only the slightest of accents.

"We're on our way home," said Alex. "See you there?"

Polite code for "Get lost," he figured. "Sure," he said. "I've got to get groceries. You want anything?"

"Rice Krispies," she said. "She's never had them, and we're almost out."

| | |

Sangita and the girls were in the kitchen, drinking tea, when he returned. Sangita helped him unpack the bags while she selected what she wanted for dinner and started chopping.

"Devi's going to teach me Nepali and maybe Tibetan too," Alex said.

Peter handed her the cereal. "Does she know she's dealing with a know-it-all?"

Alex rolled her eyes. "She's brilliant, Dad. And don't worry, Sangita said we can spend as long as we want if she doesn't get behind on her homework."

Peter looked at them both. They seemed a little giddy. Devi had a peculiarly intense gaze and a delicate scar cutting diagonally across her nose. Peter wanted to ask some sort of question, but he wasn't sure what that question might be.

"Great," he said. "That's great." He looked at Sangita, who was rinsing out a pot and smiling her enigmatic smile.

| | |

After dinner the girls went up to Alex's room and turned on some music. Peter helped Sangita carry the plates to the sink.

She held up two fingers, side by side. "Just met yesterday and already they like *this*," she said.

"You saw it coming?"

Sangita nodded as she ran hot water into the sink.

"Is this okay with you?" he asked. "I mean, Alex doesn't have a lot of friends, but I know how she is with the chosen few. You and Sonam might start missing your daughter."

"Devi eighteen, very strong," she said. "Will like mule, worse even than me. *Ke garne?*"

"She speaks English very well."

Sangita smiled. "She smart, got scholarship to international school. Son gone, we figure, better educate daughter!"

She'd mentioned the boy before. "Where is your son, anyway?" Peter asked.

She hesitated, then finished washing a plate and put it in the dish rack. "Maybe better not much saying," she said.

"Well, is he alive? Is he okay?"

"We not know," she replied, and it was clear from her tone— a mix of anxiety and resignation and emotional gristle—that that was all she was going to say about it.

SEVEN

Franz slouched behind his desk, holding his head dejectedly. A half-empty bottle of pink Pepto-Bismol sat beside a jam jar full of pens. Mina sat bolt upright on one of the chairs at the front of the desk. Peter slumped on the other chair. It was the end of the day, and although the light was fading, Franz hadn't turned on his desk lamp. The room had a dank, autumnal air, like a cornfield about to be attacked by crows.

Franz spoke quietly, without looking up. "If we don't get our funding we'll all be gone in a few months, so this may not matter," he said. "But in the meantime I don't care if you hate each other; I just care that it shows. I can't have this kind of thing going on."

Mina crossed her arms over her chest. "He's just like the Belgian," she said.

"I never even met the Belgian," Peter retorted. "For all I know, you *invented* the Belgian. Are we still in high school here? I merely asked whether ampicillin was the best choice for that kid's infection. In America I'd have used Cefzil."

The brief, fragile détente had been broken; perhaps it had been an illusion, anyway. Franz spoke again, but his words were barely audible, his voice rumbling like an ancient, discouraged oracle. They both leaned forward to hear.

"First, Mina, he's a much better doctor than the Belgian, and you know it," Franz said. She huffed dismissively in response, as if this were irrelevant. "And Peter, you should know by now that we don't have access to antibiotics that cost five dollars a pill. You've got to learn to trust Mina's judgment."

"He doesn't seem to be able to learn anything, so why should he learn that?"

Franz sighed. "Please," he said. "I will give you a special bag of cat treats, which one of my patients paid me with today."

"Where on earth did they get cat treats?" she asked.

"He works for an English lady, and she gave them to him as a tip," Franz said. "They've probably been in circulation for years, like fruitcake."

"I'll take them," said Mina.

"Cats," Peter said. "It figures. You probably live with fifty cats."

Mina turned to him, her gaze cool and level. "If *you* lived with fifty cats, they'd all be dead within a week."

"I don't pride myself on veterinary skills, like some people."

"If you paid attention you'd see by now that I know what I'm doing."

"Since half the time I don't know what *I'm* doing, how the hell would I know about you?"

"Well," she said, "at least you admit it."

Franz cleared his throat. "Glad to see we're getting somewhere," he said. He finally looked up, just barely. "Now, what's this about your daughter?"

"I just asked Mina how she'd feel about having Alex volunteer," Peter said. "Instead of welcoming the opportunity, she seemed to take it as a threat."

"As if I'd be threatened by some teenager," Mina snapped. "You're just more interested in building your daughter's character than in treating patients."

"There are ethical issues, Peter," Franz pointed out. "What if she catches TB?"

"It's a minimal risk, and she's aware of it," Peter said.

"But what if she does?" Mina asked. "Are you willing to take that responsibility?"

Peter stared at her. It hadn't occurred to him that she might actually be concerned about Alex's well-being.

"Of course I will," he said, but he faltered. "I'd have to take her home, though, I guess."

"I rest my case about tourist doctors," Mina said.

Franz waved his hand like a white flag from a trench. "Mina, please," he said. "I couldn't keep this clinic open without you, you know that."

She tossed her head triumphantly. "I know that very well," she said.

"And I can't keep it open without him, also," Franz continued.

Encouraged by the praise, they both leaned slightly in toward the desk. Franz raised himself smoothly, the way a cobra does when its prey has finally stumbled into striking distance.

"If Alex wants to help us out, she will be at your disposal, Mina. If you want to get rid of her, you can. Peter will not be angry about it, will you, Peter?"

Peter shot Mina a look. "As long as you give her a fair chance," he said. "If you ax her over some trumped-up BS, I'll be in your face."

"Just be sure she knows why she's here," said Mina.

"She'll know," Peter replied.

"Hallelujah!" said Franz, his hands upraised. "Everyone is happy now!"

| | |

Peter stalked through the door, took off his helmet and mask, and tossed them on the table. Alex and Devi were sprawled on the couch together as Devi quizzed Alex on vocabulary.

"*Ke cha,* Papaji?" asked his daughter.

"The good news is you're in," he said. "The bad news is you'll be working with a psychopath." He went to the fridge and pulled out a beer. "You might actually be right about going home."

Alex glanced at Devi. "I've been rethinking that."

Peter looked at his daughter. He fell into his chair by the couch and took a swig of beer. "Care to elaborate?"

"Well, the clinic might be a broadening-experience kind of thing," she replied. "Plus, I have seventeen years of practice with a psychopath."

"Bear in mind that broadening experiences are often unpleasant."

"Would *you* care to elaborate?"

"On today's menu we had multiple forms of respiratory distress due to lives spent breathing smoke from ox-dung fires," he said. "Three cases of extensive scabies, given Kwell. A probable case of TB."

"TB or not TB?"

"That is the question," he said, and they briefly beamed at each other. "Let's see . . . a kid with complications from measles who's now in the hospital. TB, TB, and TB yet again. Assorted infections, many in the eyes. Two streps, one with a side of staph—patient may die depending on antibiotic-resistance profile. Oh, and I ran over a fresh pile of cow shit on the way home and sprayed it all over my scooter. We don't have a hose, so now it's covered with shit *and* flies."

"Oh," she said.

"And I know we've talked about this, but bear in mind that if you work there, you'll be exposing yourself to some serious microbial risk."

"You do it every day, right?"

"I have to. You don't."

"If you can do it, I can."

He appreciated her grit, but it still worried him. "If I die, at least I won't die young," he said cautiously.

"No, you'll just leave me orphaned at seventeen in a strange country."

"Hmm, good point."

"Whereas if *I* die, you'd ship me home in a box and get on with your life. You can have all the kids you want, but I only get one shot at having a dad."

"Oh, right," he said. "I expect I'd immediately forget all about you and just start happily procreating with the first woman I met."

"Well, why wouldn't you? I would if I were you."

"You two are extremely, upsettingly bizarre," said Devi.

"See?" said Alex. "The girl's got vocabulary."

Peter took a breath; all the cheery banter about mortality was making him uneasy, and he craved some sort of segue. "So *ke cha* with you two, anyway?" he asked.

Alex smirked at Devi. "Multiple forms of intellectual distress due to the nutty way these people speak."

"Hey," said Devi.

"Nepali actually turns out to be pretty straightforward, but Tibetan is unbelievably hard. They end their sentences with verbs, but that's the least of my problems."

"That's for sure," said Devi.

"Hey yourself," said Alex.

Peter watched them and remembered Sangita's remark. They did seem unusually comfortable together for such new friends.

"How do you like the international school, Devi?" he asked.

"It's difficult," she answered. "I like physics and philosophy, though."

"Good combination," said Peter. He sipped his beer. "This Gorkha's pretty good. Have you tried it?"

Alex laughed. "You know we have. I've seen you count the bottles."

"I only count the bottles to know when we need more."

"I certainly believe that, Papaji."

"Your daughter memorized forty more words today," said Devi, in an apparent flanking maneuver. "She is a genius, I think."

"Of course she's a genius, but don't *tell* her so."

Alex air-kissed him. *"Ma teamelai maya garchu,"* she said.

"That better be as nice as it sounds."

"Sure it is, if you allow for sarcasm."

EIGHT

The two of them faced off like boxers sizing each other up in the ring. Alex was taller and still growing, but Mina, though thin, had the contained, intimidating bearing of a lioness poised to defend her territory.

Peter remembered Alex's confrontations with Cheryl, how they'd become more volatile as Alex grew older. A few months previously, for the first time, the long war of nerves had erupted in a physical skirmish. Cheryl slapped Alex, who quickly grabbed both of her mother's wrists, lifted them over her head, and pinned her against the wall. "Let me go!" Cheryl shrieked, and Alex said, "Fuck you," and then Peter, who'd heard the fight start from the other room, broke it up.

After that, Cheryl fell back to ragging on Alex about her bookishness and her appearance, not to mention whatever personal slights from Alex she imagined herself suffering on a given day, but she shrank from open confrontation to a sniping insect whine. Alex just started ignoring her and grew more confident by the week.

Alex looked durable enough there in the clinic, and Peter was proud of her. The kid was a survivor. It was she, in fact, who'd suggested they make a public display of acquiescence to Mina.

"You're to do whatever Mina wants, no questions asked," Peter said now, trying not to sound too theatrical. Mina stood by, her arms folded across her chest, eyeing the two of them skeptically.

"Sure," said Alex.

"Listen and learn. Give selflessly."

"You know me, Dad."

"See, Mina? She's ready."

Mina regarded Alex calmly. "I guess we'll find out, won't we?" she said.

| | |

What really got to her, it turned out, were the children. The fourth case of dysentery that afternoon was a baby with stick limbs and an abdomen like a soccer ball who had an abscessed fistula leading right into his small intestine. His fever was 105, he was leaking liquid shit from a dime-sized hole an inch above his navel, and his mother, of course, had no money for the hospital.

Peter was paying attention to the baby, but he was also keeping an eye on Alex. She had turned pale, and she hovered a few feet back from the table.

"Get me a bag of saline and a line, will you?" Peter said, wanting to keep her busy. She went to the cupboard, looking relieved to have a task that would allow her, even momentarily, to turn away. "While you're there, bring a bag of Rocephin. We'll hang them both."

Mina came in and held the baby while Alex hung the two bags on the IV stand and connected the plastic line. Her hands were shaking. Mina watched her, then looked at Peter.

"Pull off the cap and attach the needle to the end of the line," Peter said, and Alex did. Peter inserted the IV and taped it, then started the drip. They put the child and his mother in a room in the back. He told Mina to assure the woman that they would get the boy to Kanti, the children's hospital, and negotiate something. Mina spoke to her in Nepali and then left. When they were alone, Peter sat Alex down.

"You okay?" he asked.

"Is he going to be all right?"

"With stamina and surgery and luck, he might last the night. He also might not. If he makes it to tomorrow he'll have a better chance."

She looked like a damp sheet trembling on a clothesline. "How often do you see stuff like this?"

"Ten times a day, more or less."

She began to cry. He had had a pretty good idea something like this was going to occur, knowing what he knew of his daughter's sensitivities. Now that it *was* happening, though, he was nursing doubts, but he didn't have time to coddle her.

"I've got to go," he said, handing her some Kleenex. "Try to hang in. We'll talk later." He squeezed her shoulder and headed out to the next catastrophe.

Soon someone from Kanti came and took the child. Alex stayed in the room for a half hour or so, then finally emerged, still ashen, and tried to make herself useful again. When she saw Mina she dipped her head and sidestepped gawkily out of the way, her deference apparently genuine this time. Mina gave Peter a brief smile of understanding.

"She's a good kid," she said quietly, when Alex was out of earshot. "She'll be all right."

Before Peter could respond, she turned away and walked down the hall to her next patient. He watched her go, dumbfounded.

There were a couple of other bad cases that afternoon, and three hours later Alex was silent as they rode home together on the Hero. When Devi met them at the door, Alex took her in her arms and started weeping again. They went upstairs. Peter checked in with Sangita, who said she didn't need any help and waved him away. He poured a glass of wine, went out to the back porch, and sat down in a lawn chair under the jacaranda.

Had he done the right thing? Maybe she had enough on her plate without this. He'd also begun to wonder what went on upstairs between those two, after school and in the evenings. Were these innocent teenage sleepovers or what, exactly? Alex had had two or three boyfriends in junior high and high school, but nothing had ever become serious. Peter had figured this was a result of her dedication to her studies and to basketball, not to mention her guarded and appropriately self-protective response to such matters in general, given that her experience consisted primarily of the wildly dysfunctional relationship between her parents. But now he wondered if he'd drawn the wrong conclusion. He'd had lesbian friends since college, and he knew plenty of mainly straight women who'd experimented when they were young. He wanted to think he could take something like this in stride. Besides, she was seventeen, and more of her affection would naturally be directed to friends than to him—and for that matter, he was glad she *had* a friend.

It was getting past the point where it was really his business, but it still felt like his business. Sangita seemed untroubled, but was this her usual equanimity or just that she was too busy to pay attention? And anyway, how much of this had to do with an unexpected jealousy he'd begun to feel—that Alex had a close relationship and he didn't?

Tiny birds of some kind chirped in the tree. The wine was sweet and oaky and deep, from the Napa Valley. He hadn't even known you could get American wine here. It was unsettling that something from home, experienced in a new place, could begin to seem exotic. As if he himself had changed without knowing it, beginning with the most primitive sense, taste.

He tried to relax. Even if Alex *had* changed majors, it was a surprise but certainly not a catastrophe. Devi seemed like a good kid. At least he could let their relationship unfold under his own roof, a shelter from the bigotry of the bigger world.

He listened. Alex's window was closed, but that didn't completely block the sound. What had been sobbing now seemed to be something else.

Sangita came out. Their eyes met.

"You thinking what I'm thinking?" Peter asked quietly.

She averted her eyes. "Maybe," she replied.

"Do you know when this started?"

"Not sure."

Peter swirled his wine pensively. Silence was uncomfortable, because then they could hear. "I'm fresh out of wisdom. Say something wise."

She looked away, over the trees. "America, this how seeing?" she asked.

"Some people think it's natural, some think it's a sin," he said. "I'm in the 'natural' faction, at least in the abstract. How about here?"

"Nepalis more conservative," she said. "Tibetans . . . mmm . . . not so much care, in general."

"And you? How do you feel about it?"

"You mind?" she asked, looking at his glass. It was a most unservantly request, just the kind of thing he'd learned to like about her. And anyway, it seemed they'd become unofficial in-laws.

"Help yourself," he said, and held it out.

She took it and sipped, watching the sky and apparently savoring the wine. She handed back the glass. "Well, bright side looking," she said, sounding resigned. "Nobody pregnant, hm?"

"If it lasts, it might cut our chances for grandchildren, I suppose," Peter said. Sangita smiled at him warmly, as if she'd been considering the same thing. She turned to go back inside.

He followed her and refilled his glass as she finished fixing dinner. Her husband, Sonam, wasn't feeling well, so she left for home without waiting to eat. Peter thought it was perhaps a convenient exit, but *ke garne*? Soon the girls descended, looking rumpled and somber. They ate quietly, then did the dishes together and adjourned to the living room. Peter sat in the chair, and the girls sprawled on the couch, one at each end with legs intertwined, as had become their habit.

"We should probably talk, Dad."

"Okay," he said nervously. He knew he was going to have to appear calm no matter how he felt.

Alex crossed her arms, apparently pondering how to put it. "Will you think I'm a wimp if I don't come back to the clinic?"

This was what she wanted to discuss? He had to fall back and gather his wits. He almost laughed. "No," he said, at last.

"Are you sure?"

"Yeah, I'm sure," he said. "But, um, I think you *should* come back."

"Why?"

"Because Mina will definitely think you're a wimp."

She considered this. "Since when do you care what Mina thinks?"

The question caught him off guard. "Since she got to say whether you stay or go, I guess."

"Who is Mina?" Devi asked.

"Sooner or later you'll get to meet her," Alex said. "You can decide for yourself who she is."

Devi grinned. "Oh, you mean the psychopath?"

"That's not quite how I'd describe her, actually."

"Come on," said Peter, trying to recover his poise. "You're giving her too much credit." But this felt false, even as it passed his lips.

Alex just eyed him. "Dad, Dad, Dad," she said.

NINE

"Franz is doing this to torment us, just to show who's boss," Mina said. "You don't need my halting, half-baked Tibetan when you have your little Devi along to translate for you."

She had recovered her usual prickly demeanor, and Peter found her mercurial changes increasingly hard to navigate. If a river was frozen, you knew how to cross it; if it was warm and flowing easily, you knew how to cross it. If it went back and forth by the hour, you had trouble on your hands.

"I wouldn't call her little," said Peter. "She's taller than you."

The girls snarfled with laughter in the backseat. Peter suspected he knew why they were laughing—they were reading something into this testy exchange—but he was fairly certain they were wrong.

They headed out of town in a borrowed jeep, north on Maharajganj, past Ring Road, through the shantytowns, then up into terraced rice fields and villages. From there they wound their way up a mountain; in places the road was barely wider than the jeep and was littered with rocks as big as grapefruit, which tilted them violently from side to side. Mina drove, sitting on the right, and Alex sat behind her, hanging on to the roll cage for dear life. Every time a big rock tipped them toward the edge she got an inspiring view of a five-hundred-foot vertical drop. Her fingers were white from gripping the steel bar.

Peter hadn't been in territory this rough for a long time, and old habits quickly resurfaced. He began to scan the rock faces, looking for interesting routes up them. In Yosemite or Smith Rock he would have seen little chalk blotches on the cliffs, revealing the passage of other climbers. Here there was nothing but pristine granite. A shiver went down him as he remembered the day he'd quit climbing, the terror he'd felt. His palms began to sweat. He looked away from the cliffs to try to redirect his thoughts.

They entered a high mountain valley where the road leveled off and followed a stream. Peter figured they were up at about seven thousand feet. He felt pleased that he would actually get to ply his trade as a cardiologist for a change, though he was nervous about the patient, a Tibetan lama with heart trouble. Peter didn't know much about lamas, but Devi had warned him that the old man had a formidable reputation; she'd heard about him for years but had never seen him, since he rarely ventured from his monastery. She was excited but also apprehensive at the prospect of meeting him.

"Hey, Tibetan chick," said Alex, between clenched teeth. "You digging this?"

"I am *so* getting in touch with my roots," said Devi, but there were jitters behind her flippancy.

The jeep crabbed up a steep, muddy grade and bounced over a crest; then suddenly they were on top of the ridge. Mina braked, and they came to a halt by a small iron gate. Beyond it stood a cluster of low, square, whitewashed dwellings. Several monks in burgundy robes walked about or sat together, talking. Farther up the hill a bigger building perched on the highest part of the ridge, alight in the late-morning sun. A monk approached, waving, and opened the gate.

"*Tashi delek!*" he called.

"*Tashi delek,* Lobsang," said Mina. She jumped from the car and gave him a hug. Peter was astonished to see her so affectionate. He found himself wondering what the monk had that he didn't, and the answer came to him immediately: *vows.*

Mina gestured at Peter and the girls. "I've brought fresh meat for the lion."

"Ah, good!" said the monk, looking them over. "Lion very hungry!" He laughed as he sized up the dusty, rattled occupants of the jeep. He was about thirty, broad-shouldered, and wore a red *tzen* thrown over his left shoulder and a matching monk's skirt. His brown, callused feet were slipped into rubber flip-flops. He had just a little stubble of black hair, along with a couple of razor cuts in his scalp from the last time his head had been shaved. He was almost alarmingly good-humored.

He came over to Peter's side of the jeep. "You doctor?"

"Yes, I'm Peter," he said, and they shook hands. "This is my daughter, Alex, and her friend, Devi."

"Hi," said Alex.

"*Tashi delek,*" said Devi, attentive and respectful.

"Oh—you Tibetan?" asked Lobsang.

Devi nodded and smiled. There followed a brief, animated conversation, during which he took both her hands in his and they gazed at each other like old friends. They spoke quickly, through grins, seeming always on the point of laughter.

"You getting any of this?" Peter asked Alex.

"Not a word." She sounded irritated.

Lobsang mussed up Devi's hair as if she were his kid sister; she narrowed her eyes teasingly and said something that sounded vaguely cutting, and he jumped back, mouth wide open, fists on his hips in mock indignation. They both laughed again, and Lobsang waved her off, then came around and hopped up on the front of the jeep. Mina got back in and hit the gas. They sallied forward, bouncing up a rutted, muddy track to the base of a stone walkway that led to the main monastery building. When Mina braked, Lobsang slid off the hood right onto his feet, as if they'd done this a dozen times.

| | |

On the top floor, Lobsang opened the heavy wooden door and let them into the lama's quarters. To their right, through a row of windows, the Kathmandu Valley spread out below as cloud shadows drifted over the city and outlying farms. The windows on the other side of the room revealed the jagged ridges of the Himalayas to the north, great plumes of snow blowing off their summits.

Lama Padma sat opposite them, cross-legged, on a cushioned wooden platform with an ornate backrest. A small table in front of him held a vase with a handle and a spout, topped with peacock feathers, as well as a two-sided wooden hand drum with skin heads, a bell and its companion implement called a *dorje,* and a tall red ceramic tea mug with a lid.

The lama nodded to his visitors and smiled. *"Tashi delek,"* he said.

He was about sixty, his face etched with laugh lines. He was sun-baked and bald on top, with a wide band of close-cropped white hair around the outside of his head. He wore the same kind of red *tzen* as Lobsang, over a gold sleeveless shirt. He didn't look nearly as scary as Peter had feared; in fact, his eyes were kind and humorous, though he clearly wasn't well.

Peter looked around. The place was in serious disrepair. Jagged cracks laced the walls like veins, and a couple of small saucepans stood on the worn plank floor to catch leaking rainwater. *Thangkas,* paintings of deities, festooned the walls, and to the left of the door stood an elaborate, terraced shrine on which rested bronze deity statues, a long row of water bowls, a couple of vases of wildflowers, and dozens of butter lamps. The small golden flames shifted in the draft from the open door, as if a flock of tiny finches had suddenly changed direction in the sky. Lobsang shut the door, and the flames returned to rest on their wicks. Incense drifted up from an intricately carved box and formed a layer of whitish smoke just below the ceiling. It smelled of juniper.

Lobsang poured the lama fresh tea from a pot, then sat down quietly on a small rug to the left of the platform.

Mina approached Lama Padma and bent low, as apparently was the custom, offering a long white silk scarf, a *katak*. He smiled, took it from her, and draped it around her neck. Devi pulled a *katak* out of her pocket and did the same. As Lama Padma was putting the scarf around her neck, Lobsang said something quietly to him, and the lama's eyes lit up. He and Devi spoke together in Tibetan for a few moments, then he smiled and put his hand on her head.

They all sat on a long rug on the floor in front of the lama while Lobsang brought them tea. Peter started with the usual questions as Devi translated. The lama said that for two or three years he had had discomfort in his chest, under the sternum, as well as in the left arm and jaw. The pain was sometimes more intense with exercise and seemed to be getting worse. Lately he'd been short of breath.

"He ignore, always," said Lobsang. "To get him to see doctor, we must beat him with stick." He playfully mimed whacking the lama, and they both chuckled.

Peter watched their interactions, their easy fondness with each other, and felt himself begin to relax. The smell of the incense, the soft light coming through the windows, and the cool, fresh air all seemed to permeate his body and settle him down in some palpable way.

"Does he feel weak?" he asked.

Devi spoke to the lama, who replied softly. "Yes," she said.

"Any swelling in his feet or ankles?"

"Sometimes."

"How does he spend his days?"

When he heard the question, Lama Padma smiled.

"Sitting," Devi said. "He says meditating is his job, that is why they pay him the big bucks."

Mina laughed. Peter glanced at her; she too seemed more at ease. The stern glare had left her eyes, which looked softer and somehow larger.

"How many hours a day does he meditate?" Peter asked.

"He says eighteen or nineteen."

Peter looked at Mina in disbelief. She just nodded.

"So if you add eating and sleeping and walking in the evening, he gets how much sleep a night?"

"About three hours," Devi said. "Sometimes two."

Peter tried to understand how this could be possible. The only patients he'd ever had who slept so little were clinically depressed, which was obviously not the case here.

He turned to Mina and spoke quietly. "Angina, don't you think?" She nodded again. "Has Franz ever done any bloodwork?"

"Last year he took a sample, but the vacutainer broke on the way down the mountain and we were in a hailstorm, so we had to let it go."

"Is it all right if I examine him?" Peter asked.

Devi asked and the lama nodded, his eyes bright. Peter put on his stethoscope and checked Lama Padma's carotid arteries, then listened to his heart and lungs. He thought he heard a murmur, maybe a little click or mitral valve noise. Usually this was nothing; sometimes it was worth paying attention to.

"Did he ever have rheumatic fever as a kid?"

Devi spoke to him. The lama replied, seeming somber now. "He says he doesn't know," Devi said. "When he was growing up, most children had fevers, and many died. He lost a brother and a sister to measles, but the other diseases were not called by any names that he remembers."

Peter noticed that the lama's nails and lips had a bluish tint. "What does he eat?" he asked.

"Mainly *tsampa*, roasted barley flour mixed with hot water and butter. Some tea. Rice, sometimes, also with butter. Lamb, when it's available."

"He likes butter, I take it."

Devi didn't bother to translate. "All Tibetans like butter," she said.

"Is it all right if we do some tests?" Peter asked.

The lama nodded. Mina drew blood, and Peter hooked up the portable EKG they'd brought, which confirmed his impressions. He told the lama he probably had atherosclerosis and heart disease, and that he'd most likely had rheumatic fever as a child, which had damaged his mitral valve.

"If you come down to the valley we can arrange an echocardiogram," Peter said. "We may want to put stents in your arteries and repair the valve. Is that something you'd consider?"

When the lama heard the translation of this, he smiled.

"He says he very much wants to help you do your best, that he can see this is important to you and he appreciates it," Devi said. "But his commitment is to stay here and practice."

Mina seemed unsurprised, but Peter felt frustrated. Why had he come all this way if no one was going to take his advice?

"Unless he's willing to exercise more, he may progress to heart failure within a couple of years," Peter said. "And he should probably cut down on the butter."

Devi spoke with the lama, and he looked thoughtful for a few moments before replying.

"Lama Padma says please do not be upset," Devi said. "He says he will try to walk more."

Peter was used to patients disregarding his recommendations out of fear or carelessness, but this was new terrain. He didn't completely understand, but he couldn't deny the lama's presence and evident kindness. He felt chagrined at his frustration.

"Tell him I'm sorry," he said quietly. "I just want to get him well."

Devi spoke to the lama, and he answered. "He appreciates this," she replied. "He says he will even try to cut back on his butter, but that the whole monastery will have to pray if he is going to accomplish such a great challenge."

With that, Lama Padma and Lobsang began to laugh again.

Peter looked at Mina; she shrugged, and her expression said, *Ke garne?*

Lama Padma spoke to Devi, then. She turned to Peter again. "He wonders if you know anything about Western science."

He was surprised by the question. "Biology, mainly," he said. "That was my undergrad degree, and I try to keep up. Why?"

"He'd like it if you would think about corresponding with him," she said. "He enjoys what he's learned of this, and he'd consider it a favor."

"I'm really an amateur," Peter said. "But sure, of course."

Devi spoke to Lama Padma and smiled at his response. "He says he is an amateur at meditation too," she said. "That's why he has to practice so much."

Lama Padma and Lobsang laughed again, and once more Peter felt the calm of the place settle into him. An uncanny radiance suffused the room, as if even the light held secrets. Peter's eyes went to the window, to the sky outside, and in that moment he felt that he had been lifted right through the glass and into the open air. It was a dizzying and exhilarating sensation, as if the boundaries of his mind had expanded to encompass part of the sky. When he looked back at Lama Padma, the lama was watching him intently, a coy smile on his lips, his eyes dancing with delight.

Lama Padma spoke gently to Devi, who blanched a little and glanced at Alex.

"What is it?" Alex asked.

"He wants all of us to have his blessing before we leave," Devi said. "He thinks that soon some karma purification is coming for everyone in the room."

"Oh, no," muttered Mina.

Peter looked at her. He had come back through the window, back into himself, but he still felt a little giddy, as if nothing could really be unpleasant. "What's wrong?" he asked. "Isn't that a good thing?"

She looked at him, frank dread in her eyes. "Long-term, yes," she said. "Short-term, get ready for things to hit the fan."

TEN

Two days later Peter awakened at 2:00 A.M., curled into a fetal position with excruciating abdominal cramps. His gut made noises that sounded like a trapped badger going bonkers in a trash can—something he had actually heard once, as a kid at summer camp, and had forgotten about until now. He sprinted down the hall to the bathroom and burst in on Alex, who was crouched miserably on the toilet in her nightshirt. He backed out, and they spent the night taking turns.

They barely made it to the clinic the next morning, where Mina herded them into a room, looked them over, and said, "Tch." Peter didn't like putting himself at her mercy, but he didn't know what else to do. Alex lay down on the exam table, and Peter slumped in the chair. "Any suggestions?" he asked weakly.

Mina smiled, just slightly. "You could take advantage of this wonderful opportunity to develop compassion for the plight of your patients," she said.

Alex and Peter looked at each other and had a brief moment of telepathy, in which they both understood that they were too debilitated to kill her.

"Or we could go over to the hospital and leave samples for the lab," he said.

"The treatment is going to be the same regardless of what you've got," said Mina.

"Flagyl, I suppose."

"What is it?" asked Alex.

"A miraculous medicine that will make you feel much better," said Mina.

"By killing every living thing between your mouth and your butt, including a bunch of stuff that's good for you," Peter added. "You'll feel like you have the worst flu in history, but you'll feel better than you do right now."

"We'll get you some yogurt to take with it, and you'll be fine," Mina said. "Now, if you can get up, we have patients who are, believe it or not, sicker than you are."

| | |

That evening Sangita and Devi came over to tend to them. Devi went upstairs to be with Alex while Peter sat up on the couch.

"All foreigners, this happen." Sangita clucked sympathetically, handing him a cup of mint tea.

Peter sipped gratefully. He'd already had the first dose of Flagyl and was too nauseated to eat. Sangita sat in one of the chairs and blew on her own tea to cool it. She sipped it, set it aside, and took out her knitting. He'd never seen her knit before—possibly because she never sat still long enough.

He'd been wanting to ask about her son, but it always seemed too awkward. It bothered him that he was so little acquainted with the details of her life, partly because she knew much more about him and Alex, and the imbalance of this emphasized her status as a servant and irked him. He liked to believe that such things could be more or less egalitarian—you're working for me today, maybe I'll work for you tomorrow—but he knew this was a bullshit rationalization to assuage his conscience, because in fact he would never find himself working for her. All of which was, of course, further complicated by the relationship between their daughters.

What struck him, though, was that Sangita accepted the situation as she accepted everything, with a shrug and a *"ke garne?"* and a rueful laugh at the great jokes the universe played on people. For her part, Alex viewed Sangita as a motherly figure who happened to take a little money for her mothering, and who was in any case the mother of her lover. Devi was harder to read; Peter sensed fire in her, a temper and a keen sense of justice. As a result, he felt more comfortable with her, since they were basically two sides of the same coin. Sangita, Peter thought, would scoff at such high-minded concerns. They didn't make her life any easier, and anything that failed in that regard was by her definition a waste of time. Peter thought he understood why they all functioned so well as a kind of wacked clan.

Not that this delivered him from the anxiety the master feels in the presence of the servant he senses is his superior. Knowledge, the great leveler, offered one way out of this angst.

"Franz told me you were Tibetan," he said, looking for a casual way into the questions he wanted to ask. "How did you end up here?"

She waved her hand. "Story very boring."

He doubted it. Her general amiability to the contrary, underneath she was one of the most private people he had ever met, and he briefly recalled Franz's dismissal of his questions, saying that Sangita would tell him about herself if she chose. Peter didn't want to press her, but her reticence just provoked his curiosity further.

"I've got nothing better to do," he said. "I'm just sitting here, trying to get my gut working again."

She leveled a keen, evaluative gaze at him, then glanced upstairs, as if to be careful she wasn't overheard. "This many years ago, when Devi very young," she said quietly.

"You came over the mountains?" Peter asked. She nodded but seemed hesitant to continue. "It was bad in Tibet, under the Chinese?"

She looked at him as if he'd just asked whether the sky was blue. "My parents, killed," she said. "Older brother, a monk, they put in prison. My sister, they take her to police station and rape her, many times."

"Jesus." Suddenly Peter felt idiotic for opening this can of worms, but now it was open and there was no way to seal it up again. If he felt embarrassed or enraged or sickened, her frankness said, he'd asked for it.

"When my younger brother go for her, he get angry and shout at them. They take him behind that place and shoot him. The monasteries, they tear them all down, everything burn." Her face was flushed. She set her knitting in her lap and picked up her teacup. It shook a little in her hand.

Peter felt ashamed at his own ignorance. "You don't have to tell me if you don't want to," he said.

But the fuse was lit, and it looked as if it was going to burn right down to the charge. Sangita's whole being had transformed from her usual placid politeness into seething indignation, and Peter knew he'd misjudged her. She was more like Devi than he'd realized. Her body tensed, and her voice took on an acerbic edge. "When we come to Nepal, Sonam and I working in tea shop in Tamang, to north," she said. "We stay four years, then the owner, he sick becoming. He give shop to us, we rooms adding, put in kitchen, some trekkers then come. Everything pretty fair okay."

"Good for you," said Peter.

"Then one day these people come; I don't know word in English. . . . " She gestured as though she were carrying a rifle.

"Guerrillas?"

"Yes," she said. "Maoists. Time to time, they come to village and take money and food. Not ask, just take. Then one day my son taking too."

"They conscripted your son?"

She nodded. She set down the teacup but didn't pick up the knitting. She interlaced her fingers, then pulled them apart again and placed her hands, palms down, on her knees. "I go find leader and tell him give my son back. He laugh. He say he doing this for *my* benefit. I proletariat!"

"What did you do?"

Her right hand shot up and tucked a stray lock of hair behind her ear. "I not very polite then. I say to this man—I charity needing not, just only my son. Then they come and take tea shop, throw us all out. We Kathmandu coming."

"How long ago was this?" Peter asked.

"Six years. Devi still very angry, so I not much say."

"I don't understand why you pretend to be Nepali, though."

Her hands still shook as she picked up her knitting again. "I Tibetan," she said. "But here I speak Nepali, I know customs." She pointed to the small red dot on her forehead. "I wear *bindi*. I took Nepali name and gave daughter one as well, though Sonam this much will not do."

"But why?" Peter asked.

Tears brimmed in her eyes. "I afraid if Communists take over Nepal they will rape Devi like my sister, they will shoot us just like Chinese did."

ELEVEN

A slender girl of about fifteen was sitting on the exam table when Peter walked in. Mina was engaged in a heated discussion in Nepali with a middle-aged man who appeared to be the girl's father.

"What's the problem?" Peter asked.

"He wants to stay while we examine her."

"Why's she here?"

"Female trouble of some kind."

"Out he goes. Tell him."

The man chimed in with a deep, resonant voice. "I speak some English, Doctor," he said. "I will not leave her alone with a strange man; it is not proper in my culture. I realize you Americans may not understand, but—"

Peter interrupted him. "Mr.—"

"Bahadur."

"Mr. Bahadur, Mina will be here during the exam."

"Yes, yes, she told me this. I'm sorry, but still it is not acceptable."

"You've brought in your other daughters over the years," Mina said. "You never insisted on staying before."

Bahadur was a large man with a thick black beard and a potbelly, and he wore a traditional Nepali tunic with a Western sport coat over it. He shifted his weight from foot to foot and seemed agile, as if well oiled. His big hands moved fluidly in front of him in motions that suggested bargaining, or perhaps the deflection of blows. He shrugged as his eyes shifted between Peter and Mina.

"Before, the girls were always examined by nurses," he said. "It was not an issue."

"It's not an issue now," said Mina.

"I believe it is," replied Bahadur.

Peter and Mina exchanged a look of consternation. The girl sat on the exam table, watching with canny dark eyes, her hands beside her and her expression inscrutable. Her legs were crossed at the ankles; a little copper bracelet just above her left foot gleamed dully against her cinnamon skin. Her eyes moved from Peter to Mina to Bahadur like translucent black stones, wary and alert.

"I understand your concern," Peter said, even though he didn't really understand it. "But I will not even ask this girl the color of her hair with you in the room."

Bahadur smiled, just a bit sarcastically. "Surely, Doctor, you can *see* the color of her hair."

Peter shifted his weight to the balls of his feet, poised. Bahadur took a small step back.

"One of two things is going to happen now," Peter said. "You'll leave so we can examine her, or you'll take her to some other clinic."

"Now look—" said Bahadur, but Mina cut him off.

"You will not take me seriously because I am a woman," she said. She nodded toward Peter. "Maybe you will take *him* seriously, hm?"

Bahadur looked at the girl again, then shrugged in concession. "All right," he said reluctantly. "I only meant to be of assistance. Please come get me if I can answer any questions."

He strolled out of the room, head high with preposterous dignity. Peter left Mina with the girl and went to find Franz, who was in his office.

"Ah, Mr. Bahadur," Franz said. "The man who shoots only X's."

"How many daughters does he *have*?"

"Let me pull the charts." Franz went to the *B* cabinet and pushed away the thick tendrils of the plant that sat atop it, then rooted until he produced a stack of manila folders. He looked through them. "God, you do ask the right questions, don't you?"

"Let's hear it."

"Eight counting the one you've got now," said Franz. "I suppose it's possible, if his wife is strong."

Peter took the charts and looked through them. "Three or four of these birthdays are within six months of each other," he pointed out.

Franz looked at the folders and grunted. "I doubt she's *that* strong," he said. He threw the charts on his desk. "*Scheisse*," he said. "He's a *zuhälter*."

"A zoo what?"

"Procurer. Whoremonger."

Peter leaned against the desk. "What do we do? What are the laws?"

"They are ambiguous, unfortunately," Franz said. "I think it is technically all right for a woman to sell herself if she chooses, but no one else may take any of the money."

"She's about fifteen," Peter said.

Franz sighed. "Even *that's* complicated here because girls are often considered grown up at puberty." He pulled a pencil from his pocket and drummed the eraser against his desk. "This is probably some country girl he bought from her parents. The police don't care much for this kind of thing, especially if Bahadur pays them off, which I assume he does."

"Agencies?"

"Long backlog."

"Any ideas?"

"Let me think about it."

Peter went back to the exam room and told Mina.

"This is the *eighth*?" she said. "I should have noticed. Damn it."

"You see thirty patients a day, all week, all year," Peter said. "He brought them in one at a time, not in a herd, and a couple of times his wife brought them. It was mostly mundane stuff, anyway, like eye infections and strep."

"I still should have caught it. There's no excuse."

"Mina, you didn't even see half of them. There were other initials on some of the charts."

She turned to him. "You noticed whose *initials* were on the charts?" she asked, looking at him a little strangely.

He nodded.

Mina's voice became uncharacteristically soft. "What do you want to do?" she asked. She sounded surprisingly conciliatory. The girl leaned forward on her arms and watched them intently.

"We probably ought to start with an exam and see if we can figure out what's going on," Peter said.

Mina nodded. "She's complaining of pain and itching," she said. "There's some bleeding too, but apparently it isn't menstrual."

"Explain to her that I'll need to have a look but that you'll be right here and no one's going to hurt her."

Mina spoke to the girl, who shrugged as if she couldn't care less what happened. That little casual lift of her shoulders chilled Peter more than anything he'd heard about her so far.

The girl's vulva was red and swollen. She had active herpes lesions and a thick, foul-smelling discharge that suggested chlamydia, gonorrhea, or possibly some combination of both.

"No wonder Bahadur was nervous," Peter said. "We're not talking about a little sore throat here."

"He thought you'd catch on but I wouldn't?" Mina asked. "Jesus."

"Has she had a fever?"

Mina spoke to the girl and said yes.

"She must be miserable," Peter said.

"What's a little more agony to a girl like this?" Mina said, then sat down by the exam table. "God, I'm sorry, I didn't mean that."

"It's okay," Peter said. He'd never heard her apologize. He rolled his stool away from the foot of the table and stood up.

"Let's get her antibiotics, something wide-spectrum," he said. "Famvir for her herpes—do we have any Famvir?"

"Yes."

"And she should probably have an HIV test."

"Did you see if she had warts on her cervix?" Mina asked. "There's a lot of that too."

"I didn't see anything, but you should check if you want to."

"No," said Mina. "I'll take your word for it."

Peter realized the girl had been lying there without a flinch or a question the whole time he'd had the speculum inside her and while they'd been talking. She didn't react in any way; in fact, she was absently biting her thumbnail, as if completely disconnected from anything that happened to her below the waist.

Part of what followed was predictable. They had her get dressed and called the police. The cops took Bahadur away with them, amid much of what Franz called *sturm und drang*. Bahadur shouted threats both subtle and explicit: He would be back; he would cause great bodily harm to everyone involved; he would put the clinic out of business. Franz, Peter, and Mina watched him go from the front doorway. Just as the cops put him into their car, Mina suddenly waved goodbye—festively, with a big, cartoony smile—which turned Bahadur crimson with indignation and made Peter laugh. They went back inside and explained to the girl what would happen next.

This led to the part Peter had not foreseen. When they told her that Bahadur would never bother her again, that they would send her to a place where she would be cared for, the girl began to cry. Her tears were not of relief or joy but of fury. She screeched and struck out with her fingernails and tried to bite Mina. Peter grabbed her from behind and pinned her arms while she kicked at them. After a few minutes, she wore herself out and quit struggling, and he was able to let her go.

The girl sat in the chair, looking at the floor, wiping away the last of her tears and speaking in Nepali.

"She says Bahadur was the only man who was ever kind to her, who gave her enough to eat and kept her clean," Mina said. "She knows two girls who were sent to orphanages, and they both hanged themselves there. She said orphanages are where girls like her go to die."

"Tell her we're sending her to some people who'll try to get her into school," Peter said. He had only the vaguest sense of what such places were like, but it was crucial to get her away from Bahadur. "Tell her she can also go back to her family if she wants."

When the girl heard the translation of this she looked at Peter, spat, and launched into another angry soliloquy.

"She says why should she go home to the people who sold her in the first place?" Mina said. "They worked her half to death, and she never wants to see them again. As for school, she knows about these organizations. They promise, but most of the time they don't deliver, and you end up living in bunk beds in a freezing dormitory with fifty other girls. She wants to go back to Bahadur, where she has her own room and an electric heater."

"Tell her if she doesn't have HIV already, she'll have it soon, and that she won't be able to afford the drugs. It's a death sentence. I'm sorry."

The girl spoke again, but Mina just turned away.

"What did she say?" Peter asked.

"Nothing."

"You can tell me."

Mina looked at him with tired eyes. "She says, 'Fuck you, American doctor.'" The girl spoke again, and Mina smiled, just slightly. "She says she hopes your cock rots."

Peter turned to the window. "Is it true, what she says about these places?" he asked. "Are they that bad?"

"Some are better than others, but none of them are great."

To the east, a dozen ravens spiraled in a thermal as he watched. "You know that karma purification Lama Padma mentioned?"

"What about it?"

"I'm wondering if maybe it's finished now."

Mina sighed. "I hate to tell you, but I have a feeling you've just made a very worthy adversary," she said. "This may be just the beginning."

TWELVE

Devi led them on an expedition, the nature of which she would not disclose. It was the festival of Dasain, when thousands of animals—mainly chickens and goats—were herded into the temples of the Hindu goddess Durga and sacrificed, slaughtered with the ubiquitous Nepali *khukuri* knives.

A half hour after leaving the house, Peter and Alex found themselves ankle-deep in gore outside one of the temples. Lungs and livers and shiny serpentine intestines, all laced with crimson veins, littered the blood-soaked ground, and an assortment of amputated goat legs lay intertwined. Over by the temple, compact, muscular men skinned and butchered the carcasses with businesslike efficiency. The air reeked of thick, drying blood, a smell so viscous Peter could taste it deep in the back of his throat. Swirling, iridescent clouds of flies filled the air.

"As surprises go, I'm not liking this one very much," said Alex, who was slightly green.

"Just wait," Devi replied.

"I thought you were a Buddhist. You want to *sacrifice* something?"

Devi had spotted a young, pretty goat. She went over to the owner and started bargaining. Peter and Alex hung back, not wanting to spoil the haggle, because if the seller knew American money was available, the price would quintuple.

Alex leaned into her father, but he was a little woozy himself.

"You and your goddamn wall map," she said.

"You threw the fucking dart."

In one way, he reflected, it made sense to placate death by offering life, feeding the beast so it wouldn't come after you. Sacrifice was as old as humanity, or at least as old as religion, and these people were models of gentility compared to, say, the Aztecs. But that didn't make it any less brutal. Just when he was starting to feel a bit more at ease in Nepal, to sense how to navigate and function, the situation jolted him into outsider status again. He looked around, wondering how long this would take.

Soon Devi handed the man a wad of rupees, then tied a rope around the goat's neck and pulled it over to them. The goat was panicked; its eyes darted back and forth, and its legs shook.

"Come on," Devi said. "Let's get out of here."

She led the goat away from the killing ground, and Peter and Alex followed. People were collecting rich, dark blood and splattering it on cars and buses, even bicycles, for good luck. The goat shivered with fear until they put some distance between themselves and the temple.

"My father is still sick," Devi said at last. "It's good to save the life of an animal to remove such obstacles."

"You have a place for it at home?" Alex asked. Devi just looked at her.

"Oh, no," said Peter. "No, no, no. Our yard is too small, and I don't want goat shit everywhere."

Alex looped her arm through his and put her head on his shoulder. "What a generous man you are," she said. "So kind and accommodating."

"Also too smart for this crap," he said. "Don't forget that part."

"Of course," said Alex. "Of course you are."

| | |

"Look at how she smiles," said Alex, as she brushed the goat in the backyard.

"Goats always smile," said Peter, unenthusiastically watching the hair pile up. "It's an anatomical accident, not an expression of mirth."

"What will we call it?" asked Devi.

"We'll call it Dad," said Alex.

"There's only room for one goat named Dad in the house," said Peter.

"How about George Bush?" offered Devi.

"There's a name I want to hear fifty times a day. Third try's the charm, ladies."

Alex thought about it, then looked at her father and grinned. "It's obvious, it's perfect," she said. "Wayne Lee."

Oh, yeah, Peter thought—*this* is going to fly. "Are you forgetting she's a girl?"

"It's not like she'll know."

Peter did his best to think of the possible advantages of naming a little nanny goat after the giant meth-head biker who'd run off with his wife, but he couldn't come up with any. While he was pondering, the decision was made for him.

"Come on, Wayne Lee," said Alex, rubbing the goat's neck. "Let's feed you some nice rotten cabbage from the compost bin." Wayne Lee smiled up at her with what seemed marvelous ungulate gratitude.

Well, Peter realized, they *would* be feeding her a ton of garbage that would ordinarily have gone to compost and helped stink up the yard. And of course from a psychological point of view, it offered Alex the chance to literally domesticate one of the great demon-fears of her childhood.

The whole idea was actually pretty twisted, which was what finally won him over.

| | |

The next day Peter came into the yard and found Alex and Wayne Lee facing each other.

"You trying to prove you're more stubborn than a goat?" Peter asked. "I could have told you that."

Alex had planted her feet and was leaning in, pushing on Wayne Lee's forehead; Wayne Lee was pushing back. It was goat versus goat, and no one was budging. Devi was lounging in the sun in a T-shirt and shorts, reading a Bollywood fan magazine. Peter asked her how long this had been going on; she checked her watch.

"Thirty-five minutes," she said.

"You seriously think you'll outlast her, Alex?"

"I guess we'll see."

"Butting is what goats do for a *living*, honey. She's a professional; she's an athlete. She has a contract with Nike, and they're going to brand a little swoosh on her flank."

"Nobody is gonna brand my little baby Wayne Lee, are they, baby darling?" Alex said, making goo-goo noises. Wayne Lee stood unmoved, pushing back and smiling her little goat smile.

"Drill her on some vocab, at least, Devi. She needs it for the clinic. I want to hear body parts."

"Head," said Devi.

"*Tauuko,*" replied Alex.

"Nose, lips, hair."

"*Nak, othaa, kapaal.*"

Peter was on his way inside.

"Legs, feet, fingers, hand, stomach."

"*Khuttaa, paitala, aula, haath, peta.*"

When he was safely out of sight and almost out of earshot he was pretty sure he heard, "Clit, pussy, tits, cunt," then Alex collapsing in laughter.

| | |

He was confused about too many things. There was the situation with Alex and Devi. There was the situation with Mina. There was the question of whether he could really do any good in Nepal, for his patients or his daughter or anyone else. He wanted another grown-up to talk to about it all, and he didn't know who that person might be.

Lama Padma had expressed an interest in Western science and had asked Peter to write him about it. It occurred to him that the lama might be able to shed a little light on his own problems, and that the correspondence could be a way to open that door.

But although he was glad for the old man's informality and good humor, he didn't know how honest he could be about his own views without offending him. Nor, for that matter, was he sure how candid he could be about the personal issues; for one thing, Devi would be translating the letters.

Even so, it was an intriguing opportunity. If the lama was annoyed, he figured, they didn't have to continue.

Dear Lama Padma,

I'm glad you wanted to correspond, though I have to preface this by saying that I'm often too frank for people's liking. I guess I'll just apologize in advance, because I don't often have a very good feel for when I'm stepping over the line.

Regarding your desire to examine science in the context of Buddhist thought, I might as well tell you I don't have a lot of faith in anything that could be called a benevolent God. On a weekly basis, here in Nepal, I see babies scalded by tipped cooking pots; whole families burned when an errant spark from the fire drifts into the tinderbox; children who are sex slaves, who have AIDS by age twelve, who will be dead by fifteen. Anyone who believes in an all-powerful God must also believe he is a murderous, sociopathic monster, because what other conclusion can you draw? The only dodge is to say he's not all-powerful, in which case he's no longer God. You didn't ask my opinion, but you may as well know who you're dealing with.

In any case, as I said, when it comes to science I mainly know about biology, and you can't understand biology without understanding evolution, which is about mutation and natural selection. Mutation is the engine and happens all the time, from viruses to elephants; it's why people need a different flu shot every year (and why people who deny evolution, but get flu shots anyway, are hypocrites).

As for natural selection, I'll give you an example. A few years ago a fishing boat sank a couple of miles off Iceland. The water was frigid, the crew didn't have a raft, and only one guy made it to shore. Some scientists in Reykjavík were curious why he survived when the others didn't, and they found that he had a freak mutation—an extra layer of fat, kind of like blubber, under his skin. It wasn't that thick, but it was enough.

This is evolution in action; you have five guys who won't be having any more children, and one who can still have as many as his wife agrees to, once he warms up a little. So through the generations there are more and more people with this extra fat on their bodies. It doesn't make them stronger or more intelligent or better people—it just makes them more *fit* for that environment.

The situation is complicated in humans, though, because a lot of our evolution has consisted of adapting to one another, and certain traits may be more successful simply because they are attractive to the opposite sex. In the extreme view, we're little more than host vehicles for our DNA, and our emotions exist largely to manipulate us into behaviors that ensure our survival and that of our offspring.

As such, it's hard to conclude that there is any moral or spiritual basis for existence. I'm troubled by this, I'll admit. It's not that you become cold and unemotional, it's just that you start to see emotions for what they really are, and it's depressing. I'd be interested in knowing what you think about this.

—Peter

THIRTEEN

"I don't think I love her because she's a woman, exactly," Alex said. "I love her because she's *Devi*. I think I'd love her just as much if she were a guy."

"I understand that, I think," Peter said.

Devi had gone home with Sangita after dinner, so Peter and Alex had leashed up Wayne Lee and taken her for a walk through a nearby neighborhood.

"What do you love about her?"

"All the obvious stuff," she said. "She's smart, she's funny, she's incredibly tough. I thought *I* was an athlete, but we've been taking hikes in the foothills after she gets off school, and she puts me to shame."

"Well, honey, she's *Tibetan*."

"Even so, it's humbling, and I don't like humbling," she said. "What's so special about Tibetans, anyway?"

"They've got hemoglobin levels and a whole oxygen-delivery system that's miles beyond ours. Vertical miles, literally."

"She once said she has a mountain heart," Alex reflected. "I don't think she was talking about physiology, though."

The evening was cool. Windows turned orange in houses and apartments as lights came on inside. A big 747 drifted in over the valley, on final approach, its lights blinking red and white. The roar of its engines echoed back and forth between the hills, growing loud, then soft, then loud again, like ocean waves swirling and chuffing between cliffs.

"That is the weirdest thing," said Alex.

"What?"

"Two or three months ago I would have felt like the plane was normal and the goat was weird. Somewhere along the line I switched sides."

Peter knew what she meant. He was now able to spot other Americans a block away, and not by their clothes, because Canadians and Brits and Australians dressed pretty much the same way. (The Germans he could always tell because they had a peculiar habit of wearing shorts and sandals with dark socks, and sometimes even knee socks.) But a lot of the Americans looked kind of dead in the eyes. They would walk the streets purposefully, their wallets poised, buying brass trinkets and folk art and often seeming to genuinely experience nothing. It made Peter uncomfortable, because once he became aware of it, he realized other people probably saw it too.

There were nice Americans of course, and some of them had done a lot of good. There was a couple from Oregon who'd spearheaded the conversion of the *tempo* fleet from diesel engines to electric motors, and earnest students of Buddhism, and a woman from Sausalito named Olga, who'd started a program that gave poor villagers alternatives to selling their daughters as domestic slaves. But the tourists were a distinct breed. Peter had lived his whole life in his home country and somehow never noticed that look until he saw it in contrast to people who were different.

They passed the floodlit grounds of the Australian embassy, then took a couple of turns and found themselves on quiet, deserted streets without lights, unpaved and fronted by small shops and ramshackle houses. Wayne Lee came to full attention and picked up her pace.

"I should have brought a flashlight," Peter said. "I have no idea if it's safe here."

Alex straightened her shoulders and looked around. "Let's keep going."

He'd always liked her courage, but after a few minutes they heard scufflings and he began to have doubts. He thought he saw movement behind them, flowing dark shapes low to the ground. Wayne Lee broke into a trot, and he struggled to rein her in.

"What the hell *is* that?" asked Alex.

"I don't know, but I'm not liking it and neither is the goat."

He felt a surge of adrenaline. They were moving quickly, but the living shadows moved with them. The street branched, and one fork led back to the main road, about a hundred yards away, where there was light.

"Take a right," Peter said, but the things followed.

"Dogs," said Alex. "It's a dog pack."

"They want Wayne Lee."

They started running. The dogs closed the distance and were nearly on them when a figure suddenly darted out from the shadows. It was a boy, yelling in Nepali. They halted, and the dogs quickly surrounded them. The boy walked in a circle, keeping himself between them and the dogs, brandishing a long, heavy stick. The dogs snapped at it, but he was quick; he'd pull it away at the last second, then slap them on the nose with it.

"You have a bit of trouble, I think, mister sir," said the boy, his English heavily accented.

Peter asked him what they should do, and he told them to bend down and pretend they were each picking up a rock. They did as he said, and the dogs immediately backed off a couple of feet.

"Follow me, please," he said. "Keep your arms up, like you are going to throw the rock. You, girl, in the rear, please to face behind you. Arm up."

Crablike, they shuffled their way down the narrow lane. Wayne Lee, bleating and shivering with fear, shat prodigiously. Alex—in addition to walking sideways, keeping her arm up, and watching the dogs—did her best to avoid the goat shit, often unsuccessfully.

As they approached the lit street, though, one of the dogs lunged at the boy, briefly grabbing the stick in its jaws. The boy stepped back, which pulled the dog toward him, then shoved the stick down the dog's throat. It gagged and opened its jaws for an instant, and in that moment the boy yanked the stick back out of its mouth and smacked it on the snout. The dog snarled and lunged again, and this time the boy clobbered it hard over the skull. It yelped and scuttled back to the pack.

They kept moving, the dogs still with them, but the strategy was working; as they approached the light, their pursuers began hanging farther and farther back, and by the time they reached the paved road, the dogs had melted into the black gloom like djinns.

The three of them stood under a flickering yellow streetlight, sweating in the cool air, as the panicked goat continued to bleat. The boy's eyes gleamed in his dark face.

"Who *are* you?" Peter asked, astonished at this intercession.

"I am Raju," the boy said. He stuck out his hand, and they shook.

"Thank you, Raju. You saved our necks."

The boy was about twelve, barefoot, and he wore a loose Madras shirt that hung askew because he'd buttoned it wrong. His pants were held up with an old piece of nylon climbing rope and had a carefully stitched patch over one knee. How to account for this discrepancy? The tidy patch with its tight whipstitch, the shirt one button off. Peter wondered how long ago the patch had been applied, and what had happened to the woman who sewed it.

He realized that even as he was sizing up Raju, the boy was doing the same to him.

"It is not wise to walk here at night, certainly not with an animal," he said, sounding cheerful for a kid who had just faced down a pack of feral dogs with an old stick. He whirled the stick around him nonchalantly, and Peter couldn't help noticing how

graceful and economical his movements were, as if he'd been train-
ing all his short life with some dog-stick master for just this moment. He saw Peter watching him and smiled.

"Is there anything I can do for you?" Peter asked. His heart was
finally slowing down.

"You are American?"

"Yes."

Raju swished the stick back and forth in front of him, thinking.
"Why does an American have a goat, if I may demand of you?"

Peter smiled at Raju's formal, almost-correct schoolboy English. The boy's parents must have struggled to get him some sort
of education. "We live here now," he answered.

Raju shrugged his narrow shoulders in that unique Nepali
way—resigned to fate, making the best of the situation, the physical expression of *ke garne*. "I suppose if you are American you
may give me rupees as a token of your appreciation," he said,
sounding a little unconvinced, as if he'd only heard rumors of this
odd custom.

Peter handed over all his cash and then remembered with chagrin what he'd just been thinking about Americans and their wallets. Raju grew wide-eyed and looked around a little fearfully.

"Sir, if a policeman should see this he will think I am a robber.
This will buy my whole family food for a month."

"Good," Peter said. He asked Raju if he knew where the
Phwoof clinic was. Raju shook his head, so Peter described it to
him. "If you ever need anything, Raju, if someone in your family is
sick, come find me there."

| | |

Ten days later Devi worked with Alex to translate the response
from Lama Padma.

Dear Peter,
    Please be assured that it is not my intention to convert you
to anything. Buddhists do not posit a God in the sense of an

all-powerful being who looks down on everything and causes benefit or harm. What you think of as your dark view of life on earth is not so unlike ours, in that we consider existence in the unenlightened state to be an endless cycle of suffering. It appears to me that the genetic mechanisms you describe are nothing more than the biological machinery of that cycle, which we call samsara. As such, I find them interesting but not surprising.

Though we do not say there is a God in the narrowest sense, we do aim to experience what we call Buddha nature. This is described as *yeshe,* the all-pervasive awareness that suffuses everything, and that is our own fundamental essence. The goal of meditation is to develop wisdom and compassion to the point that the mind rests in this state at all times, sleeping and waking, without distraction, even across the threshold of death. That, put very briefly, is what is meant by Enlightenment.

I hope you do not feel too much despair at the state of things, but despair is an important first step. I could go on about this, but I think I will continue later. I have a couple of students from California now, and I have learned something about the Western attention span!

Yours,

—Lama Padma

FOURTEEN

"You recall our beloved Mr. Bahadur?" asked Franz.

"How could I forget?"

"He is quite exercised, and it turns out he is *zuhälter* of choice to a wide spectrum of government ministers and muck-a-mucks in the army."

Peter was astonished. "Are you telling me that a government with an armed insurrection on its hands is actually getting bent out of shape over the tribulations of an aggrieved pimp?"

"The power of such men lies in their ability to inflict damage," Franz said. "They can end marriages and careers with a word."

Franz had acquired a stray cat, which he'd named Wittgenstein in honor of the philosopher from his hometown. Wittgenstein jumped up onto the desk and started rubbing his face against Franz's hand, bit him affectionately, then lay down under the lamp.

"In any case, I've had to placate them," Franz muttered, petting the cat and looking slightly guilty.

"Which means what?"

Franz cleared his throat. "We have a small satellite clinic out in

Jorpati, near Boudhanath, that serves the monks and nuns in the monasteries there."

Peter considered this. "That's a workable commute, right? What would it take, an hour?"

"You'll be on call when you aren't in the clinic. It's important that you live nearby."

Peter stared at him. "I'm being *exiled*?"

"Just till things cool down."

"How about I quit and save you the trouble?"

"Admit defeat?" Franz asked. "Take your ball and go home?"

"My balls, more like it, instead of handing them to you."

Franz blinked enigmatically. "Of course, there's the matter of your daughter. I understand she's quite happy here now."

Peter couldn't believe what he was hearing. "Sangita," he said. "You sent her as a spy?"

"Not at all," said Franz. "But she cooks for me too, and with a little effort one can draw her out."

Peter got up and went to the window. The invasion of privacy notwithstanding, he knew Franz was right; Alex was happier with Devi than he'd ever seen her. If they left the country now she'd be even more upset than when he brought her over. Then there was the matter of Bahadur; was Peter just going to roll over and go belly-up for some lard-ass hustler? The more he thought about it, the more he realized there was all kinds of unfinished business here, and home seemed less appealing than ever. He put his hands in his pockets and studied the floor.

"You're a fascist," he mumbled. "A devious, manipulative Austrian brownshirt."

Franz wagged an admonishing finger at him as the cat jumped from the desk to the windowsill and slipped out.

| | |

"Mike's Breakfast," said Peter. "On me."

Alex looked at Devi uneasily. "This can't be good," she said.

She got her coat, keeping a watchful eye on her father, and the three of them headed out.

Mike's had been started by a Peace Corps volunteer in the 1970s who'd liked the freewheeling hash-head haven that was Kathmandu in those days. His restaurant was still a gathering place for homesick, hungry Westerners who craved something besides rice and lentils for breakfast. Peter and the girls took a *tempo* across town and sat at a table in the garden. Devi had never been there.

"Waffles with scrambled eggs and orange juice," said Alex, when they'd been seated.

"Pancakes," said Devi. She looked at Alex, a little unsure of herself. "With butter and maple syrup and hash browns. Okay?"

"The diabetes express," said Alex. "Go for it."

"Coffee here," Peter said. "And, mmm . . . everything everyone else is having."

When the waitress left, Alex turned anxiously to her father. "Let's hear it."

Peter explained the situation, and soon she looked as if she were going to burst into tears. "I'm sorry," he said. "We'll have a jeep, so you can borrow it once in a while."

The girls looked at each other. Devi put her hands on the table. "I want to come too," she said.

It was the most openly assertive Peter had seen her. "Don't your parents need you?"

"I think they're tired of having me around."

"She's practically been living with us, anyway," Alex said.

"Still, you'd have to ask them," he said.

"I will, but they won't mind."

Peter rested his chin in his hands. He should have anticipated this, and he hadn't. "What about school?"

"I can do homeschool, like Alex."

"Franz says it's barely an apartment—really just a big room."

"We'll pretend we're in New York," Alex said.

Peter did his best to sound reasonable. "What I mean is, you won't have any privacy."

Devi rolled her eyes. "I grew up in a family where having your own room means hanging a blanket," she said. "I'm not *used* to privacy. Too much privacy is what makes Westerners sick in the head."

The conversation was a stark reminder that new alliances had complicated Peter's authority. Of course, he could lay down the law like a bully and endure weeks of sulking while he and his daughter lived like caged rats in an ugly experiment, courtesy of a vengeful panderer. Beyond that, though, they'd be treating Tibetans without a Tibetan translator, which would only worsen the nightmare.

It hadn't occurred to him, but for that reason alone it would probably be better to have Devi there than not. Add in Alex's happiness and the effect it would have on him, and matters quickly distilled themselves into clarity. Some defeats turned out not to be defeats at all.

The girls picked at their food in silence, looking tense and unhappy.

Peter did his best to suppress a canny grin. "You'll both have to work in the clinic every day, then," he said. "You'll do your schoolwork in the evenings. Absolutely no malingering."

"Ha!" said Alex, grinning. She high-fived Devi. "Ha!"

And Peter thought, *"Ha" is right, kid.*

| | |

Peter awakened on their first morning in the new place and lay there, disoriented, thinking he had to go feed Wayne Lee. But Devi's parents had moved into the house to care for the goat while he and the girls were gone. It turned out that Sangita and Sonam had been living in a wall tent set up in the courtyard of an apartment building, which was why Devi never wanted to take Alex home with her. It was also why Sonam hadn't been able to get over his respiratory problems.

The Jorpati apartment adjoined the house of a Nepali Brahmin family; ten years previously it had been a cowshed. The family had hired workers to plaster the walls and pour a concrete floor over the dirt. They apparently hadn't bothered with rebar, and the floor was full of cracks that still emitted a vague odor of manure. It was about fourteen by twenty, not a closet but close enough with three people crammed into it. Peter had a cot in the corner near the window; on the opposite side of the room, behind a curtain, Alex and Devi shared a small double mattress on a platform made of pallets.

Devi was snoring softly, but Alex was in the first stages of her early-morning rustling. She'd be up soon. The walls were damp with all their breath. Suitcases, backpacks, the heater they'd brought, and various cardboard boxes containing food and household goods were spread out across the floor. To the left of the door was the kitchen, which consisted of a sink, a tiny fridge, a two-burner propane hot plate, three pans, and a teakettle. The bathroom was an outhouse in the owners' backyard.

Peter heard noises from outside, so he hauled himself up and pushed the curtain aside. There was a water tap just below the window, and a long line of women stood in the morning chill, waiting to fill plastic jugs from the trickle that flowed out of the spigot. Fortunately he and the girls had their own supply inside, and he'd bought a filter.

He lay down again, his hands behind his head, which was propped up on a cheap, lumpy pillow. He stared at the ceiling, laced with a complex pattern of cracks like the scratched hide of an old water buffalo. The walls of the room had been painted, but the ceiling had been left the dull bone white of rough plaster.

So much for canny victory. *I am an utter failure,* Peter thought. It wasn't a particularly dramatic revelation, just a dry, unpleasant truth, like the bitter taste that lingers in the mouth the morning after too rowdy a night. He had failed at marriage, failed at fatherhood, failed even in his battle with Bahadur. He had been too trusting; he had underestimated multiple threats; he had failed to work hard enough. He was forty-four. His old classmates had successful practices and beautiful wives and brilliant children and elegant homes in lush suburbs, and he was lying on a hard mattress on the floor of an old cowshed while women in *lungis* drew dirty water from a rusty tap five feet from his head. He had chronic diarrhea; he was afraid of getting TB; he was afraid of Alex getting TB—in fact, increasingly he was just afraid in general.

Alex mumbled in her half sleep, and outside one of the women suddenly laughed boisterously. Peter wondered at the happiness of the Nepalis, people who owned nothing but a few clothes, a cooking pot, a jug for the neighborhood water tap. They lived short, uncomfortable lives beset with pestilence, shared with parasites and mangy dogs, and still they laughed more than anyone laughed in Berkeley.

As for him, he dreaded the new clinic, dreaded the day itself. He didn't even want to leave his bed. He remembered, briefly, the radiance at Lama Padma's, the singular light that seemed to hold secrets, and the feeling of being physically carried outside of the room and into the sky. What *was* that, anyway? Lama Padma had grinned at him as if he knew exactly what was going on. To Peter it was unlike anything he'd ever felt, and at the same time the experience seemed familiar, as close to real happiness and freedom as he could imagine. But as far as he knew he might never see Lama Padma again, and he had no idea how to regain that state himself. For that matter, this business of karma purification was even worse than Mina had predicted. It wasn't just things hitting the fan; it was *he himself* hitting the fan and getting cut into thousands of pieces that blew outward to the winds.

Alex stirred, groaned, and pulled back the curtain. She scowled out into the room with fright-wig hair. "Time?"

Peter felt for his watch, which was buried amid the wallet, keys, water bottle, and other stuff on the crate that served as his bedside table.

"Seven-thirty," he said. "It's late."

She briefly surveyed the room, then lay back down and pulled the covers over her head. One arm snaked out and drew the curtain closed.

Peter didn't want to get up, but he did. Alex and Devi would be hungry. He dressed and put on his scuffed shoes. In the confusion of arrival the previous evening they hadn't turned the heater up high enough, and the place was cold. He went over to it and rotated the dial, then went out to pee.

The outhouse was built of planks, with a tin roof, but between the chilly air and the ample ventilation, at least it didn't stink. There was just a hole in the ground with a place on each side to put your feet if you needed to squat. When Peter had finished, he hung a roll of toilet paper on a nail and went back inside.

Alex pulled back her curtain again, as if she'd hoped the previous viewing had been a hallucination. "Good fucking God," she said.

"You're being punished for your father's sins," Peter said. "It's very Greek."

"I wouldn't mind Greek if we were in Greece."

Devi cried out, babbling something in Nepali, and Alex shook her and said her name. She rolled over and buried her face in Alex's flank. Peter rooted through the food bag to see what he could cook. The heater was ticking, but so far it wasn't helping much.

Alex lifted Devi's arm off her, then pulled on a sweater and a jacket. She grabbed her pants from the foot of the bed and put them on under the covers. She got up, slipped on her socks and shoes, then headed outside.

"Fuck!" echoed in from the outhouse in back, and Peter briefly wondered if the Nepali family had heard it too. He decided he didn't care and got water heating for oatmeal. Devi stirred again and mumbled. Soon Alex returned, her teeth chattering.

"This country is a real confidence builder," she said, hopping up and down near the heater to try to get warm. "Just when I think I'm starting to get it, it turns out I don't know shit."

"You'll be intimately acquainted with shit by the time we leave *here*," he said. "What happened?"

"I'm trying to squat over the thing, but it's so cold I can't even relax enough to go," she said. "And then I missed the hole, and I'm thinking, they're going to find me out here frozen to the ground by a pee icicle."

Devi rolled over sleepily and sat up. She rubbed her eyes and looked around. "Hey, not *bad*," she exclaimed, smiling. "We've even got our own water!"

| | |

An hour later they met Ian at the clinic for the official passing of the baton. He was a good-looking, affable Kiwi of about thirty who'd finished his residency the previous year and had signed on with Phwoof so he could get in some mountaineering before starting a full-time practice back home in New Zealand.

The Nepali nurse—a short, broad, fierce-looking woman named Banhi—busied herself with some paperwork as Ian walked them through the clinic, which took up two rooms on the bottom floor of a concrete building. One was an office and exam room; the other served as the triage and waiting room. Both had windows to the street made of old-fashioned opaque security glass with wire mesh cast inside it. It was chilly.

"Looking forward to going home?" Peter asked.

"Can't begin to tell you."

"What's Wellington like?" Alex asked. She'd been watching Ian quite closely.

"Splendid," he said. "It's all built on hills around the most beautiful harbor. If you're up there in the evening, with the sun going down over Cook Strait and the city lights coming on . . . It's just . . ." He looked about ready to weep at the prospect of seeing it again.

"It sounds wonderful," Alex said. She had acquired a kind of glow. "I'd love to see it someday."

Peter and Devi both stared at her, then glanced at each other, then looked back at her. *Holy shit,* Peter thought. He'd seen her flirt before, but this time she was doing it right in front of Devi. He hoped there wasn't about to be some sort of blowup.

Ian seemed to notice too. "Of course," he stammered. "I mean, you're always welcome to come visit if you . . . um, you know . . ."

"Turn eighteen," Peter offered, helpfully.

Alex shot him a look, then smiled at Ian. "Thank you," she said. "I might. Visit, I mean. *And* turn eighteen."

Ian handed Peter the keys, wished them luck, and started off down the street. His step was so buoyant he looked as if he might break into spontaneous, ecstatic dance, twirling from the light poles like Gene Kelly in *Singin' in the Rain.*

Devi turned to Alex and crossed her arms over her chest. "My, *my,*" she said.

Alex blushed. "I'm sorry," she said.

"You are such a hussy!"

"I know," Alex said, "and I really, really apologize. But you have to admit . . ."

"Well, he *was* pretty gorgeous," said Devi. She uncrossed her arms, then Alex hugged her and mumbled something in her ear. Devi smiled, then laughed.

They strolled through the clinic again and took stock. The waiting room had one old poster taped onto the concrete wall— the usual kitten hanging by its front claws from the usual branch, with the usual "Hang in there, baby!" printed over the top—but with translations written freehand underneath in both Nepali and Tibetan. The tape was old and yellow, and the poster had started to peel off the wall.

A dozen or so blue metal folding chairs with white paint spattered on them were arrayed haphazardly around the room, and in the center stood a low wooden table that looked as if it had fallen off a truck and broken into pieces, then been reconstructed by a four-year-old using chewing gum and vomit. It held a tattered copy of *Newsweek Asia,* a slightly more recent Bollywood magazine, and a thick wad of Kleenex that was suspiciously yellow in the center. Peter kicked it onto the floor, then kicked it again, to the side of the room. When Devi went to pick it up he told her not to touch it, and he was serious.

In the office–exam room–lab there were a few boxes of latex gloves, assorted syringes, an old mercury thermometer in an alcohol container, cotton swabs, a handful of surgical masks, and a pressure cooker on a hot plate that apparently served as an autoclave.

When Peter opened the fridge, though, he could barely believe his eyes. There were the usual antibiotics and painkillers, but there was also a huge supply of second- and third-line TB drugs, better stuff than they'd had at the main clinic in town. He turned to the nurse.

"Banhi, where did these come from?"

She turned to look and made a dismissive gesture. "We getting some things," she said vaguely.

"Getting how?" Peter asked.

She eyed him coolly. "Just getting," she said. "Not necessary knowing everything."

Peter looked at Alex and Devi, who appeared as astonished as he was at this blatant insolence. He felt his temper rising. "In this case, I'd like to know," he said as evenly as possible.

She responded by closing the ledger, throwing on her coat, and stalking out without even glancing back at him. The steel front door slammed behind her.

"What the hell was that?" Peter asked. "Are we dealing with some sort of Mafia here?"

"I don't think the Mafia's too interested in Nepal," Devi said.

"Well what, then?"

"Don't have a stroke, Dad."

"She's obviously a bitch," said Devi.

"Probably been talking to Mina about you," Alex added. She stretched out on the exam table. It was built of plywood and two-by-fours, and had a thin vinyl pad on it that appeared to be stuffed with animal hair, some of which was coming out at the seams. "It's like lying on a dead goat," she said.

Peter was still fuming. He sat down on the stool and rested his chin on his hands. "I was one of the best cardiologists in California," he said.

"Or maybe a dead yak," Alex said. "A black yak, whacked by the little-known Nepali Cosa Nostra."

"Smacked in the back by a Mafia hack," said Devi.

"I was supposed to speak at a colloquium at Stanford last week, in fact," Peter continued, ignoring them. "I would have become pals with the new dean of the medical school, and as a result you would be starting next fall on a full ride."

"Dream on, Dad." She turned to Devi. "I've seen this syndrome once or twice before with him. You might want to take a seat."

Devi sat on the table by Alex's feet.

"In your first year you would write a memoir of your experiences called *Alexandra on the Farm,* which due to its tastefully suggestive and inspiring content would quickly land you a place on *Oprah* and become an international bestseller," Peter said.

"The farm?" asked Devi.

"Stanford's nickname," said Alex.

"There are animals there?"

"Extremely well-bred ones."

"The film rights would sell for three million dollars," Peter continued, ignoring them, "and you would be played by . . . um . . . Who would be playing you?"

Alex spoke with only a hint of sarcasm. "Keira Knightley, I expect."

"Fair enough. Of course, sooner or later Keira would want to meet me. Just, you know, to express her appreciation for what a great job I'd done raising you and all. Dinner and drinks, a long walk on the beach. Nothing fancy."

Alex looked at him a little askance. "I'm pretty sure Keira Knightley has a boyfriend."

"She does?"

"God, Dad, don't you ever read?"

FIFTEEN

Several Tibetan monasteries had been rebuilt near Boudhanath after the destruction by the Chinese across the border. People still routinely fled from Tibet across the high passes, and Peter was seeing a lot of frostbite. He was usually able to save fingers, but sometimes the refugees' toes would turn gangrenous and require amputation. For that, he gave them bus fare and sent them into Kathmandu, to Franz.

Alex's Nepali had become serviceable, and she and Devi worked together with the Tibetans so Alex could get closer to fluency in Tibetan too. Alex and Devi were tireless, putting in ten-hour days every day but Sunday, and soon acquired a devoted following among the children.

One night after work, Devi cooked *momos,* Tibetan dumplings stuffed with ginger, lamb, and garlic. Alex picked up a calendar and realized they'd forgotten Christmas—missed it by five days, in fact. She wanted a tree, but Peter had no idea where to find one without poaching it. They did have a green marker, though, so they drew a tree on an empty rice bag and tacked it to the wall. Peter told them they'd open presents the next night, on New Year's Eve.

The heater wasn't really up to the task, given the drafty window and the concrete floor, and they were always cold. Peter found a shop that had a thick rug, big enough to cover the entire floor, with a good pad for underneath.

On New Year's Eve he brought the rug home. They moved their stuff into the yard, unrolled the rug, then brought everything back in. The girls were delighted and promptly stretched out on it, luxuriating in the thick fibers and cooing their approval. The room felt warmer immediately, just by having their feet shielded from the heat-sucking concrete floor.

Peter decided to give the girls some time to themselves, so he walked down the road and called Franz, who picked up on the second ring.

"Home alone on New Year's?" Peter asked. "Serves you right for banishing us to the outlands; we could have kept you company."

"I'm not alone," said Franz.

"Oh, you're right, I can hear the cat. I expect that's the closest you're getting to pussy tonight, boss."

"Fuck you, American doctor."

Peter smiled. "What's the news at court? Any chance Duke Bahadur will be mollified by spring?"

"I'm taking care of his girls for him, gratis, thanks to you."

"Well, you old whore."

"Everyone he touches ends up as some kind of whore, apparently. He has even more connections than I knew."

"Meaning what, exactly?"

"He's still pissed at you, so I've got a feeling you're going to find out," said Franz. "Oh, and by the way, that girl you sprang? She's already back with him, and she *is* HIV-positive."

Peter felt the holiday cheer bleed right out of him. "I'm sorry to hear that," he said feebly.

"Happy New Year, Dr. Do-gooder," said Franz, then hung up.

Peter had been trying not to think about futility, but it had acquired such multifarious manifestations it had become impossible to ignore. Recurring trachoma, because you could treat the patient but you could never kill all the flies. Kids dead from diarrhea, because you could give them antibiotics but you couldn't clean up the rivers. Endemic TB, because for every case you treated there were ten that never came to a clinic, that lived with it and died with it, while the bacteria just kept evolving resistance. For that matter, a kind but stubborn lama who could have had his heart repaired but who preferred to stay at the monastery and meditate. Peter could see why docs burned out here; it was like medical Whac-a-Mole. For every case he hammered, ten more sprang up that he couldn't do anything about. There was no end to it, no sense of having finished or accomplished anything. It was starting to feel corrosive, as if it might burn its way through his skin and begin consuming him from the inside.

| | |

He scheduled visits at a couple of the monasteries up the hill and took stock of his paltry supplies. Stuffed into the old leather doctor's bag that had belonged to his father was a stethoscope; a thermometer; a Ziploc full of latex gloves; a speculum; a couple of dozen sterile-wrapped syringes; an otoscope; and his favorite reflex hammer, gift of Bollixall Pharma, with its titanium handle and orange rubber head. Medications from the clinic stock—ampicillin, sulfa, Cipro, cortisone (injectable and inhalable, for anything from anaphylactic shock to asthma), albuterol, insulin, and a few other things. And of course the amazing array of TB drugs.

Peter hadn't thought of his father in a long time, but the bag brought the old curmudgeon to mind. Peter and his sister had grown up in Jackson, Mississippi, where their father was a dermatologist. Even though his father was otherwise embarrassingly conservative, as a young man in the late 1950s he'd raised eyebrows by being one of the first white physicians in town to accept black patients.

"Once you learn something about skin, you'd have to be an

idiot to think it makes any difference between people other than maybe in melanoma," he told his son, when Peter was about ten. "And if that's your metric, *they're* superior to *us*."

Holding the old leather bag now, Peter felt more fondness for his father than he had in some time, and wondered if his father too had felt his work was futile. Mississippi in those days had almost as much poverty as Nepal did now, and he must have wrestled with some of the same issues.

The jeep had only a canvas top, and the morning they left, it was cold as they careened through the mud on terrible roads. Devi was excited about seeing other Tibetans, though—or as she put it in her blunt way, Tibetans who weren't afraid to *be* Tibetan, as her mother was.

They drove through the front gate of the monastery and found their liaison, a robust, red-cheeked nun who showed them to a small room where they would treat the other *anis*.

The room, like the whole building, was unheated. It was furnished simply with a cot, a chair, a small writing table, and a shrine with water bowls, lamps, and photos of the Dalai Lama. Down in the valley the days did warm up; it might be thirty degrees in the morning, but it would hit the mid-fifties by afternoon. Up at elevations like this, it stayed cooler. Having a row of butter lamps and three people crammed into the room helped, though. It was more than a matter of comfort; Peter liked his patients to feel safe, and it always seemed that they were more relaxed and talked more easily if they were in a warm place.

Alex and Devi unpacked the various kits. Devi was worried that the *anis* might balk at being examined by a male doctor, but the abbot, Lama Yeshe, had assured the nuns that there was no misconduct in this and encouraged them to keep themselves well.

Soon the first *ani* appeared, a broad-hipped woman in her late thirties. She'd had recurrent diarrhea ever since leaving Tibet. Peter asked about it, and the nun said there was no blood in it, and that between bouts she felt all right, though a little weak. Without access to a real lab, Peter had to treat empirically, so he gave her

Flagyl and figured that would likely take care of whatever she'd picked up.

The second nun was much older, possibly in her seventies, and had a skin rash over her lower back, buttocks, and legs. It wasn't clear what was causing it, but it didn't appear to be serious. Peter suggested she try to bathe every day with gentle soap, then gave her a big tube of cortisone cream.

Next came Ani Dawa, a pretty but tough-looking young woman in her twenties. She'd had a hacking cough for three months. Peter did his best to listen through her three or four layers of clothing but finally had to ask, through Devi, if she would mind paring down a bit. Ani Dawa laughed and unwrapped herself, leaving in place just the T-shirt that served as her bottom layer.

When he lifted the shirt in back he noticed the scars. They were eight to ten inches long, slightly curved, red, and shiny. There were about a dozen of them, from mid–shoulder blade to her sacrum. He met Devi's eyes briefly, then continued with the exam, listening to Ani Dawa's lungs and then, from the front, to her heart. There was a little bit of a wheeze, but otherwise her lungs sounded clear, and her heart was strong.

"Is this the first time she's had the cough?" he asked.

Devi spoke to her and said, "No, she says she gets it every winter. This year has been worse than before. Sometimes it keeps her up half the night."

"Any phlegm or blood?"

"Sometimes phlegm."

"What color?"

"She says clear or white."

"Is she weak?"

"She says not so much. Sometimes she gets tired just from all the coughing."

Peter asked Alex how much of the Tibetan conversation she was able to understand.

"Half, maybe," she said.

Peter told Devi he wanted Ani Dawa to have a TB test, but he was pretty sure that wasn't the problem. They got out the kit and pricked her forearm, then told her what to look for so they'd know what to do when they came back.

He told her it was probably mild asthma. "This place is cold and damp," he said. "When I know for sure she doesn't have TB we'll give her an inhaler."

Devi relayed this, and Ani Dawa rewrapped herself. Peter looked at Devi again, the question in his eyes, and Devi nodded, just slightly. "She may not want to talk about it," she said quietly.

"I'd like to know what happened."

Devi spoke and, for a moment, Ani Dawa shrank back. She said a few words, her eyes going from Devi to Peter.

Devi said, "She's afraid you're a spy for the Chinese."

Devi and Ani Dawa spoke at length, then, and the nun was evidently reassured. "She says that when the Chinese came to her *gonpa* in Tibet, she was still very young, about fourteen. The Chinese soldiers would take the nuns into a room, one by one, and do things to them there."

"What kinds of things?"

"The pretty ones they raped, and if the nuns got pregnant they would force them to have abortions. But the abortion doctors were careless, and several nuns died from bleeding. They also tortured them in various ways. Ani Dawa was burned with cigarettes, and one time with a hot iron; that's how she got the scars. They kept asking her, 'Where is your Buddha now? Why doesn't he come save you?'"

Peter looked at the nun, who seemed a little agitated. She stopped and quietly recited a mantra for a few moments, then finally spoke again.

"She says they wanted to get the nuns to renounce the Buddha, but the soldiers didn't understand anything about it," Devi said. "She tried to explain to them that you cannot renounce what is inside you, but she quickly realized it was useless. The soldiers had very little schooling, and most were completely ignorant."

"This happened to all the nuns?"

Devi spoke, and Ani Dawa nodded. "She says yes," Devi continued. "Many died. One girl about her age was raped with an electric cattle prod over a period of two or three hours and later died from her injuries. That really upset Ani Dawa, because she and this girl had been particularly close friends."

"What about the monks?" Peter asked.

"She says the Chinese brought the monks down from the neighboring *gonpa*. All the soldiers would crowd into a room, where they'd put a mat on the floor, and they would get drunk and their commander would start picking couples, one monk and one nun. They would force them to have sex on the mat; all the soldiers and all the other monks and nuns had to watch. If a monk was too frightened, or for some other reason couldn't get his penis hard, they would make him wait and try again later, and if it happened again they would take him out and shoot him. They shot eight monks in one night because they either couldn't or wouldn't break their vows."

Alex stood by the door, her hands in her pockets, looking at the floor.

"She says do you want her to go on?" Devi said. "She says there is much more she could say, but she knows there are other nuns waiting, and she doesn't want to take all your time."

"I just want to know how she is now. How her mind is, I mean."

Devi asked her, and Ani Dawa thought about it a little while before she spoke.

"She says the hardest thing for her was that she began to hate the soldiers, especially after they killed her friend," Devi said. "She had fantasies of taking one of their rifles and shooting them all. She knew she could do it if she had a chance. And when she realized she was dreaming of this, actually planning it if an opportunity presented itself, that was when she knew they'd broken her, and then she was really troubled."

"I don't understand," said Alex. "It seems pretty natural."

Devi spoke to Ani Dawa. "She says of course it is natural; it is samsara, but she does not wish to remain in samsara. It did not break her vows to be raped, because this she could not control. But when she found herself planning to kill them, *this* broke her vows. The soldiers had stripped her of what was most valuable, her compassion for other beings. Then she knew she had to escape, because if she didn't, she would be just as bad as they were; she would be of no benefit to anyone."

Peter took her hands in his. He felt an unsettling mix of emotions, sorrow for her, anger at the soldiers. He didn't know what to say.

"Is there anything else I can do for her?" he asked.

Ani Dawa bowed slightly and spoke to Devi.

"She says no," Devi said. "She says thank you, American doctor."

When they'd seen all the *anis,* they went up the hill to the main *gonpa* to treat the monks. The stories were much the same. Several told of being soaked with water and forced to stand outside all night in freezing cold. Others were locked for days at a time in nearly airless boxes so small that they had to sit hunched over inside, with their knees up near their ears. Reports of cattle prods, bones broken by truncheons, and various other tortures were commonplace.

What amazed Peter most about these stories, though, was how they were told. Many of the monks would recount unbelievable horrors with the detached good humor of a fond uncle relaying an amusing prank pulled by a couple of unruly nephews. One, who'd been shut up for weeks in a dark box, said the soldiers had inadvertently helped him, because of a secret meditation practice he did that benefited from such confinement. Others, though, clearly had more trouble coming to terms with what had happened, and they seethed as they described what had been done to them and their friends.

Late in the day, shortly after they'd finished, a frigid wind blew in from the north, bringing low gray clouds and the smell of rain. Peter could see the translucent curtain descending as the front approached, so they packed up quickly and started back to the jeep. Just then he saw a familiar face.

"Lobsang!" he called. The monk looked up, and a broad smile burst across his face. They walked toward each other, then Lobsang opened his arms and wrapped them all in a bear hug. Peter asked what he was doing there.

Lobsang explained that Lama Yeshe, the abbot, had asked Lama Padma to come down and help conduct a long, multiday ceremony. Lama Padma had also agreed to teach.

"I have medicine for him," Peter said. "I was going to drive up to see you tomorrow."

"Oh, road very bad," said Lobsang. "We almost slide off mountain two, three times." He laughed a little ruefully and suggested they wait until spring.

"I have it with me," Peter said. "I'll go get it and give it to you before we leave."

Just then the first sleet pelted them. Lobsang looked up and appeared concerned. "I wonder . . ." he said. He then spoke to Devi in Tibetan; she translated that he was worried about them driving on with the weather changing. He said Lama Padma was planning to speak to the monks and nuns that night, and they would be welcome to attend if Devi could translate for them.

| | |

In the shrine room, Lama Padma sat cross-legged on a dais while several other lamas sat on slightly lower platforms along the wall on both sides of him. The room itself was large, about forty feet square, with high ceilings. Everything looked fresh and well maintained, unlike Lama Padma's dilapidated place. All the woodwork was painted in bright colors, and the walls were covered almost completely by huge, intricately detailed *thangkas*. Long, low benches held the monks' texts, bells, and *dorjes,* as well as a few small hand drums of the type Peter had seen at Lama Padma's. There were sections for larger instruments as well: long horns whose broad mouths rested on stands in front of the benches; shorter, handheld horns with intricate silver trim; and large, flat drums with green-dyed skins on both sides, which hung from floor-standing frames and were played with a long, curved stick.

The room was lit by hundreds of butter lamps along two sides, and incense smoke filled the air. The monks and nuns had crowded in, segregated by sex on the right and left sides of the room. Even though it was cold out, with the lamps and all the bodies, the room quickly grew warm. Peter and the girls sat in the back. Lobsang brought Lama Padma a cup of tea, then sat down on a pad on the floor at his feet.

Lama Padma lifted the lid of his mug, sipped, then set the cup down and began to speak. Devi translated quietly as he spoke, using "I" when he said "I" instead of her usual interpretive "he." Only occasionally did she hesitate, and Peter found that it was almost like having subtitles.

"I would like to thank you for inviting me," said Lama Padma. "It is a slightly unusual circumstance this evening; only recently have I begun to teach a few Westerners, and now I'm worried that if I go off into some story about yaks, they won't understand and the real meaning will be lost."

The monks and nuns chuckled at this. Lama Padma smiled and sipped his tea.

"I think tonight I will just cover some basics, and if the older monks start snoring, we'll poke them," he said. "Please be sure you are coming to this teaching with the proper motivation. This is the desire that, above all else, we will reach Enlightenment not just for our own benefit but for all beings. Without this, you might as well go work on a road crew, where at least your sweat will do some good." He paused for a moment, looking mischievous. "In fact," he added, "I have a road in mind!"

The audience, apparently aware of the state of the track up to Lama Padma's place, laughed heartily at this. Peter had always imagined the monastic life to be ascetic and humorless, and the bonhomie took him by surprise.

The lama considered his next tack. "We Buddhists always talk about suffering," he said. "What we mean is obvious to many people, but I sometimes worry that Westerners won't get it, because in many ways their lives are easy. But some come here with pure intention; they are generous and want to do good. They travel, and they see the profundity of human troubles, and their minds open to how things are. People everywhere are afflicted by old age, disease, and death. Those in prosperous countries may be shocked because much of their lives they are insulated from these things. They have good doctors, good jobs, clean water, and they think, What's all this talk of suffering? Isn't it very morbid?"

A few of the monks turned and glanced shyly at Peter and the girls.

"Then they go to the doctor one day and learn they have cancer," Lama Padma went on. "Or maybe their wife is killed in a car accident. Or they lose their job and their money disappears, and soon they are living alone by the road. Everything that gave them comfort is stripped away. No one is spared from impermanence."

Lobsang got up and filled the teacup, then returned to his seat.

"So, then, what to do?" Lama Padma asked. "We are caught in this cycle. It is as if we are strapped to the tire of a truck, and one moment we see the sky and think, How lovely the world is! and the next moment we are crushed into the mud, and we think, How terrible the world is! It just goes around and around."

Devi looked at Alex and smiled.

"This wheel of suffering arises from the mind. We talk about being in samsara, but really it's the other way around: Samsara is in *us*. Our responsibility is to loosen the grip of attachment and aversion, and you do that through meditation practice. You train the mind to see through this masterpiece of illusion we call existence, and you do it with love in your heart for all beings. So this is good, because most of you are already doing what you should be doing. And for those of you who aren't—why are you living in a monastery? You could be having much more fun someplace else!"

That night Peter lay on his bed in the monastery's guesthouse, listening to the wind blowing outside. Sleet hit the windows in little ticks, as if someone were tossing sand against them. Devi was sawing logs, as usual, but Peter sensed an alertness in Alex, in her bunk against the opposite wall.

"You awake?" he whispered.

She sat up. "I feel like I just drank about eight cups of coffee."

It was something about the place, or the people in it, an ambient energy. Alex came over and sat on the edge of Peter's bed. He asked how she was doing, with the relocation and the cramped quarters and life in general.

"I'm okay," she said. There was a pause. "You're going to think this is weird."

"It takes a lot to shock me these days."

She hesitated. "I kind of miss Mom."

It did shock him, but he didn't say so. "You feel what you feel," he said.

"What if what you feel is weird, though?"

He smiled. "Everybody thinks what they feel is weird."

She went back to bed and eventually relaxed into sleep. Peter lay awake, watching a blue patch of moonlight crawl along the wall, incrementally changing its dimensions as it moved. When it reached the corner of the room it flowed through it, over the course of a half hour or so, then continued on.

He was thinking about Ani Dawa. Who were these people, that they could forgive such atrocities? He wondered if he understood human nature at all. Only a few days ago he'd lain in bed, just like this, contemplating his pathetic life, all his defeats and fiascoes. Yet his petty sufferings weren't even on the same scale with those of these people. He didn't have much money, but he always had a way to make more. He wasn't healthy, but he had the means to go somewhere and *get* healthy. He wasn't homeless, he hadn't been raped or tortured or shot, he hadn't been imprisoned, and he hadn't lost toes to frostbite in a desperate attempt to escape. He felt idiotic and self-indulgent in his unhappiness.

Now Devi stirred. She crawled gently over Alex and sat on the edge of the bed. "Are you still up?" she whispered.

"Yeah," mumbled Peter.

"We should take a walk."

"It's freezing out."

She got up and started dressing. "I think it may be important."

He'd grown to trust her instincts, so he got up too. They pulled on their coats and shut the door behind them as quietly as possible.

The worst of the storm had passed, and hoarfrost blanketed the ground in the moonlight. They crunched across it in the direction of the main shrine room.

"What's this about?" Peter asked, his breath ghostly before his face.

"I don't know," she said. "I just woke up and had this feeling."

They let themselves into the shrine room. The overhead lights were out, but dozens of butter lamps provided enough light to see. The room was empty except for one person; Lama Padma still sat on his platform, sipping from a cup of tea. When he saw them he brightened and waved them over. Peter sat on the carpet by the platform, and Devi offered three prostrations, then joined him. Lama Padma spoke.

"He says what a lucky coincidence we should come by," Devi said, smiling. "He says your letter piqued his curiosity, but it's hard to get mail back and forth from his monastery, so if it's okay with you he'd like to talk about some of this now."

Peter nodded. The whole situation was a little uncanny, but Lama Padma seemed his usual good-humored self.

The lama spoke again. "He's interested in how ideas about this evolution you describe have affected society in the West," Devi said. "Are there moral or spiritual implications?"

Peter appreciated the lama's curiosity, but it was a funny thing to bring up at one o'clock in the morning. Then he remembered how little Lama Padma slept, and it made more sense. Peter was still feeling both jazzed and sleepy, so he tried to clear his head and collect his thoughts.

"Mainly, I guess it's useful in understanding what motivates us," he said. "I feel strange saying this to a monk, but from an evolutionary perspective, mainly what drives people is sex. And what's underneath it is the subconscious desire for viable offspring. Once you understand that, a lot of things make more sense."

The lama spoke, and Devi said, "So you're saying that the desire people feel is just how their bodies get them to act in certain ways?"

"Exactly," Peter said. "The guy thinks he wants to get into her jeans, but really he wants to get into her genes."

"Then how does morality play into this?"

Peter rubbed his head and realized his hair had gone all wild as he'd lain in bed. "Consider what sexual practices have been frowned upon in most cultures, at least until recently," he said. "Homosexuality, incest, masturbation, sex during menstruation, abortion, contraception."

The lama raised his eyebrows and spoke. "There's some thread between all these?" Devi translated.

"They all have one thing in common," Peter said. "They reduce the chance of viable offspring. I think we've manufactured morality out of our own instinctive desire to reproduce, then thrown a heavenly cloak over it, hoping people won't peek too closely at what's underneath. We even write books with things in them like 'Be fruitful and multiply,' then ascribe the quotes to God."

The lama spoke. "But what does this mean to people?" Devi said. "Does it make them intolerant, or more forgiving, or what?"

"Even if you're aware of what's driving you, it doesn't necessarily make you able to resist it," Peter said. "It's all very emotional, and that's the nature of the beast; we're the saddest kind of slaves because we actually believe we're free."

As Devi translated, the lama said, "Ah," and then sipped his tea, looking pensive. He spoke again.

"He agrees that we tend to be captives to our emotions," Devi said. "But he wants to emphasize that compassion is the one emotion that has the potential to free us, because it isn't based on a desire for our own happiness."

"Free us from what, though?" Peter said. "From the kind of slavery I was talking about?"

"More than that," Devi said. She listened to the lama for a few moments, then went on. "One of his Western students described the fall from grace in the Bible, and he says it's like that, except that instead of a legendary event it's a real one that happens in people all the time. What really chains us is ordinary mind, the inability to rest in pure awareness. That we're always falling away from that, and that's how we lose our true freedom."

Peter rubbed his eyes. "It seems like you guys are way ahead of us," he said. "I mean, this monastery is full of people who've taken vows that remove their DNA from the gene pool, who devote their lives to the welfare of others. That's an extremely rebellious act against the forces of instinct."

When Devi translated this, the lama's eyes lit up and he laughed.

"Yes," Devi went on. "He says every monastery is really a hotbed of subversives!"

Then the lama turned to Devi. They spoke together in Tibetan for a little while, and tears came to Devi's eyes.

"What?" Peter asked, a little anxiously. He hoped this wasn't about more karma purification.

She looked down and wiped her eyes. "He asked me if I was just sitting here translating, or if I was paying attention," she said. "And then I realized this whole thing wasn't just about having an intellectual discussion with you."

Peter looked at Lama Padma, who was watching Devi with kind interest. "So I was the decoy?" Peter said.

Devi smiled. "Only partly," she said. She glanced shyly at the lama. "He just thinks I have potential, and I might want to pay attention to that."

SIXTEEN

In the morning, Devi appeared introspective, quietly holding her-self apart from them as they loaded the jeep. When they were briefly alone, Peter asked her what was on her mind.

She stopped and looked at her feet shyly. "I think I might like to stay here for a few days," she said. "Maybe spend some time with the *anis*."

Alex walked up with her bag then, and overheard. "Devi," she said. "Please tell me you're not thinking about joining up." She smiled, but her concern showed.

Devi shrugged. She was clearly wrestling with her feelings. "I'm just curious," she said.

Peter watched her. "You should stay if you want," he said. "We can pick you up next week."

Alex looked at him, her eyebrows arched in surprise. But Devi's face filled with color, and her eyes teared up. It was as if he'd ca-sually offered her a diamond. "Would that really be okay?" she asked.

"Call me on your cell if you want us to come sooner."

"Thanks," she said, and put her arms around him.

| | |

On the road back, Alex was quiet for a long time, staring out the window. It began to rain.

"Let's hear it," Peter said, finally.

"How could you just let her leave like that?"

"She's a grown-up," he answered. "For that matter, so are you."

She crossed her arms and stared straight ahead. "So I'm not allowed to be upset?"

"She's got to figure out her own life. I thought you'd be sympathetic."

"I'd be plenty sympathetic if it didn't include her becoming a nun."

"Give her time," he said. "If you try to tie her up, she'll fight you all the way."

She made a dismissive puffing noise. "Since when are you the great oracle on successful relationships?"

He looked at her, genuinely stung by this. "I'm not," he said. "But sometimes I know what *not* to do, and if there's something really important to somebody you love, you don't want to tell her she can't."

"Oh, like Mom and meth? Tolerance worked real well there, huh?"

He felt the hackles rise on his neck. "I put her into rehab three times, and three times she went back on that shit."

"So then you do it a fourth, if you have to."

"Another thing you learn along the way is when to quit." His voice was hard. "If Devi wants to meditate, it might take her away from you, but it isn't going to destroy her. Don't pretend you don't see the difference. You're not that stupid."

She fought back tears. "Maybe I should just walk back."

"Good idea," he said. "It's only eight more miles, and it's not raining *that* hard."

"Goddamn it, Dad!"

"What do you want from me? I'm not her father."

"You dragged me out to this godforsaken place, and the one consolation was that she'd be here! Now I don't even have that!"

"You think I'm having a great time? Just weeks ago you wanted to stay. Don't make it sound like this is all my damn fault."

"It *is* your fault," she said.

"It is not!"

"It is!"

"Enough!" he shouted, and she recoiled and sobbed harder. They were both too angry to say any more or even look at each other. Alex snuffled the rest of the way home, and when they got there, she got out of the jeep and went inside ahead of him, without glancing back. The silence continued through dinner. When Peter finally cooled down a little he wanted to say something consoling, but he didn't trust his temper. Alex went to bed early but slept fitfully. Peter read until after midnight, then finally turned in, exhausted.

SEVENTEEN

The next day Bahadur appeared at the clinic with three girls.

"Doctor," he said, with an unctuous smile. He seemed to enjoy viewing Peter's reduced circumstances.

The girls crowded onto the exam table like birds on a wire, dangling their feet and surveying the room nervously. Two of them were beautiful, but the youngest was gangly and plain, and wore an old pair of plastic glasses held together at the bridge with masking tape.

Peter looked at them. "What are you doing here, Bahadur?"

Bahadur handed him a letter. It was from Franz, instructing Peter to cooperate with whatever Bahadur asked him to do. The survival of the clinic was apparently at stake.

"Now that I'm getting used to how things work around here, I trust there's something in it for me?" Peter said.

"I suppose that depends on what you want, Doctor."

"Tell me what *you* want, then we'll negotiate from there."

"Very well," Bahadur said, smiling. "These three girls are to be sold as virgins. I will need a letter that they are intact and without disease."

"You can't seriously be asking me to do this."

Bahadur tapped the letter in Peter's hand and smiled. "Banhi tells me you're quite impressed with the TB drugs and the quinolone antibiotics," he said. "What a shame for your patients if they ran out."

Peter stared at him, processing this. He'd just been talking to Lama Padma about bogus morality, but there was one form of morality he believed in, which was that you didn't deliberately participate in things that harmed people. Now he was being asked to do just that, and if he refused, still others would be hurt because they wouldn't get the drugs they needed. It wasn't enough that he'd failed at everything else; now, if he wanted to keep practicing medicine, he even had to fail at the Hippocratic oath.

Alex loitered in the doorway, her arms crossed over her chest, her expression of distaste suggesting that Bahadur might be the only person in the world more repugnant than her father.

"Escort Mr. Bahadur to the waiting room, if you would," Peter said.

Her mouth fell open. "You can't tell me you're going along with this."

"I don't really have to tell you anything, do I?"

"This is disgusting, Dad. You'd lose your license for this at home."

"Well, we're *not* home, are we?"

"Pretty clearly not."

"Then do as I ask, please," he said.

Bahadur observed this exchange with interest, then sauntered out into the waiting room and plopped his ample buttocks down on one of the creaky chairs. Alex went behind the reception desk.

"Would you like something to drink?" she asked, and Bahadur looked up in surprise.

"You're certainly more polite than your father," he said. "What do you have?"

She looked him straight in the eye and said, "Nothing." Then she sat down, put her feet up on the desk, and opened a magazine. Bahadur hissed with exasperation.

Peter shut the door.

Banhi translated as he spoke to the girls. Two turned out to be seventeen; the plain girl with the glasses was fifteen but seemed brighter and more inquisitive than the others. Peter doubted she'd have an easy time dealing with clients, which meant her life as a prostitute was likely to be even rougher than usual.

"Ask how much their fathers sold them for."

Banhi translated and reported the news impassively. "About twenty thousand rupees apiece."

"Less than three hundred dollars."

"A year's income for a family," Banhi said.

"Ask them if they know what they'll be doing."

Banhi shot him the sort of look you'd give an idiot. "Of course they know."

"Ask them, please."

She spoke to the girls. They replied shyly, their eyes downcast, playing with their fingers.

"They say yes."

"Ask them if this is something they've agreed to do. If they might rather return home, or go to school."

"Doctor, this is all established," said Banhi. "You are making Mr. Bahadur wait."

"Bahadur wasn't paying your salary last time I checked," Peter said. Then he looked at her again. "Or is he?"

She reddened and her expression changed, which told Peter everything he needed to know. He was aware of what the clinic paid her, that it was barely enough to live on, and now he felt guilty for rubbing her nose in it. They were both collaborators at this point, anyway, so who was he to judge?

He lowered his head, showing a little deference. "Just ask them, will you?"

She spoke a little less sharply to the girls, who replied one at a time.

"The pretty ones say they cannot go home, that their fathers have refused to take them back," she said. "They say they know of

Bahadur's other girls, that he has a good reputation in the towns they come from, and that they will be well paid."

"Are they frightened?"

"They are a little afraid, but they have no education and don't think they would like school very much."

Peter looked at the girls. They were so shy they wouldn't even make eye contact with him. They would have to grow up fast.

"Do they know about AIDS?"

"Whatever they know is almost certainly wrong."

Peter nodded at the plain girl. "What about her?"

Banhi spoke to her. The girl answered quietly, her eyes downcast, and Banhi shrugged. "She will get used to it."

"What did she *say*?"

"Her name is Usha. Her parents have three younger children, and there is not enough food. She likes to read."

"She can *read*?"

"An answer much more complicated than I asked for," Banhi said. "Shall I have them undress?"

"Not yet."

Peter went out to get Bahadur, who stood at the window, watching the pale yellow smoke that belched from the rendering plant down the road. Peter smiled, shook his hand, and led him outside. Bahadur appeared suspicious of this gesture of truce. They strolled down the street, where the smell of rancid flesh soaked them like an invisible mist. A thrumming tornado of flies darkened the air over the plant.

"Your American teenagers are most disrespectful," said Bahadur.

"It's a big problem," Peter said. "Whenever she's discourteous to child slavers I ground her, but she just won't mend her ways."

Bahadur narrowed his eyes. "Did you want something from me, Doctor, or do you just prefer to deliver your insults in the open air?"

"The skinny one, Usha."

"The spectacles are charming, are they not? A certain kind of man goes wild for such things."

"You know she has no future as a whore," Peter said. "Why did you even buy her?"

Bahadur sighed. "Everything is relationships," he said. "She has two sisters who will be beautiful. I help her father by buying her, then in a couple of years I will make good money on them."

"Who knows what will happen in two years?" Peter said. "I think you've made a bad investment."

Bahadur eyed him skeptically. "Perhaps you would like to try her yourself. Is that it, Doctor?"

"I'll give you six hundred dollars for her. You double your money."

Bahadur was incredulous. "You want to *buy* her? For permanent?"

"Six hundred U.S., in cash."

"Now I am more comfortable."

"Why?"

"When you smiled at me before, I became worried. Here we say, 'When the snake shows his teeth, it is best to step away.'"

"I understood that the first time I saw *you* smile, Bahadur."

Bahadur shoved his hands into his jacket pockets, and they walked on past the plant. Squadrons of flies broke off from the huge vortex and attacked, swarming around their heads and biting viciously. Peter slapped at them, but Bahadur ignored the assault, letting them land on his face and head without flinching. Once or twice he casually waved them away. When they'd passed the plant, he sat on a low rock wall and pulled out a pack of *bidis*.

He slid open a matchbook and dug out a wooden match, then held it so the head pointed slightly back toward himself. He shoved it quickly down against the friction strip, extended his jaw as he lit the cigarette, then hollowed his cheeks as he sucked in the smoke. He growled a little. His jacket rustled as he shifted his weight. His dark, half-lidded eyes appeared disengaged.

"Do you know what would happen, Doctor, if the authorities learned that an American was attempting to engage in human trafficking?"

"Don't threaten me," Peter said. "You've been telling people I'm CIA. What if it were true?"

Bahadur flicked his ash. "Doctor, forgive me, but it is very obvious you are not CIA. The local station chief is a client of mine, as are two of his subordinates, and they all have the same look in their eyes. It is a look you do not share, I am happy to say."

Peter ground the toe of his shoe into the dirty sidewalk. There was some kind of splattering of yellow grease or fat off to the side. "You're going to make me beg, aren't you?"

"If this is begging, you could use some pointers," Bahadur said. "Perhaps you should pay attention to how the locals do it."

Peter took a shallow breath and let it out. "I suppose it's out of the question for you to just do the right thing?"

Bahadur guffawed. "This is Spike Lee movie?" he said. "The *right thing* is for you to pay me what she will earn over the next few years, which is perhaps twenty thousand dollars."

"That's crap, and you know it. She won't earn a quarter of that, and you'll have to feed and clothe her."

Bahadur took a last drag on his cigarette, then threw away the butt. A street kid picked it up immediately and trotted off with it.

"Then perhaps seven thousand," Bahadur said. "Special one-time discount."

"Nine hundred."

Bahadur raised his palms skyward, as if to catch rain. "You cannot take her to the United States," he said, his voice a falsetto of bewilderment. "I am a judge of men, and I do not think you actually want sex with her. So what will you do?"

"I'm trying to figure that out."

Bahadur put his hands back on the wall by his legs. "Let me explain how this will go, Doctor. You will pay me all this money, then you will come to the end of your stay here, and in three months the girl will be back with me, just like the last one. It is a waste of everyone's time. So maybe for you I will say five thousand."

Peter wanted a deeper breath, more air, but the smell was just too foul. "Fifteen hundred."

Bahadur smiled. "I fear we are so far apart we will have to call in the UN soldiers with their pretty blue helmets to help us."

"Two thousand."

"Impossible, completely." Bahadur shrugged. "Forty-five hundred is the best I can do."

Peter stared at him. "Twenty-five."

Bahadur waved his hand. "Three thousand, final," he said. "Take it or leave it."

"That's ten times what you paid for her."

"And a third what she'll earn me."

"A third what she'd earn you if she were *pretty*," Peter said. "Twenty-six."

Bahadur lowered his head and appeared to contemplate this. "I fear these flies will give me some horrible disease, and then I will have to come to you for help," he said. "I cannot imagine anything worse." He sighed. "Twenty-eight-fifty," he said at last.

"Sold," said Peter.

Bahadur smiled broadly, revealing jagged rows of crooked brown teeth intercut with gold. His tongue darted out between them, pink and wet. "You realize, of course," he said, "that if you insist on creating additional demand in this way, I will be forced to increase supply. Even an American cardiologist cannot buy every girl in Nepal."

"Congratulations," said Peter. "You've proven there's absolutely nothing good or beneficial I can accomplish."

Bahadur shrugged. "Life offers so few opportunities to humiliate rich Americans," he said. "One must seize the day."

Back at the clinic, Peter examined the two girls Bahadur was keeping and gave them a clean bill. As Bahadur was about to leave, he took out a battered suitcase and emptied it onto the counter. It contained a two-month supply of all the TB drugs the clinic needed, a variety of antibiotics, good French IV solutions, latex gloves, and sundry other supplies.

"Perhaps I have neglected to give you my card," he said, handing one over. It read:

BEAUTIFUL ESCORTS, SERVICE TODAY

(977) 98 1 555-BEST

A Business Doing Pleasure with You!

EIGHTEEN

The problem with buying a human being, Peter realized, was that then you owned her, which turned out to be a little awkward. He called the NGO to which he'd taken the first girl, but they'd met their quota for the next two months and had no place for Usha.

There was nothing to do but take her home. Though Alex had mixed emotions about the whole thing—she was still aghast about the other girls, but Peter had apparently redeemed himself slightly with this gesture—she agreed to bunk with Usha until Devi came back. When they came into the house Usha stood still, looking confused and tense, then spoke to Alex in Nepali.

"She hopes you're not planning on having sex with her tonight, because she has her period," Alex said.

"Candid, isn't she?"

"Evidently."

"Explain the situation, will you?"

Alex spoke with Usha for a minute, then turned to Peter. "She thinks you're nuts, but it's fine with her."

Peter started getting dinner together, but Usha—either worried by what she considered her own dereliction of duty or horrified that this crazy foreigner would inadvertently poison them all—insisted on helping. Together they made a dinner of *dal-bhat,* and Usha ate like a girl possessed. She was a good four inches shorter than Alex. Her face was gaunt, her hair stringy, her overall demeanor that of a spavined dog, but she seemed reasonably good-natured, and she clearly appreciated the food. As they ate, Peter reflected that seven months previously, as he had moved about his comfortable Berkeley office seeing patients, he would have been surprised to hear that come February he'd find himself in a tiny concrete room in Jorpati, Nepal, having acquired, in approximate order, a divorce, a motor scooter covered with ox shit, a lesbian near-daughter-in-law, a small brown goat, dysentery, a housekeeper who doubled as an informant, a medical supplier who doubled as a pimp, and a sex slave with whom he had no intention of having sex. Oh, and yes, instruction from a Tibetan lama on the endless mutability of things.

Usha helped Alex do the dishes, then she lay down and went to sleep almost immediately. Peter made tea and was pleased when Alex poured herself a cup, came over, and sat beside him.

"How much money you figure you're losing by working here, Papaji?"

A thaw, mercifully, he hoped. "That's what makes us different from them," he said. "I can go home and make more. Hope totally changes the psychological terrain."

Usha began to snore. Alex rolled her eyes. "What is it with these people? Do they all snore? Is it some special mutation?"

Peter suppressed a smile. "Of course, I feel obliged to point out that you snore."

"I do not. Though *you* snore like a goddamn ape."

"Liar," he said. They were both grinning for the first time since the fight.

She looked over at Usha. "Think about it," she said. "Her parents actually *sold* her."

"It's a tempting idea sometimes, I'll admit. The only thing that holds me back is knowing how little I'd get for you."

She batted at him, then got up, changed into her sweats, and crawled in with Usha. Soon she too was snoring. A few minutes later, one of them—Peter wasn't sure which one—farted. The place was like a barracks.

He got into bed and turned out the light. The night came in: the dripping of the outside water tap, dogs trotting by and rooting through trash, beggars shuffling down the road and yelling at the dogs to keep them away. Someone was chanting a late-evening *puja,* the bell ringing out into the night in rhythm with the liturgy.

Soon he drifted off, but he awakened again when he heard something near the bed. Usha stood there, blue bands of moonlight across her T-shirt.

"Dhanyabaad," she said quietly.

He pulled himself up on one elbow. "Don't mention it," he said. "We'll figure something out. Get some sleep."

| | |

Alex took Usha under her wing and showed her how to help at the clinic. The next week they drove up to get Devi. They found her in a concrete courtyard with four or five of the *anis,* playing a pickup game of basketball. Some American foundation had apparently decided that the monks and nuns had a pressing need for exercise, so they had sent over six soccer balls, three basketballs, and a backboard and hoop. Lama Yeshe had overseen the construction of the half-court for the nuns and had helped the monks build a small soccer field.

Devi's face lit up, and she ran over and gave Alex a hug. Alex introduced Usha to Devi, who regarded the newcomer quizzically and not all that happily. Alex quickly whispered that it was fine and she'd explain later, then strode out onto the basketball court.

"You girls need instruction," she said. "You don't even know how to dribble."

"So show us, if you're so smart," Devi said.

They walked toward the court with Usha in tow. Devi said something, gesturing at Alex, and the *anis* pretended to be overwhelmed with awe—laughing at her in a shy, funny sort of way. They tossed her the ball. Alex took it, dribbled once, and swished a three-pointer from the edge of the court. The nuns stopped laughing. They threw it to her again; she took it on the run, drove to the basket, then leaped and sunk a layup. She snagged the ball, dribbled out to the end of the court, and threw a hook shot over her shoulder that hit the backboard and then the rim before falling through. The *anis* stood still now, watching with big eyes, until Devi said something and they laughed again.

"She said this is what passes for spiritual practice in America, and that I have great *siddhis*," Alex told her father. "She said I'm a *tulku*—a reincarnate master—of basketball."

They wanted her to teach them, so she gathered everyone together. Peter was proud, watching her. They got two balls going and stationed someone behind the backboard to act as goalie so they wouldn't have to spend so much time trotting down the hill after missed shots. Soon more nuns showed up and got into the drill, rotating through shooting, dribbling, and catching runaways. Shortly thereafter the third ball was in play and the *ani gonpa* looked like it had been transformed into a basketball camp, except that all the women had shaved heads and wore maroon robes, and they ranged from roughly Alex's age to maybe sixty. But even the oldest ones were startlingly spry.

The nuns already knew about high-fives, and when it was getting close to dinnertime, Alex worked the crowd, slapping one palm after another.

She came back to Peter, her face flushed, her smile brilliant. Devi collected her things, and the four of them piled into the jeep. Usha stayed quiet and held herself a bit apart from the other two girls.

NINETEEN

Bahadur had been satisfied with his payoff, and word came from Franz that they could soon return to Kathmandu. Peter didn't really want to kick Sonam and Sangita out of the house, but it turned out they'd saved enough by staying there that they could finally rent a small apartment in the complex where they'd previously pitched their tent.

One morning, a young Canadian couple showed up at the clinic in Jorpati. Anne was a freshly minted pediatrician, and David was a burly, seasoned RN.

Banhi gave them a steely once-over, her arms across her chest, her jaw set like a bulldog's. She finally grunted her approval and returned to sterilizing instruments in the pressure cooker.

Peter walked them through the clinic and watched the sheen of their idealism fade.

"Um . . . there's no *autoclave*?" asked Anne, her voice rising in disbelief.

"It's surprising how well the Presto works."

"Those trucks," said David. "They're hauling *hides*?"

"Water buffalo, mainly, yes."

The two looked at each other, and Peter could see the silent conference.

"The taxi driver just ripped us off," said David. "We can't walk ten steps without getting accosted by street kids. I understand we'll be getting most of our drugs from a pimp."

"When was the last time you had patients who were genuinely grateful?" Peter asked.

They thought about it. "It happens from time to time," said David.

"Patients who decide to name their next child after you? Patients who want to give you their best goat?"

"As far as I know, there aren't any extra Annes out there because of me," Anne admitted.

"As a rule we aren't offered a lot of goats in Toronto," said David.

"Here it happens all the time," Peter said.

David gazed downward at the floor, his shoulders elevated as if shrugging off a cold rain. "This pimp," he said. "Can he get us other kinds of stuff? Like, say, disposable syringes or at least a decent autoclave?"

"Depends on how badly you want it," Peter said.

"I mean, what if we pay out of our own pockets?"

Peter felt a surge of warmth. "You'll do fine," he said. "Just offer him a tenth of what he asks and haggle up to about twenty percent."

| | |

That evening Peter said goodbye to Banhi, closed the clinic, and went to a small bookstore, where he found some children's books in English. The three girls had formed a casual alliance, but now that Devi was back, Usha set up a separate bed and apparently understood the situation. Alex and Devi went out for dinner by themselves, as a sort of farewell to Jorpati, so Peter and Usha had some *dal-bhat* and sat together on his bed, leaning against the wall. He

read to her the way he'd done with Alex when she was young, following the words with his finger and relating them to the pictures.
Usha was a quick study, and, perhaps because she was already lit-
erate in Nepali, within an hour she recognized some of the words
and pronounced them as he got to them. She was especially good
with animals, and got "dog," "cat," "goat," "chicken," and
"cow" right away. He was so proud of her that it surprised him.

The girls came back, sated and happy. Devi, who seemed even
more radiant than usual since her stay at the monastery, suggested
they go to the great stupa in Boudhanath. She told them to bring
as much money as they could.

As they walked the narrow streets they could see the huge,
spired dome towering over the houses and buildings, glowing in
the fading light.

More people moved with them down the dusty road, released
from the day's work, fingering the Buddhist rosaries known as
malas and quietly reciting *Om Mani Padme Hum*, a deep rumble
of sound that seemed to well up from the earth as much as from
the people on it. From houses and nearby monasteries came chanting, bells and drums, and the long Tibetan horns used in *pujas*.
The horns were so deep and powerful they seemed to bend air and
rupture it, blast it outward toward the mountains in palpable
waves.

It seemed they'd waded into a warm current and needed only to
let go and allow themselves to float calmly downstream. Alex's
eyes were wide and luminous. She slipped her cool hand into her
father's as they walked. Usha and Devi strolled together and talked
quietly in Nepali.

The dome was alight with butter lamps on ascending levels,
shimmering as breezes brushed the flames, the crowning spire
reaching upward a hundred feet. Multicolored prayer flags fluttered against the darkening sky, lit from below by the lamps.
Around the perimeter, merchants closed up their shops for the day
as children and animals played in the dust. Rows of beggars sat

waiting, patiently insistent. A legless old man on a small, wheeled cart said, "Rupees? One rupee, please?" Devi gave him one, and they moved on.

"Give all your money away while we're here," she said. Peter slipped some rupees into Usha's hand so she'd have some to pass along.

They entered the slow, clockwise whirlpool of people circling the stupa. Mainly they were Tibetans and Nepalis, but there were foreigners too, Americans and a few Germans. Several sturdy-looking Tibetans progressed via prostration; wearing wooden blocks on their hands and long leather aprons, they extended themselves on the ground, arose, and moved forward like inch-worms.

Devi spun the prayer wheels as they walked. A gust extin-guished a dozen butter lamps, and they stopped to relight them. Clouds of incense arose from sticks piled into wooden boxes. As they moved on, a couple of monks walked beside them for a while, tossing rice; other people threw flowers or lit candles. One woman sat with a small burlap bag, throwing barley to the birds, which would fly in, peck a few grains, burst away again, then return. An-other woman, hidden from view, sang high, haunting notes in a language none of them recognized, and Peter wondered if she had made it up. One kid pedaled the circuit on a rusty, dented bike.

A small family sat off to one side, burning juniper and incense and praying, offering the blue smoke itself, which swirled upward above their heads and fanned out, scenting the air and dissipating into the night sky. A small boy looked up from the flames, his face half bright, half shadowed; his eyes were big and dark, his expres-sion neutral, neither smiling nor frowning. Devi blew him a kiss, and he staggered back a step, as if the kiss carried force.

There was a blond, Scandinavian-looking woman in a ball gown so vividly blue it seemed electric, with matching elbow-length gloves and a tiara. She tottered forward barefoot, holding a champagne glass aloft in one hand as if toasting, her hair radiant in the twilight. Some of the locals looked at her in disgust, some in awe, but Alex just grinned.

A small girl of about six lugged a green thermos half as tall as she was. She went from beggar to beggar, pouring them tea that smelled of cinnamon and cloves. Some of them ignored her, some blessed her, but all drank the tea. Peter and the girls passed them, and coin by coin, bill by bill, their money dropped from their hands as their pockets emptied and they grew lighter.

They finished one circuit and ascended to the stupa's second level, and then the third, and from this vantage they could see out across the city, its wires and streetlights, and the tiny bright squares of windows. Away to the west lay the illuminated galaxy of Kathmandu. Up the hill to the north, one of the monasteries gleamed in the hard light of the rising moon, a butter lamp on every windowsill. Behind it rose the Himalayas, their snow crowns ghostly blue, hovering in space above the foothills. And above them, the north star and the Big Dipper, bright and nearly un-blinking in the high, cold atmosphere. Juniper smoke and incense and the smell of people mingled in the air, and always came the low recitations, *Om Mani Padme Hum*. Devi had told them it translated as "the jewel is in the lotus," meaning that Enlighten-ment was to be found within one's own heart, in the flower whose roots are anchored in the mud of everyday existence.

A mud that was not just about fertility, as Peter had told Lama Padma, but also about mortality. He wondered where he and Alex would be when their time came to die. This would have seemed morbid in the United States, but it was natural and practical to think about here, where death was a constant in every household. People's parents died, their husbands and wives died, their broth-ers and sisters and children died. Peter remembered seeing Satyajit Ray's Apu trilogy in college. The characters were dropping like flies, but Ray wasn't painting a particularly dark picture; he was just showing Bengal as it was. Western democracies had had a tech bubble, but they were also having a health bubble. Bengal and

Nepal were how the whole planet had been a hundred years earlier. Half the epidemiologists Peter knew were on Xanax, because
they understood that if enough strains of staph or strep or TB developed multidrug resistance, or if avian flu jumped species, the
world would be just like the plague years again, with bodies
stacked, rotting in the streets, the cities emptied.

Alex would be eighteen in April, just a couple of months away.
She had started her slow walk away from him, and even in her
presence he missed her. What he faced now was not her physical
mortality but the first of the small, unavoidable deaths that lay before it. His daughter, a woman in love, opening the door that led
from his house.

He recalled a Leonard Cohen song that had come out a few
years earlier. There was a refrain: *"Say goodbye to Alexandra leaving, then say goodbye to Alexandra lost."* He'd loved that song,
the complexity and melancholy of it, even though he was never
completely sure what it meant. He'd waited years for it to acquire
resonance in the context of his own life, but now he was beginning
to get it.

They came back down and circled the stupa twice more, Devi
leading them, Usha by her side, Alex and Peter walking behind
with their arms around each other, flowing with the crowd. They'd
given away all their money. They had nothing to do but this. When
they had finished and started for the street, Devi turned back
toward them, her face illuminated by the butter lamps, her eyes
dark oceans. She stopped and took them in her arms.

TWENTY

"I have another volunteer for you," Peter said.

Franz wandered among his potted plants with a green plastic watering can, giving them each a little shower and inspecting the undersides of their leaves. During Peter's absence the office had begun to resemble an abandoned temple, its musty bookshelves overrun with tendrils. On the shelf under the south window, Wittgenstein lay in the sun, watching with large green eyes and twitching his tail.

"Who?"

Peter explained about Usha. "She's smart," he said. "She wants to be a doctor."

Franz shrugged. "If you can sell it to Mina it's fine by me. But speaking of stray children, a boy's been by, asking for you."

"He knows my name? What does he want?"

"He won't say. He goes by Raju."

Peter remembered then: the boy with the stick who'd fended off the dogs. "When was he here last?"

"A few days ago. I told him you'd be back today."

When Peter asked Mina about Usha, she arched an eyebrow skeptically. "You *bought* her?"

"As an alternative to where she was headed."

Mina startled him by laughing. "It's fine with me," she said. "Bring her in tomorrow."

| | |

That afternoon Raju appeared. Peter shook his hand and explained to Mina what had happened.

"What's going on?" Peter asked. "Are you sick?"

"No, sir. My father is ill these two months and now will not get up."

"Why did you wait so long?"

"I came to find you, but this other man, he said you were not here. It was not possible for me to walk to Jorpati so I have returned just now."

Peter and Mina exchanged a look. "You didn't need to see me personally," Peter said. "Franz or Mina could have helped."

"I understand this," Raju said. "However, when my father heard you are being American, he declaimed he will see no one but you."

Peter expected Mina to say something cutting about how this illustrated the deleterious effect of foreign doctors, but she didn't. She just said they'd be done soon and asked Raju to show them the way.

"You want to come?" Peter asked.

"If he's the oldest son, he may be the only one in the family who speaks English."

In the car, he watched her out of the corner of his eyes. She chatted with Raju, who seemed to take an immediate liking to her. She seemed transformed—looser and more open. Peter had thought of her during his exile, when he was plumbing the depths of patience and sanity, and had realized that much of her prickly aversion to him was probably justified. Nepal had exposed him for a fraud, and he too was calmer now, partly because his pride had been so thoroughly crushed under the wheels of experience that he no longer had much left to defend.

As if she could read his thoughts, she asked, "How goes the karma purification?"

He looked at Raju, who was staring rapt out the window, and it occurred to Peter that the boy might never have ridden in a car before.

"I feel like a mashed bug, but I'm still crawling," Peter said. "How goes it with you?"

"Still crawling along," she replied. Their eyes met briefly, and they smiled. Peter felt as if the roof had suddenly been torn from the car and there was nothing over their heads but wind and sky. He took a deep breath of sweet air.

Raju lived in a small, third-floor walk-up in a concrete building over a shop. They followed the narrow stairway up to a flat roof, where an old woman was washing clothes in a red plastic tub and hanging them on a line. A small shed constructed of discarded lumber, cardboard, and tin hunkered to one side, slightly askew and fragile-looking. A thin young girl sat there, feeding stale bread and scraps to a handful of pigeons.

"That is my sister," Raju said. "She is very smart with birds, and twice a month we are allowed to eat one."

The girl squinted at Peter with a mixture of fear and curiosity, as if she'd never seen such an exotic creature on her roof or anywhere else. The apartment was next to the pigeon coop, and Raju lived there with two other sisters, who were sitting in the corner, playing a game, and a younger brother about two years old who shrieked with delight when he saw the strangers. The woman doing laundry was the grandmother; Raju said his mother had died the previous year. Peter thought back to the patch on the boy's pants and the misbuttoned shirt. Now he understood.

Raju introduced them to his father, who was sprawled on a thin straw mattress and propped up against the wall on a couple of pillows made of rags stuffed into old rice bags. Raju spoke to him animatedly in Nepali, apparently indicating that Peter was the long-awaited American doctor. The man smiled faintly, and the grandmother appeared in the doorway.

"Mr. Shrestha," Peter said, and shook his hand. Everyone in the family had rich, brown, lustrous skin except him; he was a pale, deathly gray. His abdomen was grossly distended, his limbs and neck like withered sticks. Peter asked him about his symptoms as Mina translated. It became clear fairly quickly that he had cancer, probably colon cancer that had metastasized; he hadn't been able to shit for nearly two weeks, and he'd stopped eating. He was obviously in a lot of pain and would most likely be dead in days. Mina and Peter looked at the grandmother, at the children, and then at each other.

"American doctors can heal anything, yes?" said Raju. "This is why we wait."

"Stay here with your father, will you?" Peter said.

They took the grandmother outside onto the roof. She wiped the tears from her eyes as Mina explained the situation. She agreed to learn how to give her son injections for his pain, but there were no other relatives she knew of, and she didn't think she could care for the children much longer.

"Where are they going to go?" Peter asked Mina.

"The Teku orphanage, probably," Mina said. "This kind of thing happens all the time. At least it's fairly new; it isn't out of Dickens or anything."

"Jesus."

"What are you going to do, Peter? You've already got Devi and Usha on your hands."

He wanted to herd everyone out of the city and burn it down, so they could build something decent and start over. "It's just that I've been thinking a lot about futility lately."

"I don't want this to sound harsh, but you shouldn't even do that much to take care of them while you're here."

"What are you talking about? Why not?"

"Because you'll have to turn them over to the orphanage when you leave, and it will be even worse for them if you get involved with their lives and then dump them like a litter of stray cats."

He didn't want to hear this; it was just another affirmation of Bahadur's Law. Even so, he knew she was probably right.

Raju took the news about his father badly. "I had always thought if I found you again . . ." he said. He cried and held his head.

"I'm sorry," said Peter.

"There are no machines or special medicines, nothing that can be managed?"

"It's too late."

Raju sat against the wall and sobbed a sort of kittenish mewing, as if it were his intention to make as little motion or noise as possible. Peter put a hand on his shoulder. After a few minutes, the boy wiped his eyes with the heels of his hands, looked at each of them in turn, then stood. "My sister needs help with the pigeons," he said, and started over to the coop.

"Raju—" Peter said, but Raju just waved his hand behind him, a wave that was at once a goodbye and a dismissal, as if Peter and Mina were unworthy of a look back.

They taught the grandmother how to administer the morphine and left her a supply, then packed up to leave. But as they were going, Raju came back and caught them at the top of the stairs. He sounded resentful, as if he regretted having to ask anything further but saw no alternative.

"My father said that when it was time, he wanted a proper cremation at Pashupatinath," he said. "Could you help arrange this? There is no money and I don't know what to do."

"Of course," said Mina.

Peter wrote his address on a piece of paper. "Come find me there if I'm not at the clinic."

Raju folded the paper, put it in his pocket, and went back inside without looking at them again. Peter and Mina headed downstairs. Each time Peter's rubber sole hit the concrete steps, the dry squeaking noise sounded to him like a small whispering voice. He looked out from the side of the stairwell; the sky was a clear blue, with a few bright clouds, and washing hung from lines on rooftops and balconies, shifting listlessly in the humid breeze. Peter tried to focus on these scraps of beauty, but as he continued downward his feet repeated the word over and over: *despair, despair, despair.*

| | |

A week later Raju was waiting by Peter's front gate when he got home from work. Peter called Mina, who came over and picked them up.

On the ride to Raju's, it hit him how weary he was. Funerals had always served to remind him of his failures—and, for that matter, the failures of the universe to provide people with the longevity they could conceive of and therefore naturally wanted for themselves. When the families of his patients asked him to attend, he usually found an excuse to stay away. It felt cowardly, but in this he allowed himself cowardice.

Of course then there was Raju, who had put himself in harm's way to save them and asked little in return. When Peter arrived, Raju was trying to be stoic, but he was obviously distraught. Peter imagined what it must be like to be orphaned so young, with sisters to care for. He put an arm around Raju's shoulders, and the boy leaned into him.

"I'll talk to the people at the orphanage," Peter said. "I'll give them money and make sure they look after you. When you're older I'll send you money too."

But Raju looked skeptical and didn't reply, and Peter realized that once again he'd become the stereotypical American, trying to fix a bad situation with cash when something better was called for. But he couldn't be a father to the boy; all he had to offer was a little temporary consolation. He felt that his debt to Raju was beyond mere gratitude for saving them from the dog pack, because Raju had offered his protection selflessly, with no thought of personal safety or recompense. He had seen their trouble and reacted with natural generosity and courage—it was more the *how* than the *what* that mattered. How could such a debt be repaid?

It was after sundown, and a few friends of Raju's father had collected. The men wrapped the body and put it on a rough litter made of bamboo and rope. One produced a straight razor and a bar of soap, then all the men took turns shaving each other's heads, dipping the razor into a bucket. When they'd finished, one of them shaved Raju's head; his locks fell to the surface of the roof and were carried away by the breeze.

Then, chanting prayers, the men hoisted the litter onto their shoulders and started down the narrow stairs, followed by Peter, Mina, Raju, and the oldest daughter—the pigeon girl—whose name was Arati. The grandmother would stay home with the younger children, who were huddled together in a heap, weeping, their eyes big with fear. As the men negotiated the litter around a tight corner they almost tipped the body off, but one man caught it in time, and the others chuckled quietly at the mishap. Raju stared ahead, his expression inscrutable.

After they'd gone a couple of blocks, Peter realized they were planning to walk all the way. A couple of the family's friends, one playing a small hand drum and the other a bamboo flute, led the little procession through the darkened streets. Raju and Arati walked in front, just behind the body, holding sticks of incense, and Mina and Peter brought up the rear. The pace was slow down into Naxal, and they often had to maneuver around *tempos,* trucks, and cattle. But an hour later, as they headed east into Gyaneshwar and crossed the bridge over the Dhobi Khola, traffic began to thin out.

The stars were shining, and the evening grew cool as they went on, the men seemingly tireless under their load. They made their way by streetlight, or by the illumination from an occasional passing motorbike, but there were dark stretches where they proceeded primarily by the glow from the rising moon. People walking the other way stepped aside and bowed their heads briefly as they passed. The drum and flute rang out into the night, their music plaintively marking the progress of the journey. Once, from a side street, a black dog appeared and began to howl.

They passed Ring Road and, after another hour or so, entered the long approach to the Pashupatinath Temple. When they reached the bridge into the main grounds, the men stopped. The leader, the one playing the drum, came back and spoke to Mina. He was a tall, emaciated fellow in ragged clothes. His freshly shaved head gleamed in the dim light.

"You aren't allowed into the temple grounds because you're not Hindu," Mina explained to Peter. "But if you want to donate something for wood and flowers for the cremation, you can."

"How much?"

"Give them four or five thousand rupees. It will be important to Raju that it's done right."

Peter handed the money to the man, who nodded and spoke to Raju. Raju took the man's hand, and they crossed the bridge. Mina showed Peter to a nearby bench, where they sat and waited.

"How are you holding up?" she asked.

"I probably should have eaten."

She pulled a small bag of cashews out of her purse, opened it, and shook some into his upturned palm. "It's going to be a long night, I'm afraid."

The men carried Shrestha's body into a nearby building to prepare it. Mina told Peter about the temple, which had been established in the fifth century, comprised several buildings over more than an acre, and was dedicated to Shiva. The Bagmati River, which flowed beneath the bridge, was sacred, though Peter could see by the light from the temple lamps that the banks were littered with old papers, cardboard, and other trash. Monkeys screeched in the trees overhead.

On the other side of the river, a stone terrace abutted the base of the building into which they had taken the body, and stone steps led down to the water's edge. This was the ghat where the body would be burned.

They sat quietly for a while, then Peter turned to Mina. "Would you want to be cremated here?" he asked.

Mina sounded bemused. "What kind of a question is that?"

"I just wondered."

She hesitated. There was a commotion in the trees as the monkeys squabbled over something. "To tell the truth, I've always had the feeling I will die far from here," she said. "I don't know why. I can't think about it without getting morose, so mostly I try not to."

This surprising sign of vulnerability moved him. They were in moonlight. The torches on the temple grounds flicked orange light onto their faces. Mina looked tired, her head inclined, her eyes downcast. She leaned forward and took some of her weight with her arms. Peter could smell her perspiration, her fatigue, and a certain distinct scent that was just Mina, animal and familiar and even a little sweet.

It was time to say something; he felt it as surely as he'd ever felt anything. He didn't really know *what* to say, but he couldn't let things go on like this. His heart pounded.

"If you should die far from here, but not far from me, what would you like me to do?" he asked.

She looked at him, shifted her weight, uncrossed her legs. "Please tell me this isn't some kind of joke."

"Of course it isn't."

She half smiled, a smile that was part skepticism and part indulgence. "I thought you hated me."

"I thought so too, for a while. In fact, I was pretty sure the feeling was mutual."

She was pensive for a few moments. "I did hate you, I think."

He thought he understood her reasons now, but he wanted to hear it from her. "Why?"

She exhaled between pursed lips, a *fffff* sound. "It's embarrassing," she said. "But almost every doc who's come through the clinic has tried to get me to . . . you know."

"Are we talking about romance?"

She waved her hand. "Oh, no, they didn't want love; they didn't even particularly seem to want friendship."

"Just bed the beautiful native girl so you can tell your buddies back home?"

"Something like that," she said. "The Belgian wasn't a very good clinician, but the real reason we got rid of him was that he was such an incorrigible lech. I just figured you were the same."

He leaned forward and rested his elbows on his knees. "I wasn't looking for sex, but you were right about one thing: I thought I knew more than I did," he said. "I didn't know anything. I would have torn out half that girl's septum on the first day if you hadn't walked in."

"That's also true," she said, smiling. "You were a sorry case."

"So what changed, what happened?"

She sighed. "*You* happened, I guess. You started listening to me. You bought a girl to keep her out of slavery. You're paying for the funeral of a man you don't even know."

"I didn't do any of that to impress you."

"I get that," she said. "But why? Nobody's that saintly."

He thought about it. "Alex had a rough time growing up," he said. "She has a lot of natural compassion, but she had to put so much energy into defending herself, early on, that it just got trampled. I guess I wanted her to see that it's possible to live another way, that you don't have to harden your heart to survive."

"I get the feeling you weren't just targeting her for that lesson."

He shook his head. "I knew it had happened to me too. Just with the everyday grind of living, I'd developed this carapace. Nothing surprised me, nothing delighted me anymore."

"There must have been easier places, though."

He smiled, thinking of the map and the dart. "We picked Nepal because she has terrible aim," he said, then explained.

"So this wasn't your first choice."

"Personally, I was rooting for Tuscany. Of course, Tuscany wouldn't have had you in it."

There was a great hooting of birds, back and forth, among the trees. Mina shivered a little.

"I missed you while you were in Jorpati," she confessed. "I was kind of horrified when I realized it."

"It was mutual," he said. "The missing, I mean, not the horror. I couldn't remember the last time I'd really missed someone."

She turned to him, her eyes large. She rested her hand on his, lightly. "You still want an answer to your question?"

"Sure."

She took a breath and let it out slowly. "Cremate me then, I suppose, wherever we are," she said. "Keep some of my ashes with you, while you're alive, and scatter the rest."

"If that's what you want."

"And if you're first?"

He thought about it. "I'll have whatever you're having."

She laughed, briefly and quietly. He loved hearing her laugh.

A little evening chill came up off the river. The temple doors opened, and the men brought the body out to the ghat. They built a pyre on the stone, then placed the litter on top and piled more wood around it. Raju and Arati sat on the ground to one side, their arms around each other's shoulders. One of the men went down to the river and scooped up water in a small silver container. He brought it back up to the body and poured some of the water into its mouth, then flicked the rest over it with his fingers. He pulled the wrap up over Shrestha's face, struck a match, and lit the straw and kindling all around the body. Smoke curled up into the light, and a cool gust fanned the flames quickly. Within a minute the pyre blazed. The children began to keen. One of the men went over, squatted down behind them, and took them in his arms.

In the firelight, Peter noticed a man sitting cross-legged on the ground nearby—a sadhu, a Hindu mystic. He wore a garland of flowers and had a long graying beard and dreadlocks. His forehead bore three white bands of paint, horizontal, each about the width of a finger.

"Offer him some money to pray for the dead man," Mina whispered.

Peter went over and placed a couple hundred rupees in front of him, then pointed to the burning figure. The sadhu nodded, very slightly, without looking at him.

An hour later, when the fire had burned down and there was little left but glowing coals and a few fragments of bone, the men indicated that they would finish the night watch and scatter the ashes into the river in the morning. They suggested Peter and Mina take the children home.

Just up the road Peter hailed a *tempo,* one of the last out at that hour. Raju and Arati began to cry again. Mina and Peter reassured them as best they could, but Peter knew their words sounded as hollow to the kids as they did to him.

They took the children home; then, exhausted, drove Mina's car back to Peter's house. They arrived a little after 3:00 A.M. to find a jeep parked in front. Two soldiers waited, one sitting sideways in the rider's seat, the other standing by the archway to the front gate with one foot against the wall. As Peter and Mina pulled in, a bright orange dot bloomed in front of the standing soldier's mouth as he sucked on a *bidi.* He pulled it from his mouth and exhaled the smoke, yellow under the streetlight. He threw the cigarette into the street, pushed himself off the wall, and came toward them.

"Oh, Christ," said Mina. "I forgot to call my parents."

"Your *parents?* You're thirty-six."

"I'm thirty-six and unmarried, and living at home," she said wearily. "In other words, to them I'm still a rebellious teenager."

Mina's father, though retired, could still muster up a few troops for private duty if he paid them on the side. They spoke to Mina in Nepali, and it was easy enough to get the gist. The conversation grew heated. Mina turned to Peter in exasperation.

"They insist I ride in the jeep with them, even though my car is right there."

"Tell them there's no way I'm letting you get into that jeep, no matter who they work for."

She repeated this in Nepali. The soldiers got angry, responding forcefully and gesticulating. "They say it is not up to you to allow or not allow anything," Mina said. "They have orders, and they plan to follow them."

"This is nuts, Mina."

She was near tears. "Welcome to my father's world."

"Tell them if they take you in the jeep, I'll follow in your car so you can get to work in the morning. Tell them I have a phone with me. They'll get the point."

She spoke to them. "They say your travel plans are your own concern," she said. "They suggest that you not follow too closely, in case there is some sort of accident that results in your being injured."

"Tell them I did my residency in Los Angeles, and I'm perfectly capable of sitting six inches off their bumper at eighty miles an hour with a cup of coffee in one hand."

Mina rolled her eyes. "I'm not going to translate that, Peter. Anyway, how will you get back?"

He took a breath. "I'll find a *tempo*, and if there aren't any, I'll walk."

"It will take you the rest of the night."

"The rest of the night is only three hours."

The soldiers finally agreed. Peter took Mina in his arms. She pulled away a little.

"My father will hear about this," she said.

"Good."

"Are you trying to make trouble for me?"

"Absolutely."

She smiled, and they kissed. She lingered on his lips, then finally they loosened their grip on each other and she stepped away. She got into the jeep, and the soldiers shut the door. Peter followed to her house, an old Rana temple that had been converted into apartments for her extended family. He could see a silhouette waiting in an upstairs window. They got out of the cars and met by the gate.

"That him?" he asked.

She nodded. "He knows I've been old enough to do as I please for a long time," she said. "But that doesn't stop him from thinking of me as a little girl. If there were any justice in the world, he would have worked himself into a stroke by now."

TWENTY-ONE

Peter had been wondering about the changes he'd seen in Devi since her stay among the *anis*. She still laughed easily and kidded around with Alex, but something was stirring beneath the surface.

Wayne Lee bleated out back. The afternoon light fell through the kitchen windows as Peter chopped vegetables.

"Anything interesting happen at the monastery?" he asked, as neutrally as possible.

"Lama Padma asked me to translate for his California students while I was there," she said. "Then word got around and more Westerners started showing up. By the end of the week I was sitting up in front with him and translating for, like, twenty people."

Peter was astonished. "You must be the most modest person on earth," he said. "Why didn't you tell me?"

She shrugged and got up to wash the beans. "It's not really anything to be proud about," she said. "It's actually really nerve-racking. All these people are waiting, so you have to think quickly. There are a lot of specialized terms in Tibetan, and the same thing has different meanings in different contexts. I got stressed trying to keep it all straight."

"What, for example?"

"Well, Alex told me once that Eskimos have about a hundred different words for snow. But Tibetans have all these words for *consciousness,* with a lot of subtle variations. Sometimes it's hard to know which one they mean."

"You're happy, though?"

She smiled. "It's what I like best, I think. Studying dharma, being with the lama. It feels like coming home."

"If you've found your calling at eighteen you've got the rest of us beat."

She fished through the drawer and picked out a knife. "You didn't decide to be a doctor when you were young?"

"I'll tell you a story," he said. "I've never told Alex about this, though, and I'd appreciate it if you didn't either."

"Okay," she said, a little warily.

"After college I had an old Kawasaki with a cargo box on the back, and I spent a couple of years bombing around California and Oregon, climbing rock. I was lean and callused, and went pretty much unwashed for days at a time, but I don't ever remember being happier."

She looked at him. "But you quit? Why?"

He hesitated. "It was just time to," he said.

He remembered very well why he'd quit, though. He'd been free-climbing a 5.9 pitch at Smith Rock, three hundred feet off the deck, when first one shoe slipped off the rock, and then a hand, and he swung slowly out away from the face like a door opening. He struggled to get a hand or a foot back on the rock, but he couldn't move without risking his only foothold. He was adhered to the cliff face largely by force of will, and his leg was starting to shake with the strain.

His climbing partner, Dave, was talking to him in an urgent voice, but Peter couldn't understand a word. Usually, if you fell while climbing, it was sudden. You either spidered out your rope or, if you were free-climbing, cratered before you knew what hit you. He'd never expected it to be slow like that, to give him time to contemplate what was happening. The last of his strength drained from his arm, and his shoe started slipping, ever so slightly, off the nubbin that held it. He had maybe two or three seconds left and there was no longer anything to lose, so he managed one last effort, a dynamic swing over and a big reach, and somehow found a tiny handhold, just enough for two fingers, and then a foothold, and then he was facing the rock again. He carefully reattached himself and settled for a second, trying to get his breath. Stars twinkled at the corners of his vision, and for a few moments he thought he might pass out. He hung there, panting, for two or three minutes, afraid to move, as Dave talked to him from somewhere over on the right.

Peter looked and saw his friend ensconced in a big, comfortable-looking crack. At first Peter wasn't willing to give up any of his holds, but he knew that sooner or later he'd have to. After another couple of minutes Dave talked him over, hold by hold, and then Peter got a foot, and then a hand, and then another foot into the crack. He brought in the last hand, astonished at this sudden deliverance.

The rock was warm. There was a breeze, and soon the sweat started to evaporate and cool him down. Dave advanced upward, then Peter moved up a little, too, and found another hold. Dave went ahead, talking to him in what seemed to be the language of birds. After a half hour or so they reached a ledge from which it was possible to traverse off the face and scramble down the back side of the cliff.

This kind of thing happened to all climbers sooner or later. If you were dedicated enough, you shrugged it off and kept going. Peter was not. That afternoon was the first time that he'd really understood, viscerally, that he was mortal, believed it in a way he could not dismiss as something distant and abstract. Once he'd felt the great, dark maw open under him, he lost any interest in tempting it further. He sold his gear rack the next week, but the nightmares he kept for years.

Standing there in the kitchen with Devi, all this came back so vividly that his palms began to sweat. This beautiful young woman was chopping carrots, and he was here, alive.

"So if you just got tired of it, why didn't you want Alex to know?" she asked.

"You've seen her play basketball," he said quietly. "Climbing wasn't something I wanted her fanatical about."

TWENTY-TWO

That first week of April in 2006, when antigovernment riots broke out in Kathmandu, Peter went home and brought Alex and Devi in to the clinic. Mina, Usha, and the clinic's two other nurses were already there. Anne and David drove the jeep in from Jorpati. By sundown they were swamped with the injured. When the house was full they laid people on mats in the backyard. They stitched lacerations, set bones, tamponaded broken noses, wired jaws. Rubber bullets had broken ribs and shattered facial bones, even blinded a couple of people.

Early in the day, the various opposition groups had joined together and called for a general strike. Tens of thousands of protesters pushed through the city, shutting down everything and eventually converging on the Royal Palace. There had always been an understanding that there would be no physical threat to the palace or the king, so this threw the army into a panic.

Peter and the girls scurried between the litters, doing their best to triage as people cried out and moaned and called for help. Franz shuffled around, checking for broken bones, and Mina moved through the ranks, squatting and talking to people, trying to figure out what had happened to them. They transferred the really serious cases—compound fractures, bullet wounds, internal bleeding, and the like—to hospitals when they could, but one woman had miscarried, hemorrhaging badly, and three others died before any ambulances came. They started transporting people in oxcarts, *tempos,* and taxis. It was train-wreck military medicine.

They worked straight through the night, stopping in turns for food or coffee. At seven o'clock the next morning, when things finally started to settle down, Franz turned on the news. It was soon clear that the bloodshed had been unnecessary. The day before, the king had heeded his generals' advice and taken his family to his country estate in the south. He hadn't even been at the palace.

"Jesus," said Franz. "All they had to do was tell them."

The phone rang.

"Leave it," said Mina. "It won't be good news."

Franz picked it up anyway. *"Scheisse,"* he said. He listened for a few moments, his eyes roving anxiously about the room. "They had to do this today? They couldn't wait? Right. So where are they?"

He reached for a pad and jotted down a few notes, then hung up and turned to them. The call was a radio relay from the north. Two climbers had fallen on Annapurna and had been badly injured. They'd been moved down to a village a few miles from base camp, but they would have to be evacuated.

Peter was so exhausted his hands were shaking. "This should be the RNA's job, or at least CIWEC's," he said.

"The CIWEC staff will be as done in as we are after last night," Franz said. "Anyway, they can't get a chopper."

"How are we supposed to get one if they can't?"

Franz looked at Mina.

"Oh, no," she said. "I'm barely speaking to the old fascist as it is. Every time he hears rifle fire he does a little jig. I'm not asking him for any favors."

The room fell silent. "All right, then," said Franz. "I'll tell them we can't go." He reached for the phone.

"Wait," said Mina. "Just wait a minute."

| | |

The colonel's one condition was that his daughter not take the trip herself. Franz needed her, anyway, so Peter conscripted Alex as well as Devi, who had grown up near there and knew the dialect. Usha would stay with Mina while they were away.

Mina drove them to the airport. "You've got all your gear together?" she asked, sounding nervous.

"Sure," he said. "Why?"

"Because time travel is real around here," she said. "When you get out of the Kathmandu Valley you're going to find yourself in the Middle Ages."

At the drop-off, Alex and Devi got out and pulled their knapsacks from the trunk. Peter leaned over, and he and Mina kissed. The girls grinned at him when he got out of the car.

"You're living in a glass house," he said. "Not a word."

They crowded into the chopper and put on headphones, which allowed conversation at a level slightly below the primal scream. The young pilot, Krishna, had trained in Germany, where the RNA sent most of its fliers. He fired up the engine, lifted off, and turned north.

As the morning warmed, strong updrafts started to knock the chopper around. Peter alternated between being flattened into his seat and feeling like he'd just been pushed out of a tenth-story window. Even Devi was a little green.

They followed valleys whenever they could, but occasionally they had to go up over ridges—high, serrated knife edges from which snowmelt fell in rainbowed plumes down to lush terraced fields. At the valley bottoms, rivers glinted, reflecting the sky. Alex, of course, hated to fly, and this was much worse than a 747.

The Himalayas looked like gigantic frozen tsunamis, white-capped wave sets that receded into the distance under a luminous vault of blue. In geologic time they *were* tsunamis, shoved up by tectonic forces that rippled granite instead of water. If such mountains had a message, Peter reflected, it was simply that they would outlast all humans and anything they built, for the waves were still growing in size.

The chopper's engine clattered and roared, sounding unreliable, as if important parts might be working themselves loose. After about a half hour they crossed a particularly jagged ridge, then banked sharply to the left. The helicopter leaned forward with a whine and began to fall. Alex grabbed Peter's hand, and he put an arm around her, as if that would protect her when they hit the ground and were atomized.

Their descent slowed as they neared the earth, though, and the g-forces pressed them into their seats as they came in over a field where there was a metal hangar of some kind. Krishna swooped in, hovered, and set the chopper down. He cut the engine and opened his door.

"Sorry so steep," he said, over his shoulder, when the rotors had slowed. "Important not to run out of fuel! Walk around while we gas up, if you like." He lit a cigarette and stepped out onto the concrete pad. According to a hand-painted sign on a corrugated tin building nearby, they were in Pokhara.

Alex unbuckled herself, opened her door, then stumbled out and vomited. Peter squatted beside her and patted her back.

"You okay?"

"Not really, no," she said, and threw up again. Peter got her a water bottle, then looked into the cockpit and went over to Krishna.

"The gauge reads a quarter of a tank," he said angrily. "You think you could take it a little easier?"

Krishna pulled his cigarette from his mouth and exhaled, blowing smoke all around them in the mountain breeze. "Believe me," he said, "it is necessary to fly this way."

"Why?"

"Let us hope you do not have to find out, sir."

| | |

Krishna lifted up just enough to clear the fueling shed, then made a long, low run over the valley at treetop height. When they'd cleared the town and were approaching the foothills, he yanked back on the stick, and the chopper climbed fast. Alex swallowed and closed her eyes, and Peter's gut was churning. They cleared the first ridge and continued northwest through a series of valleys toward Annapurna. All around them, the mountains spewed great plumes of snow into the jet stream.

A half hour later, with the great mountain looming before them, they dove again, down into valleys. After a few minutes there was smoke and a little village below, and Krishna leveled off just over the ground and set down in a dry rice paddy. The villagers came running as soon as the prop wash died down, then led Peter and the girls to a small house where the sherpas had carried the climbers.

There were three of them—not two, as they'd been told—an American and two Australians, and they were in bad shape. Peter examined the first guy as Alex and Devi stood by. There was a bulge in the right pants leg. Peter felt it gingerly, and the guy screamed.

"Compound fracture, right femur," Peter said. He felt for a pulse at the ankle. "The artery's intact. We won't try to set it here." He told Alex to start an IV, then hang a bag of saline and a morphine drip. When the morphine had cut in, he'd come back and splint the leg.

The American had broken a forearm and a foot in the fall, and his fingers were badly frostbitten. The other Australian had acute mountain sickness with pulmonary edema, and possibly cerebral edema as well; it was hard for Peter to gauge the source of his disorientation, given everything he'd been through in the past day. He would be dead within hours if he didn't get to a hospital.

Peter gave the one with mountain sickness a shot of a diuretic, then got them all on oxygen and started IV rehydration. The villagers helped carry them to the chopper. Peter was supposed to ride with them, then catch a lift back to pick up Alex and Devi the next day. But the three stretchers took up the whole cargo area.

"Is there some way to squeeze me in?" he asked.

Krishna shook his head. "Too much weight," he said. "I will return for you tomorrow."

They secured the doors and got out from under as Krishna revved the engine and lifted off. He headed across the river, then climbed the ridge and continued up before banking sharply southeast.

A fine needle of white smoke shot up with a hiss from the trees near the top of the ridge, in the wake of something fast and metallic. As Peter watched, the glinting dart converged on the chopper, which exploded in a brilliant orange burst. Alex screamed, and the villagers were suddenly shouting and running. People were pulling at them insistently, speaking fast in Nepali. Peter looked back toward the ridge. Tiny pieces of metal, some of them still burning, spiraled down into the trees.

Devi yelled that the guerrillas had come. Peter grabbed Alex with one hand, Devi with the other, and hauled them back toward the village. A man came up to them and pointed to the hill behind the town. Peter nodded, and the villagers led them up a trail to a small cave, then got them inside and ran back down the hill. Peter and the girls hunkered behind some rocks at the cave's entrance. Alex was weeping with fear, and Devi just lay there by her side, her eyes big, watching. Soon they saw movement in the trees.

The guerrillas appeared out of the jungle, carrying rifles and grenade launchers on their shoulders. They waded the shallow river and approached the town. There were maybe twenty of them, men and women both, dressed in camo and T-shirts, one or two in jeans, wearing boots or running shoes or even flip-flops. They were young—most of them looked sixteen or seventeen—and they appeared to be in no hurry. They laughed and called back and forth to one another as they sloshed out of the water and onto the bank.

Peter understood now why Krishna had flown the way he had. Even so, it hadn't been enough.

Down below, the guerrillas talked to the villagers. Soon they started up the hill.

"Should we try to run?" Alex said.

Devi shook her head. "They will shoot us if we do," she said. "Better to wait and see if we can talk to them."

"Devi, get chummy, then," Peter said. "Let them know you're local. Alex, you do not speak a word of Nepali, understand?"

"What do you mean?"

"I want them to say whatever they want around you. Keep your eyes down and don't give anything away. You're the only way we'll have of getting information."

A couple of minutes later, a grim-faced girl about Alex's age stood at the entrance to the cave and leveled the barrel of an AK-47 at them.

TWENTY-THREE

They hauled them down the hill to one of the houses and ran-
sacked their packs. They took Peter's wallet and watch, Devi's
flashlight, Alex's water bottle and Luna bar. One of the boys patted Peter down and went through all his pockets. He seemed
happy to get the Swiss Army knife, a special promotional model
given away by Pfizer that contained a corkscrew, a no. 7 scalpel
blade, a folding reflex hammer, and a tracheotomy tool. The
knives had prompted speculation among Peter's colleagues about
the proper order for using the tools (most favored starting with the
corkscrew) as well as sarcastic consternation over the omission of
a Lexus key.

A couple of girls gave Alex and Devi the same treatment, but
they didn't have much on them except a few spare rupees, which
were immediately confiscated.

Peter and Alex sat on the dirt floor untended, then, while the
guerrillas took Devi into the back room and grilled her. Alex whispered what snippets she overheard. The guards had been coming
downriver to take food from the village when they saw the RNA

chopper come in. They figured the village was harboring soldiers, so they sent a couple of guys up the ridge with a rocket launcher.

"They were ready to shoot everybody as collaborators when they came into the village," she whispered. "Devi is explaining why we're here."

The guerrillas who were waiting joked around with one another and appeared to hold the villagers in vague contempt. They found a boom box in one of the houses and started an impromptu dance outside in the dusty square. Two or three of them seemed to be drunk. Others were directing the villagers to prepare a communal dinner.

The interrogators finished with Devi, brought her back into the main room, then went outside to join the others.

"They're not going to kill us," Devi said, but she was paler than Peter had ever seen her.

"Did you tell them who was in the helicopter?" Peter asked.

"They said if the pilot was RNA, they just did their jobs," she said. "They figured the American and the Aussies were stupid to be out here in the first place."

The woman who owned the house came in to get some food for the meal. She and Devi exchanged a few terse words, then she left.

"These guys are eating all their food, and the boom box is using up the batteries they need to get the weather report," Devi said quietly.

Peter gathered that the guerrillas faced the classic dilemma: What do you do if your Popular Front is unpopular?

A half hour later, when dinner was ready, they herded everyone into the square so they could eat together. An older boy, apparently the squad leader, took the opportunity to hold forth loudly and at length on what Devi reported to be the glories of the revolution. A couple of the older village women used the distraction to whisper to her. When they discovered that her uncle was the cousin of someone's now-deceased stepfather, they started sneaking extra food to all three of them. The guerrillas either ignored this or didn't notice, because they were partying like the teenagers they were. A couple of them fired their rifles into the air, until the leader—whose name was Ramesh and who looked three or four years older than the rest—scolded them about wasting ammunition. As the evening wore on, though, Ramesh kept making eye contact with Devi, and Peter began to nurse concerns.

They were put in a small hut that night, overseen by a guard who apparently spoke enough English to keep tabs. Devi said that the guerrillas expected the RNA to come looking for their pilot, so now that they'd stuffed themselves and filled their packs, they'd be leaving before dawn.

"Unfortunately," she said, "that includes us."

"They're taking us with them?"

"Their boss is back up in the mountains, ten or fifteen miles from here, and he's sick. They want you, mainly."

| | |

The first couple of miles, they marched upriver through icy, knee-deep water so they couldn't be tracked. Ramesh led the way with Devi's flashlight; someone else brought up the rear with another light. The banks were steep and covered in giant rhododendron bushes ten or twelve feet tall.

Shortly before sunrise, when the sky was just turning light, they left the river and started up a steep mountain trail to the north. At dawn, the sun ignited the high peaks and sent reddish light flowing down the snowfields like lava. This triggered a flood of frigid air, which convected down the valley and blasted them with a cold wind, bitter and lip-cracking dry. Around 8:30 they stopped to rest. Peter kept expecting to hear the *whop-whop* of chopper blades from down the valley, but it never came. They'd left in such a hurry that Krishna might not have filed a flight plan, and if Franz didn't remember the name of the village, no one would know where to look for them.

Alex shrieked. She'd lifted her pants leg to scratch and found her calves and ankles covered with leeches.

They all had them, but the guerrillas viewed them as a minor occupational hazard and laughed at the American girl's dramatic revulsion. They picked them off one another and started back up the mountain.

"Nobody seems to be searching for us," Peter said quietly to Devi. "Any idea what's going on?"

She snorted. "The RNA puts on a good show, but everybody knows how disorganized they are," she said. "Their communication system is worthless."

By what he guessed to be about 10:00, Peter was winded and getting tired, and it occurred to him that they were probably up near fifteen thousand feet—about the same as the summit of Mount Whitney, as high as he'd ever climbed. He was by far the oldest person here, and he felt like it. He knew what the dangers were, of course. The water almost certainly contained a terrifying array of microbes, amoebas, and protozoa, but there was nothing else to drink. He could develop mountain sickness, as could Alex, though Devi was probably safe since she'd grown up nearby. He could, if he was really unlucky, have a heart attack or pop a hole in his lung.

After another couple of miles Peter was stumbling and finally had to sit down. The guerrillas eyed him scornfully. His shirt was soaked and he was panting, but nobody else had even broken a sweat. He told Devi to explain to them that if they wanted to help their leader, they might want to be sure he arrived alive, which meant going slower.

They held a brief conference and decided that most of them would continue on. Ramesh was willing to bring them himself, Devi whispered to Peter, but another guard insisted on staying as well. There seemed to be some sort of rivalry between the two men, and although Peter couldn't gauge exactly what it was about, he hoped it didn't have anything to do with Devi or Alex. In any case, the second guard brought up the rear, and the small band soon set out to guide Peter and the girls to the camp, which lay six miles ahead and two thousand feet up.

They came out of the trees and rhododendrons at about noon and, despite the altitude, it was hot. They stopped in the shade by a stream and picked off more leeches. Ramesh opened his pack and brought out a piece of flatbread, which he smeared with goat butter and passed around. The other guard broke Alex's Luna bar into five pieces and handed them out. Peter was about to dunk his head into the water when Ramesh waved him off.

"He says if you do that you'll end up with leeches in your ears and nose," Devi said. "They're tiny until they start sucking."

Peter shuddered, remembering the girl at the clinic. And the clinic, in turn, reminded him of Mina—who, he realized, expected him to be on the chopper, and who would now assume he was dead. Depending on how this went, she might end up being right.

They pressed on toward the pass as thunderheads grew in a clear afternoon sky and heat lightning flashed inside them. Low, rumbling booms echoed among the ridges. An hour later, without dropping any rain, they dissipated.

Devi walked up ahead, speaking with Ramesh in Nepali from time to time. Peter couldn't tell what their connection was, but she was smart, and he trusted her. They crossed the pass in mid-afternoon and started down. A couple of hours later they came to a village compound tucked in among trees and cliffs. It would be almost invisible from the air, Peter realized.

There were maybe a hundred and fifty guerrillas, most of them as young as the group that had been on the raid. Cattle and goats dotted the small terraced fields outside of town, and smoke curled from chimneys in the early-evening light. Devi said that this had been just another village before the local Maoist leader had appreciated its strategic location and taken it over. Most of the original inhabitants had fled, but those who remained had been put together in three or four small houses so they could be watched.

On small peaks and rock outcrops surrounding the town stood

batteries of machine guns, rocket launchers, and even a couple of small surface-to-air missiles, which must have been hauled up the mountain with considerable effort. Almost everyone carried a gun—M-16s, Kalashnikovs, and Belgian submachine guns they'd captured from the RNA.

Peter and the girls were paraded through town, but Peter sensed more curiosity than hostility. There were probably people here who had never seen a Westerner before, and Alex was drawing considerable attention from the young men. She wrapped her arms around herself and walked with her eyes on the ground ahead of her nervously. They passed a crude mural on the side of a building that showed the outward-gazing faces of five men: the Nepali guerrilla leader Prachanda, along with Marx, Lenin, Stalin, and Mao—a sort of communist Mount Rushmore.

At the base of a hill behind town, Ramesh and the other guard handed them off to four men, all of them with Kalashnikovs, who led them up a steep path. They came to a modest house with a sweeping view of the valley. The guards gestured for them to take off their shoes and go inside. The house was just one big room, with a kitchen area in the back and windows overlooking the village. There were a couple of bookshelves, a few chairs, and kerosene lanterns hanging on hooks, but otherwise it was spartanly furnished.

Commandant Adhiraj sat at a table, eating dinner with a couple of his lieutenants. He was in his early forties and clean shaven, with graying hair. He had narrow shoulders but strong-looking hands and was significantly heavier than anyone else Peter had seen in the village. Someone, at least, was eating well.

Peter had once seen a photo of the young Pol Pot and been amazed that a man with such kind eyes could have turned, over time, into a killing machine. He'd had a similar reaction to a picture of Stalin, who looked like a kindly uncle. He half expected Adhiraj to present in some similar vein, then, with at least a pretense of joviality, perhaps a warm welcome to join the dinner. Instead, the commandant looked up when they came in but said nothing. His dark eyes, behind wire-rimmed aviator glasses, were widely spaced, intelligent, and cool. He was deliberate and unhurried as he turned his gaze to the man on his right, then went back to his meal.

He reminded Peter of a tough, pragmatic, and rapacious American businessman he'd once known. Adhiraj had similar eyes, distant and even slightly hostile, and his small mouth and pursed lips suggested impatience and the kind of temper Peter didn't like seeing in someone with easy access to automatic weapons. He was probably an effective administrator, which was the last thing Peter expected from a man who was supposed to be instilling the masses with revolutionary fervor. This would, however, explain how he had, within ten years, helped his leader Prachanda build a movement from a ragtag band of juvenile delinquents and outlaws into a formidable force that had nearly overrun the country.

When Adhiraj finished eating and his lieutenants had departed, he wiped his mouth and spoke to his guards. They brought Peter to the table and motioned for Devi to come over so she could translate. Alex sat in the corner and pulled a book out of her pack—the only possession they'd allowed her to keep.

Adhiraj spoke to Devi. "He wants to know if you are really an American doctor," she said.

Peter nodded. "Ask him what the problem is."

Adhiraj responded impatiently that he'd felt unaccountably weak for some time. In the past few months he'd fall asleep in the middle of the afternoon, usually a couple of hours after eating. He'd also been getting sores on his feet that took a long time to heal.

"Is it all right if I examine him?"

Adhiraj nodded. Peter found nothing noteworthy except his heft; he was only about five-eight but must have weighed more than two hundred pounds, which by Nepali standards was tremendously obese.

"Is he thirsty?"

"He says yes, he is thirsty very frequently now."

"How often does he urinate?"

When Adhiraj heard the question he looked at Peter with vexation, as if it were in poor taste to embarrass him in front of the girl. Finally, he spoke.

"Every couple of hours," Devi said.

Peter explained that he was pretty sure Adhiraj had diabetes. Devi translated, and the commandant appeared surprised. He spoke sharply to Devi.

"He says this is ridiculous," Devi said. "No one here has diabetes. He has heard of it only occasionally in people who move to the city and grow old. He considers it a disease of decadence, which is why so many Americans have it."

"Look," said Peter. "Everyone in this camp is younger, leaner, and fitter than he is."

Devi's eyes widened. "You want me to translate that?"

"Tell him."

She spoke, and Adhiraj shrugged without taking noticeable offense. "He says he spends most of his time behind a desk now," Devi said.

"He's gained a lot of weight recently?"

"He says yes. Even three years ago he was much thinner than he is now."

"Tell him so many Americans have it for the same reasons he does," Peter said. "It isn't decadence, just too much food and too little exercise. His body can't process glucose the way it did when he was younger and more active."

Devi spoke to him. "He says he really isn't interested in all this medical theory. He wants to know what he is supposed to do."

Peter said it was simple: He should eat less and exercise. Beyond that, there were drugs available in Kathmandu that would help. "If he has someone there who can get them for him, that would be good," he added. "I'll give him the information."

Adhiraj got up and walked to the window, then gestured for Peter to join him. The lights of his village spread out below like a little fiefdom. There were a couple of bonfires in the streets, with dark figures moving around them. Across the valley, the snow-capped peaks were losing the last of their alpenglow.

"It's beautiful here, is it not?" said Adhiraj.

Peter looked at him, startled. "You speak English?"

"Sometimes it is useful to maintain a pretense," he said. "But it appears you are who you say you are, so I doubt I will gain significant intelligence from you." Adhiraj called the guard in and told him to take Devi away. "Your daughter may remain here," he said. "But I wish to speak with you about something more important than this diabetes."

The guard took Devi out. Adhiraj and Peter went back to the table while Alex continued reading in the corner, careful to keep her eyes on the page. Adhiraj poured wine for both of them and sat down. Peter, still standing, took a sip; it was, surprisingly, a reasonably good merlot. Adhiraj seemed more relaxed now that his day's work was over, and he leaned back in his seat. He gestured at the other chair. Peter sat.

"I would like to know how the Americans see our movement," he said.

Peter wasn't sure how frank he could afford to be. "I don't mean to offend you," he said, "but these days people are a lot more concerned about Iraq and Afghanistan."

Adhiraj sighed. "I had thought perhaps this was true."

"It's not necessarily a bad thing," Peter said. "If there was oil here and the CIA considered you a threat, this village would be a crater by now."

Adhiraj smiled. "You must be considered very left-wing in your country, Doctor."

"I think I'm pretty much in the middle of the road where the rest of the world is concerned."

Adhiraj pressed his index finger to the table and rotated it back and forth, idly, as if crushing a bug. "Here we say that those in the middle of the road get hit from both directions."

Peter had another drink of wine to steady his nerves. It was a little like a job interview, he realized—a casual pretense obscuring how much was at stake.

"My followers are, for the most part, about the age of your daughter," Adhiraj continued. "They have enthusiasm, but they are not particularly knowledgeable."

"You could change that without a lot of trouble."

Adhiraj smiled. "The ignorance or the enthusiasm?"

"The ignorance."

"Too much thinking makes indecision," he said. "We cannot afford it. Did you know that the annual per capita income in this country is less than three hundred dollars?"

"I did know, in fact."

"And yet everyone in the royal family is able to afford a Rolls-Royce or a Bentley. I would think such a thing would offend the American sensibility."

Adhiraj was expressing opinions pretty similar to Peter's own, and Peter hoped he could steer things into sympathetic terrain. "It would have, until about the end of World War Two," Peter said. "Since then, we've had royalty too. They're largely above the law, they run things how it pleases them, and most of them don't pay taxes."

Adhiraj appeared surprised. "What sort of royalty is this?"

"Corporations," Peter said, "and they're worse than King George ever was. If a war is good for business, we have a war. If single-payer healthcare is bad for profits, we don't have it. They control the debate and the airwaves, and it turns out to be surprisingly easy to scare people into going along."

Adhiraj smiled thinly. "Perhaps we have some common ground, after all," he said.

Peter was relieved to hear it. He was enjoying the wine and the chance to talk. He was also glad that Adhiraj seemed open to frankness.

"It's not like I'm in your camp either," he said, leaning back and crossing his legs. "Communism is how all our tribal ancestors lived for thousands of years, and it's a beautiful idea. But it ought to be obvious that when the population grows beyond a certain point, it doesn't work anymore."

Adhiraj raised his eyebrows. "Why do you say this?"

"It's human nature. When you live in a small group, it pays to act for the good of everyone because you get personal benefits from it."

"Of course."

"But when you no longer know those people, it makes more sense to look after your own self-interest, within reason. So then someone has to force people to participate in this fake bureaucratic altruism, and you end up with Stalin and Mao and Kim Jong-il."

"So a society is either tribal or capitalist?" Adhiraj asked. "You consider those the only two options?"

"There's capitalism and there's capitalism," Peter said. "It doesn't have to be a shark tank, like the U.S. You can provide medical care, tax the rich, and get the money out of elections so the politicians do their jobs instead of whoring themselves to the highest bidder."

Adhiraj emptied his wineglass and set it down. "And this would be your advice to me, should we succeed?"

Alex, over in the corner, cleared her throat ever so quietly. Peter knew it was directed at him, but he didn't know why. He stopped to consider where this was going. He felt a little light-headed, admittedly, after the long day and the wine, but Adhiraj seemed genuinely interested in what he had to say, and he doubted any harm would come of being honest.

"My *first* advice, I suppose, would be to stop pillaging and killing people," he said. "Folks out there aren't real happy with you, as I'm sure you know."

Adhiraj stared. "And yet my recruits grow by twenty or thirty every month," he said, his voice even. "We are in a position to win the war before summer's end."

"Of course," said Peter. "Your recruits seem loyal to you now."

"*Seem* loyal?"

"Look, you take poor kids with no chances and you promise them food and shelter. That kind of obedience you can get from a dog. But if you kick out the king you're going to have to *govern* this place, and it would be good if people were on your side out of choice rather than necessity."

Adhiraj poured the last of the wine into his glass. "An interesting perspective, Doctor," he said. He abruptly stood, walked to the door, and called his guard. He spoke to the guard briefly in Nepali.

"Please follow this man," Adhiraj said to Peter and Alex. He turned and walked back to the table.

Peter, perplexed, looked at his daughter. She had turned pale. The guard led them down the hill to a small one-room house in the village. What had gone wrong? Was Adhiraj so thin-skinned?

There were nine or ten other people in the room, sitting against the walls or lying down. As soon as they were inside, Alex found Devi and put her arms around her.

"What happened?" Peter asked. "What did he say to the guard?"

Alex looked at him, her eyes frightened. "He said you were the most dangerous kind of bourgeois intellectual," she said. "Why did you have to keep talking like that?"

Peter was floored. "I was trying to establish some common ground with the guy," he said. "I figured it would help us get out of here."

"You had too much wine, and you were *lecturing* him."

"I had half a glass!"

"We've barely eaten, and we're at twelve thousand feet, Dad!"

He realized that he *was* drunk, if only a little. "Well, what are they going to do?" he asked.

Alex was crying and shaking now. "He told them to take us across the river and shoot us in the morning, so no one learns where this place is."

Alex lay in Devi's lap. Her diarrhea had started a few hours before. Peter figured she'd picked something up from the stream, or that her fear had sent her gut into spasm, or both. Off in the distance someone rang a bell, and from all around the village, dogs began to howl.

Peter sat against the wall, arms crossed on his raised knees, his head dropped forward onto his forearms. He had failed again—again!—and he was astonished at his own stupidity. He hadn't said anything to Adhiraj he didn't believe, but that wasn't the question; the question was judgment. If he hadn't been loosened up with wine he would have had the sense to keep his mouth shut. Of course, this was what Adhiraj had in mind; he'd outflanked him, deftly and easily, learned whether he would be useful or not with fifty cents' worth of alcohol. While Peter was feeling so shrewd for having Alex eavesdrop on the conversation, the commandant had pulled the oldest and simplest of maneuvers, and Peter had been gullible enough to fall for it. He had just vowed to be more careful and less trusting, and then he'd let his guard down yet again, out of stupid ego, out of infatuation with the cleverness of his own ideas. He wanted to shoot himself—he was so furious that if he could have gotten ahold of one of the rifles he thought he might really do it—but in any case he didn't have to worry because now the job would be done for him.

He couldn't face Alex and Devi, and not surprisingly, they didn't seem to want to have anything to do with him. Devi had forgiven him in a way, referring simply to his miscalculation, but her grudging tone made it even harder to absolve himself.

After Devi dozed off around midnight, Alex came over and sat beside him to share what warmth they could.

"I'm so sorry," he said. "It was beyond stupid, what I did. I don't expect you to forgive me, but if I can ever make it up to you, I will."

"I don't think you're going to have a chance, Dad," she said quietly.

They sat in silence for a while, listening to the rustling and coughing in the room, the sounds of the night from outside.

"I want you to tell me something," Alex said.

"What?"

"Whenever I've asked you how you and Mom got together, you've always evaded the subject. I want to know the story."

"You may not like it," he said.

"What difference does it make?" she asked, her anger flaring.

He took a breath. "Your mother and I hooked up at a bar when I was in my residency at UCLA," he said. "I was exhausted all the time, and lonely, because I was too busy to have any kind of a social life. In those days, when she was young, Cheryl was actually pretty fun. We spent the night together and went out a few more times, but I had to study constantly between thirty-six-hour shifts at the hospital, and your mom was a party girl who went bar-hopping four or five nights a week."

Alex sighed. "You guys just hooked up? It was a lust thing?"

"Not *just* that," he said carefully. "We got along okay. But we had really different lives, and it didn't take long to figure out we weren't a great match."

"How long were you together?" she asked, as if she already knew the answer. This was going about as badly as he'd feared.

"A couple of weeks, really, was all. A month or so later I got the phone call."

"About me, you mean."

"I had it checked out, of course, given how she lived. But I was definitely your dad."

She sat up, wobbly as she was, and moved just slightly away, so that their bodies no longer touched. "So you didn't exactly want me. I wasn't like some great plan you'd made."

"You asked for the truth."

"Jesus. I see why you didn't want to tell me."

"I didn't want you until I met you, Alex. I saw you when you were about three hours old, and that was it."

"That was *what*?"

"You think I've stuck around all this time out of some sense of duty?"

"It sure looks that way."

"I never wanted you to know the whole preamble, because it didn't matter at that point in my life. I didn't even know what love *was*. Then I saw you, and I did."

She shifted. "And what about Mom?" she said, her voice a little softer. "The truth."

He thought about how to put it. "Cheryl needed a certain amount of convincing," he said. "She wasn't sure she was up for it."

"That doesn't exactly come as news," she said. "But why did you stay together so long? You thought that unlike half the kids in the country, I was such a little wuss I couldn't stand a divorce?"

"You're not a wuss. But if I'd divorced her it would have meant shared custody. You'd have been spending time alone with her and her friends."

"Did she even want me? I'd have thought she'd be happy to dump me on you."

"She loved you, Alex, but love isn't always enough. I could tell it wasn't going to stop her from screwing you up royally if I wasn't around to intercede."

She wiped at her eyes. "You stayed miserable all these years to protect me?"

"I could take it. I just wasn't sure you could."

"Well, what was different this time?"

"After Wayne Lee came back, I knew I could finally get you away from her. That's all."

She coughed, weakly, a few times. "Well, thanks for telling me, I guess," she said, sounding exhausted and bereft.

Devi stirred. Alex put her hand on Peter's, just briefly, then crawled back over to lie down with her. Peter could tell from her breathing that she was soon asleep again. When she was, and he was squatting there in the cold, alone, without her to hear him, his throat tightened and his face grew hot, and he began to weep. He tried to stop it but he couldn't. It felt as though it would empty him. He sobbed as quietly as he could, for fear of waking her again, as in darkness the tears fell from his blind eyes into dust.

TWENTY-FOUR

At dawn, Peter heard angry voices. He had dozed off, and he awoke feeling as if his bones were made of glass. He crawled to the doorway and peered outside. Three of the guerrillas were arguing with Ramesh, the boy who'd led them up the valley. Alex awakened groggily and moved over to the wall. Peter crawled back to her.

"What are they saying?" he asked.

"Ramesh wants the job," she said wearily. "He says he's older, so the least they can do is let him have the honors."

Peter turned to Devi. "They'd probably let you join up, if you asked," he said. "You could save yourself, buy some time."

She looked at him as if he were a fool. "You want me to join the people who are going to kill the two of you?"

"You don't have to be sincere," Peter said. "You just have to live."

"Peter," she said, her voice dropping, "there's something happening here that you don't know about."

But then Ramesh was at the door, grim-faced, apparently having prevailed. The compromise was that one of the guards would accompany him—the one who'd been his rival the day before at the river. He was a real Gurkha warrior, six feet tall and all muscle, the biggest Nepali Peter had ever seen.

Alex opened her arms up to her father, as she had when she was a child. He held her. He was terrified, his heart beating wildly, but she was so exhausted that she seemed calm. Peter looked over at Devi, but there was no chance now to find out what she'd meant.

"Now time," said Ramesh. He clapped his hands together, then unslung his rifle from behind his back.

He and the other guard led them out. Adhiraj stood outside, in the dawn chill, sipping from a mug of tea. Peter briefly calculated the distance between them, wondered if there was any way he could get to Adhiraj and pull his pistol from his belt before being shot. But there were half a dozen AKs pointed right at him; he'd be dead before he took two steps.

"I have decided that your daughter is to remain here," said Adhiraj. Peter stared at him, dumbstruck.

"Stay here for what?" Devi asked.

"I have my reasons," said Adhiraj.

"If you lay a finger on her—" Peter said.

"Relax, Doctor, I have much better uses for her than that."

Devi snorted. "What he's saying is that with an American girl here, the RNA won't dare bomb them."

"You would prefer she died with you?" said Adhiraj.

"She'll stay," said Peter. "Of course she'll stay. Let her live."

Devi stepped forward. "She is a clever girl," she said to Adhiraj. "She will betray you and escape. You should kill her while you have the chance."

"Devi!" cried Alex, her eyes big and wounded.

But Devi ignored her and continued. "I'll join your band, and to prove myself, after we cross the river I'll shoot them myself."

Peter slapped her hard across the mouth. "What the hell are you doing?" he yelled.

The blow sent her reeling, but Ramesh caught her. She wiped at her bleeding lip dismissively with the back of her hand.

"You do not understand the situation," she hissed at Peter. "Once again, you have misjudged."

Peter looked at her, stunned, but he still had no idea what she was talking about.

"You really expect me to put a rifle in your hands?" Adhiraj asked.

Devi indicated Ramesh. "He can stand behind me and shoot me if anything goes wrong."

Adhiraj scrutinized her with narrowed eyes. "All right," he said at last. "You're the kind of girl we can use. But you'll only have to shoot the doctor. Your American friend stays here."

"I'm telling you, you can't trust her!" said Devi.

"That I will judge," he said. He made a motion with his hand and spoke to the guards in Nepali. Two of them led Alex away. She turned and glanced back at Peter, tears running down her cheeks. Ramesh and the big guard, Bidur, leveled their rifles at Peter. Ramesh barked something at Devi, and they headed out of camp.

After about twenty minutes they came to the river. Peter was panting in the cold morning air. Ramesh and Bidur started arguing again. Peter and Devi stood a little off to the side as he bent over and tried to get his breath. Little sparks filled the edges of his vision, and he was angry.

"I don't understand how you could do this," he said.

"I've tried to tell you that things are not as they seem."

"Fuck you," said Peter. "They're exactly as they seem."

Devi's face hardened. "Don't you want to know what they're arguing about?" she asked.

"Not really."

"Bidur wants to shoot you here," she said. "Ramesh says that your body will attract vultures, and then the RNA may find the camp. He wants to go on to the next river canyon, and Bidur says it's too far, a waste of time, that no one will come."

A watershed argument, Peter reflected bitterly. Again, Ramesh convinced the bigger man. They continued down the trail, which was steep and covered with scree. The world took on a clarity Peter didn't ever remember seeing, at least not since he was a child. Suddenly everything was simple. Now he was alive, breathing clear air in sunlight, and soon his universe would end. It felt almost like a relief, except for his daughter.

They crossed a ridge and came down to a wide stream, where another argument broke out. Ramesh wanted to ford and shoot him on the other side, but Bidur had had enough. The water was fast and cold, the channel full of boulders. Ramesh pointed out the big eddy on the other side and said that Peter would sink and decompose, so that if his bones washed down in the monsoon no one would know who he was.

But Bidur refused to go on. He unslung his rifle, leaned it against the cliff, and turned away from them to piss. Ramesh immediately raised his rifle and fired. Bidur's brains and blood spattered the rocks behind him, and his body collapsed to the ground.

Peter cried out in terror. He looked at Ramesh, who put his rifle down and turned toward Devi. She came to him and they embraced, as she repeated the word, *daju, daju*. Peter knew this term: older brother. And Ramesh, he had heard that name. It belonged to Sangita's stolen son.

Devi turned to Peter, tears in her eyes. "This is why I wanted her to come," she said. "We have planned this from the beginning, when we found each other again."

"For Christ's sake, why didn't you tell me?"

"I tried, but we were never alone! You think Adhiraj would leave us in a crowded place like that without a single spy?"

Peter felt strength begin to pour into him. "We've got to go back for her."

"No," said Devi. "They will shoot us all for real then. As things are, she will live. We'll find another way."

"We can't just leave her; she's sick!"

"They need her for propaganda," Devi said. "They will take care of her."

Peter tried to clear his head. He could barely believe all of them were still alive.

"I would not suggest this if there were some other way," Devi said. "But twice now you have misjudged and put her in danger. Let me decide this time."

Her eyes were calm and firm. She knew this territory, and Peter didn't. Ramesh stood beside her.

Peter bowed his head. "Okay," he said. "What do you want to do?"

Ramesh dragged Bidur's body across the stream. Peter and Devi followed; they tied a couple of big rocks to the body and let it go. It sank into the eddy, which was opaque with glacial silt, and vanished.

"Where do we go, if we don't go back?" Peter asked.

"They will miss us soon," Devi said. "We have to get as far away from here as we can."

TWENTY-FIVE

The trail was used mainly by goats and their sure-footed herders, and it snaked its way upward along the sheer face of the canyon wall. Frequently it shrank to a faint path no wider than a foot, with overhanging rock to which they clung with their hands as they traversed along sideways.

By early afternoon they had crossed over the next ridge and started down into the adjoining valley. Peter's lungs burned, but at least the floating sparks had left his vision. After thirty or forty minutes they stopped by a stream to rest and refill Ramesh's canteen. They were drinking so much, with the exertion and the altitude, that they emptied it with each ridge crossing. Peter figured they were picking up terrifying organisms from the water, but until now he hadn't thought they'd live long enough for it to matter.

Ramesh's English was halting. He'd studied as a boy but had had no occasion to use it since he'd been press-ganged by the guerrillas at sixteen. He and Devi spoke together in Nepali, then Devi translated if it was something she thought Peter should know.

Ramesh wasn't familiar with this part of the country, though; he usually just went up- or downriver to small villages. They decided to work their way southeast, across passes and down into valleys, in an effort to get to Pokhara, which was fifty or sixty miles away. Ramesh said that by now the guerrillas would have realized something was wrong and sent pursuers. They were likely to be the sons of local herders; they would know the trails, and they would be well provisioned and move quickly. If they came across a ridge and found the three escapees exposed on the cliff-side trail across the canyon, they would shoot them down.

The skies were clear, and there would be a three-quarter moon. They decided to try to stay awake, and since it would be too dangerous to make a fire even if they had the means, they would keep moving all night.

They followed the goat trail down into the canyon. The river was bigger than the first two they had crossed, a good thirty yards wide, rocky and cold. They scouted upstream and down until they found the safest-looking ford, then cut staffs with Ramesh's knife and picked their way across. It was waist-deep in the center, and the current was so strong it nearly took Peter's legs right out from under him.

By the time they reached the other side it was late afternoon, and they were chilled to the bone. Sunset would come early and fast behind the peaks. They figured if they could top the next ridge and make their way by moonlight they'd have a decent enough lead when morning came that they might be able to stop and sleep a couple of hours after the day warmed up. The trail was a little wider here, sometimes two or three feet across, and it seemed like a highway after the terrain they'd just come through. They made the ridge by what Peter figured was eight or nine o'clock. It was a high pass, and they looked back over the day's route, probably twenty miles by land but only about five as the crow flies. Two ridges back they saw tiny bobbing lights, so distant they appeared to be fireflies.

"Flashlights," Peter said. "Four of them."

"Five," said Ramesh, and Peter saw that he was right.

Ramesh said that there would be at least two guerrillas for

every light, so Adhiraj had probably sent ten or twelve guys after them.

"They're on the same trail we're on?" Peter asked, and Ramesh nodded. "How long before they get to where we are now?"

Ramesh figured that if the pursuers kept moving, they'd catch up by sunrise. There had been one particularly tricky stretch that he wasn't sure they'd be able to do at night, though, even with lights.

"If it stops them, they will have to go back to the river and camp," Devi said. "It may give us time."

They pressed on, down and up, across the ridge, down and up again. Fording the rivers was dangerous, partly because the moon was blocked by the ridges and the canyon bottoms were pitch-dark.

By dawn Peter was staggering with exhaustion, and even Devi and Ramesh looked ready to drop, so they found a boulder patch to conceal themselves and lay down in the sun to dry out and sleep.

It was nearly midday when Peter stirred awake. Devi and Ramesh still lay curled in the sun at the base of the boulders, Devi snoring softly. Peter tried to sit up and was immobilized by stab-bing pain from his hips and knees. It felt like hot cotton had been glued to the inside of his throat.

He rolled to his side and pushed himself up on one arm, which set off a heartbeat-driven hammer at the base of his skull. Altitude. The air was thin and dry. Everything was too bright. He stretched out a foot and jammed it into the sole of Devi's boot. She moaned. He did it again, and she flopped an arm. She opened an eye and rolled onto her back, then sat up.

"What time is it?"

She shook Ramesh until he awakened. When he realized how late it was, he swore in Nepali, then started gathering his things. A few minutes later they were walking again.

Peter didn't remember ever being so hungry. He didn't walk so much as lurch from one leg to the next, swinging his weight for-ward like a sack of meat in a kind of staggering dance. Every step electrified a hot cable of pain that ran from his foot to his knee, then to his hip. The headache grew worse.

They crossed another river and refilled the canteen. After a half hour, walking up the other side of the canyon, they came to a land-slide. Peter had seen it as they descended the opposite side but hoped it wouldn't be too bad.

It was. The trail had been obliterated for a hundred yards, and they faced a sheer wall. Peter looked around, and then he looked up.

"If we're going to get out of here, we've got to go over the top," he said. He could barely believe he was suggesting this, but he didn't see any other way.

"How?" Devi asked, incredulous.

"I'll show you," he said, bending over to get his breath.

Devi and Ramesh gazed up at the canyon wall, then looked back at Peter as if he were crazy. He had never wanted to climb again, certainly not without a rope, but he figured this was maybe a 5.6 pitch—easy in rock shoes with their sticky rubber soles, tricky but not impossible without them.

"This is going to be hard," he said, "but they may give up here, or spend a lot of time backtracking to find a way around."

They wouldn't be able to climb with the rifles, so Ramesh and Devi heaved them out over the cliff; they turned end over end as they fell, then splashed into the river and disappeared.

Peter scanned the rock face, looking for the easiest routes, even if they were indirect and took longer to climb. He started out and showed them how to do it, keeping their weight on their feet, let-ting their arms go straight as they gripped with their fingers so they could dead hang—hold their weight with their bones and tendons instead of exhausting their arm muscles.

He started up a fairly easy crack, with good foot placement and large grips—"buckets"—for his hands, and followed it to a small ledge about thirty feet above the trail. They watched how he did it and followed him up. There, they rested briefly in the shade.

"We're going to have to ration the water," Peter said, panting. "Take as little as you think you can get by with." He knew but did not say that if they got stuck halfway up, trapped by an overhang or a smooth slab beyond their skills, there was no way they'd be able to downclimb without falling or getting shot. It was cool here, but he'd started to sweat, considering the many ways this could go bad. He had failed at everything, and somehow, miraculously, he was still alive; but he knew he absolutely could not afford to fail at this.

The crack disappeared into an open face with big granite nubbins sticking out of it, like a classic gym route. Peter showed the other two how to move up it, climbing the nubbins almost like a ladder, shifting the weight from foot to hand to foot, sort of flowing up the rock. He was trying to hide his anxiety, but he kept reliving that barn-door swing, and he had to measure his breath to stay calm. His palms were sweating, and he wished he had some climber's chalk to dry them out. He tried to get a little dust on his hands whenever there was a ledge, and told the others to do the same. He kept his eyes on the rock ahead and didn't look down.

They worked their way up until they got to another crack—a big, capacious crack that went diagonally up the face for forty or fifty feet, past where Peter could see. He could tell that Devi was starting to struggle.

"You're using your arms too much," he told her. "Legs, legs, legs."

"I'm trying," she said, but she was out of breath with the effort.

He showed her how to slide an open hand sideways into the crack, then make a fist and wedge it in there. "You can lie back into it, let it take your weight, while you move from foothold to foothold," he said. "Then you relax the fist, pull out your hand, and jam it in a little higher up."

When they got to the next ledge they rested again. Ramesh was agile and surprisingly strong, but the exertion was taxing him. Devi's forearms were so pumped she could barely make a fist anymore. For the first time, Peter was glad Alex wasn't with them; she would have been too weak to climb, and anyway, she probably had a better chance of surviving than they did at this point.

"How much farther?" Devi asked.

"I think we're about halfway. Maybe another hundred, hundred and fifty feet."

They were at the foot of a greasy slab cut through with strata of loose, crumbly stone—chossy rock, in climber's lingo. Peter traversed out to try to find a route. There was nothing to the right; he ran out of footholds after about ten feet and had to go back to the ledge. The other direction was a little better, but he didn't want to go too far up because he didn't think he'd be able to downclimb back to the ledge. He wanted water, food, rock shoes, and some easy holds, and he didn't have any of them. He was responsible for two other lives, they were exposed on a blank face, night was coming, and he was starting to shake from dehydration and hunger and fear.

He climbed back down to the ledge. "We'll split the last of the water," he said, his voice hoarse. Devi leaned against the wall, trying futilely to knead some blood through her swollen forearms.

A sharp crack echoed through the canyon. They looked out; the guerrillas were directly across from them with rifles raised.

"Six," said Ramesh. "Some must have gone back."

There were two or three more shots, but they were too far away; none of the bullets hit within twenty feet of them. When the guerrillas understood the situation they lowered their guns and trotted down the trail toward the river. Even allowing for the river crossing, they'd be directly underneath them in twenty or thirty minutes.

Breathing hard, Peter made a difficult traverse out to the left. The other two followed, matching where he put his hands and feet. They found a gentler grade that he thought they could manage just by smearing and crabbing up. They were all gasping for air, and the guerrillas had made it halfway to the river.

When Peter got to the chossy patch, the first hold he grabbed broke off in his hand. The second one started to work loose before he'd put any weight on it. Ramesh and Devi waited as he tried to figure out what to do. The layer ran all the way along the face. He couldn't see how to get past it without a rope.

"We'll just keep going left," he said finally, though the strategy had its limits. After another twenty or thirty yards the loose layer was broken up by a small boulder that stuck out of it a couple of feet. Rotten rock but big. Peter was able to get a hold on the side; he walked his feet up the wall and mantled onto the top of the boulder, then swung up his legs. The stone was so crumbly it didn't even feel like the boulder was anchored in the wall; if he shifted his weight the rock shifted with him, like a huge loose tooth.

"One at a time on this thing," he said. The granite above it was solid again, so he moved up and found a concavity he could get about half his butt into. With his feet stuck with friction and his hands on nubbins to the sides, he could just hold on there.

Devi stalled. She couldn't do the mantle move, and she was just hanging there, kicking her feet, trying to get leverage. The boulder shifted ever so slightly. Ramesh saw what was happening and somehow got one hand on his sister's foot, then helped boost her over the lip. From there she came up to Peter, but there was nowhere for her to rest, so he moved out of the jug and gave it to her. He faced the wall and rested both hands and feet on nubbins. He was shaking and couldn't get his breath.

Ramesh pulled himself up onto the boulder, then pushed off it, onto the wall. The boulder moved again, the nose dropping with a sort of fitful sigh as it dislodged a few pebbles and finally came to rest. There was a gap between it and the wall at the top now. One good rain would bring it down. This, Peter realized, was where the big landslide below had come from. They were spidering across the surface of the next one, and if the rocks gave way they would carry the climbers thousands of feet to the valley floor.

The chossy layer abruptly angled up the wall and to the left, so they couldn't keep traversing without crossing it again. There was nowhere to go but up. The angle of the slab was decreasing, though, and they were able to nubbin-scramble up for a good thirty feet before they came to another ledge, over which hung a little rock roof. The wall straightened out to vertical on both sides. Peter sat down on the ledge and looked around. There was nowhere to go, and it was getting too dark to downclimb. They were trapped.

He looked at the two of them and tried to figure out how much to say. A night here would almost certainly be fatal. If they huddled back against the wall, the ledge would provide some cover from gunfire, but the temperature was already dropping and the wind would soon pick up. They'd be frozen by morning, and even if they somehow survived the night, trying to climb back down would likely get them killed without any help from the guerrillas.

Devi leaned into him, shivering. "Why is it so cold?" she asked.

"Cool air coming down with the sunset." He draped an arm around her. He couldn't see the guerrillas.

"No, there's a draft," Devi said. "Up behind us. I can feel it on my neck."

He told her he'd go look, though he didn't see how such a thing could be possible. He stood up, and then he could feel it too; cool air was leaking out of somewhere. He climbed up to where the slab that formed the roof met the main wall. He found a gap in the rock about eighteen inches high, so he climbed up and put his hand inside. There was nothing in it but air. He tired quickly, hanging there, and had about enough strength left for one quick look, so he pulled himself up and stuck his head in. He couldn't see anything until he craned his neck around and looked up. He was staring up a perfect natural chimney, a squarish vertical pipe of rock that ascended maybe twenty feet and ended. The walls were rough and dry, perfect for friction climbing, and about four feet apart. Beyond it there was nothing but deep purple sky and a faint star.

They stood, precariously, on the ledge. Ramesh, the thinnest of the three, pulled himself up and wiggled through the hole. Devi went next. She got her hands inside and was kicking her way up the rock when there was another rifle shot, this time from directly below. Peter ducked as a flake of granite spun out from the wall by his head. There was another shot, then a short burst, and suddenly Devi was screaming and blood spattered the wall.

She fell onto the ledge and was just about to go over the side when Peter grabbed her and pulled her back close to him. He pulled up her pants leg. The bullet had entered her calf just above the ankle and exited halfway around to the side and below the knee. She was bleeding, but the blood was dark and steady, venous rather than arterial. Peter took off his shirt and tore it in two. One half he wrapped around the exit wound, the other around the entrance. Devi kept screaming, and bursts of fire shattered the rock to the sides of the ledge and in the overhead roof.

Ramesh peered briefly out of the hole in the rock, then pulled his head back in when the next explosion of bullets came. Peter called him and signaled that he would have to grab his sister's hands and pull her up. Ramesh nodded. Devi stopped screaming and turned white; she was going into shock. Peter put his face right in front of hers.

"Don't go away," he said. "You've got to stay right here with me."

She looked at him, her face pale, her eyes out of focus, as if she couldn't quite make out who or what he was.

"Devi!" he shouted, and her eyes seemed to clear a little. "We're going to get your weight on your good leg, and I'm going to help you stand. Okay?"

She nodded. The blood had already soaked the two pieces of shirt. Peter got his arms around her waist and lifted her. She put her right leg down.

"Now, to the wall," he said. There was another burst of gunfire and she crumpled into a ball, but she was scared, not hit. Peter got her to her feet again and put her hands on the wall.

"We're going to do this fast," he said. "Ramesh?"

Ramesh put his face to the opening and nodded. Peter lifted Devi up. She raised her arms, and Ramesh reached down and grabbed her by the wrists. He pulled and Peter pushed, and in a couple of seconds she was through the hole.

A long eruption of automatic fire chipped away at the rock around the ledge, so Peter sat down against the wall and waited for it to end. As soon as it did, another burst started up.

There was a pause, a clink, then a *ka-chunk*, then another spurt of fire. Peter listened. He was pretty sure the first sound was the expended clip being pulled out. The second, heavier sound would be a new one being slammed in. The pattern repeated itself twice.

He could hear Devi crying in the chimney and Ramesh talking to her. There wasn't enough time to be sure he had it right. He gathered himself into a crouch below the hole and signaled for Ramesh to move Devi out of the way.

Three long bursts, bits of granite flying everywhere, then the lighter, clinking sounds. Peter sprang for the hole, got his hands in, and levered himself up. Just as he got inside, the next fusillade came from below. A rock chip caught him on the ankle and cut him, but it wasn't serious. He heard shouting, and he and Ramesh peered out. The guerrillas were running back down the trail toward the river.

"Another way knowing, I think," said Ramesh.

Peter showed him how to stem the chimney, placing a hand and a foot on each side and using friction to work his way to the top. "You go first," he said. "If we fall I don't want you under us."

Ramesh nodded and spread out his hands and feet, then started up. Peter turned to Devi. "Get up on my back," he said. She nodded, a little too dreamily for his liking. She didn't look good. Blood had filled her shoe. As soon as they were on top he'd be able to get pressure on the wounds.

"You've got to hang on tight," he said. "I need to use my hands to climb. If you let go, you'll fall, and you don't want to land on that leg."

She nodded again. Peter got down on all fours, and she climbed on his back. He showed her how to grip each of her forearms with the opposite hand so she had a lock around his neck without choking him.

"Stay with it," he said. Blood was dribbling out of her shoe and splashing to the ground. Ramesh had already stemmed his way to the top. He climbed out of the opening, then Peter started up. Right foot on the right side, left foot on the left side, braced by the hands. Devi was hard to carry, and he was quickly shaking again and drenched with sweat. At about ten feet, her grip loosened and she almost fell. She began to sob. Peter's legs shook from the stress and the weight, and his crappy soles wouldn't stick to the rock. He had to keep moving or he'd start to slide, and if he slid, the shoes would come off the rock and that would be the end.

Devi almost lost her grip again. "Come on!" Peter said. "Hang on another couple of minutes."

He had ten feet to go, then five, then three. Finally they were at the top. Ramesh reached down, grabbed Devi again, and pulled her out. Peter climbed out after. They were on a cold ridge at probably eighteen thousand feet. The moon shone, and a freezing wind was blowing. Ramesh and Devi were in T-shirts, and Peter was now shirtless. They were all soaked.

Peter got pressure on Devi's wounds, and in a few minutes the bleeding had slowed enough that he thought they could move her. He had started to shiver violently. Down the hill they found a little rock shelter where some boulders had piled up. They crawled in under it, all of them now shaking with cold. Peter wasn't sure they'd get through the night. He and Ramesh pulled more rocks in around the opening so they were almost completely walled in, with a little gap for air. The space was just big enough for them to lie in a pile together, and after a few minutes it began to warm up a bit. Peter hoped Devi would still be alive when dawn came.

TWENTY-SIX

He awakened to sun shafts penetrating the rock cave. He tried to say Devi's name, but he was so cold and dehydrated he could barely speak; his voice emerged with a gravelly asthmatic whine. He nudged her gently with his hand. She was pale and still, but finally her eyes blinked open. Ramesh awakened, then he and Peter removed the rocks from the front of the shelter. They crawled out, and Devi followed, dragging her bad leg behind her. Once in the sun, Peter gently removed the blood-stiffened rags and examined her wounds. They were dirty, and the leg was starting to swell.

"We've got to get you somewhere. . . . " he said, but then his voice gave out and he started to cough. There was frost in the shadows, and he couldn't stop shivering. Neither he nor Devi had eaten in nearly three days. Luckily, the sun was bright and the wind had died. He thought he'd warm up if they got moving.

It looked as if they could head down a relatively gentle slope toward the southeast, the direction of Pokhara, without crossing more than one or two more ridges. The goat trail seemed wider, better used, so it was possible someone lived up here. Peter helped hoist Devi onto Ramesh's back, and they set out, switching her between them every ten minutes or so. She was nearly deadweight.

Peter was reduced to flat, animal endurance. His brain seemed to have shut down, but he was no longer particularly afraid. He mainly thought of finding food, warmth, and rest. Devi's lower wound started bleeding again from all the jostling, so they took a break, and he put pressure on it until it stopped.

He wasn't afraid of the guerrillas anymore either. Getting shot sounded like a relatively quick and painless way to end this ordeal. He supposed he should feel sorry for Devi and Ramesh, but he no longer seemed capable of emotion. He only wanted relief, whether by escape or by death, and he didn't care all that much which it was. He was vaguely aware that his mind wasn't working well, that he was dazed from cold and the lack of food and water, that he was in danger of making more bad decisions to add to his long legacy of them. Even so, it was hard to convince himself to care, and anyway, how much worse could his decisions get?

Ramesh stumbled on, his eyes hollow and his movements stiff. Whenever they shifted Devi between them she gave a little cry of pain. Each time Peter heard it, it stabbed at him. Still, her cries began to anger him, and once he almost told her to shut up, though he knew this was mainly from guilt. They had to find water and a way to get warm or they wouldn't survive until nightfall.

They descended to ten or twelve thousand feet by mid-morning, and the air lost some of its chill. Trees and stunted rhododendron bushes covered part of the rocky hillside. Peter's legs shook so much when he carried Devi that he had to stop every dozen steps and rest. Ramesh could haul her for a few minutes without stopping, but he was fading quickly. If their pursuers found the same trail, Peter knew, they would catch up before day's end.

Around noon they smelled wood smoke; it was sweet, better than the scent of any flower. They came to a sloping open meadow, and at the high end of it, up against the trees, stood a shack with a crooked stovepipe guyed out at the top. A thin blue curl of smoke emerged and dissipated in the breeze.

When they had covered most of the distance to the shack, they smelled water. Peter had never known how strong the smell could be; dehydration and the dry air brought the scent to him as powerfully as if it had been blood, and it surpassed even the smoke in loveliness. They found the spring twenty or thirty feet from the house. He set Devi down gently by the little pool, and she immediately began cupping the water into her mouth. Ramesh didn't even bother to use his hands; he just buried his face and started swallowing. Peter did the same. The water was cold and sweet, with a metallic mineral tang. After a few minutes of this—drinking, then stopping for air, then drinking again—Peter felt some of the fatigue and nausea begin to lift. They lay back in the sun, and after fifteen or twenty minutes he finally stopped shivering for the first time since the previous afternoon. His muscles ached so much from all the contractions it was as if he'd spent the time hooked up to electrodes.

A dog barked. The door to the hut swung open, and out shuffled a withered crone, bent over and crippled from arthritis, bracing herself on a crooked stick. She scolded the dog, a huge mastiff. It whined, put its tail between its legs, and sat down at her feet. The woman peered at them, then called out some sort of question.

Ramesh, surprised, said to Peter, "She Tibetan." Then he pointed to Devi and spoke to the old woman. The woman dropped her stick and scuttled forward. She helped Devi sit, then Ramesh and Peter picked Devi up and carried her inside, with the old woman close behind. The mastiff stayed out, on a long chain beside the cabin.

The woman pointed them to a tiny straw mattress in the corner, where they laid Devi down. The woman was barely five feet tall, her bed not much longer than she was, and Devi's feet hung over the end. It was blessedly warm inside, though, and the woman brought Peter a rough cotton shirt. He donned it gratefully and started unwrapping Devi's wounds. The woman put two pots onto her woodstove. She poured water into both of them, then cut up potatoes and put them in one of the pots.

Devi had a fever, and now that she was hydrated she began to sweat. Peter asked Ramesh to find out if the woman had any clean cloth. The woman nodded and brought out a large white T-shirt. It was one of those nonsensical Indian or Chinese knockoffs: It read "GG Comet" and had a picture of a smiling kitten flying through space, with a crescent moon and stars in the background. Peter gestured that he wanted to rip it, and the woman nodded. When the second pot had boiled and cooled a bit, she brought it over and set it down on the floor by the bed. Peter took part of the shirt and dipped it in the hot water.

"This is going to hurt," he said, and Devi nodded dreamily. He began cleaning the wounds. Devi cried out, and the old woman sat down and held her hand.

As he worked, Peter grew more concerned; the wounds weren't gangrenous yet, but they were starting to smell, and the leg grew more swollen by the hour. Ramesh held Devi's other hand, and together the three of them got her through the debridement. When Peter had done the best job he could, he tore the rest of the T-shirt in half, soaked it in the water, and wrapped the wounds. As soon as he was done, Devi fell asleep. They covered her with a blanket.

Peter turned to Ramesh. "Village, how far?" he asked.

Ramesh spoke to the woman. From what Peter understood of Ramesh's broken English, there was a road about a six-hour walk down the mountain, and a town a few miles down the road.

"We need to eat and rest first, if she doesn't mind us staying a little while," Peter said. Ramesh nodded and spoke to the woman. She got some dried meat from her cupboard and added it to the water where the potatoes were boiling, then started heating more water in the second pot. When it was hot, she took roasted barley flour and a tin of butter from the cupboard and made *tsampa*. They started with that, then a half hour later, when the potato-and-meat soup was done, they ate again. Devi awakened briefly, and Peter fed her a little soup, but she soon fell back asleep.

The old woman pulled five earthenware jars out of her cupboard and picked dried roots and leaves out of them, then spread them out on the wooden counter. She directed Peter to chop up several tough, white roots that looked like human fingers. She broke up a couple of different kinds of leaves into a mortar and began grinding them with a pestle, then added something flat and chalky. Peter chopped some thin roots that resembled ramen noodles. The woman went out to the meadow to gather a couple of flowers she wanted, and when everything was assembled to her satisfaction she put it all into a terra-cotta pot, then ladled in enough water to cover the herbs. She put the pot on the stove, gave it a stir with a wooden spoon, and sat down, cross-legged, on a cushion by the bed.

She pulled out her *mala* and began reciting a mantra that Peter had heard before, when he was treating the monks and nuns. It was for the Medicine Buddha, a deity who appeared dark blue in *thangkas*. "*Om Bekhaze Bekhaze Maha Bekhaze Ratza Samu Gate Soha,*" she mumbled, over and over. In a few minutes the pot had risen to a gentle boil and a wisp of steam emerged.

Peter, exhausted, lay down on the floor by the mattress. From this viewpoint the hut looked a little bigger but not much. Most of the things in it appeared to have been hand-cut from the woods or made of clay most likely dug from some nearby riverbank. The small woodstove, a kerosene lamp, and a few cooking utensils were from the outside world, but the sink was carved from a hollowed-out section of log, and water drained from it through a bamboo pipe. A rough-hewn table with a chair stood against one wall. There was a small shrine made of wood against the other wall. It held butter lamps, water bowls, a couple of deity statues, and photographs of both the Dalai Lama and Lama Padma as a younger man.

"Ask her, does she know Lama Padma?" Peter asked. He was so exhausted that even lying down it took effort to form the words.

Ramesh spoke to the woman. "They friends, young times," he said. "Same teacher."

"What's her name?"

"Tsering Wangmo," said Ramesh.

"Tell her I said thank you."

Ramesh spoke to her, and Tsering Wangmo smiled and nodded. Soon she got up and took the herbal decoction off the stove. When the herbs had cooled she gestured to Peter, and he got up. He unwrapped the cotton cloths from Devi's wounds, soaked them in the herbal mixture, and rewrapped the leg. Tsering Wangmo inspected the bandages, appeared satisfied, and sat to continue her mantra. Peter lay down again. He wondered how the old woman had ended up here. He had many questions, but they would have to wait.

He awakened to sunlight streaming in, to birdsong and an open door. It was just after dawn; he had slept all afternoon and straight through the night, right there on the floor. Tsering Wangmo was outside, feeding the dog.

Devi was awake, and her fever was down. The leg was still swollen but hadn't gotten any worse.

Peter raised himself on an elbow. "How are you?"

"A little better, I think," she said groggily. "She changed the dressing every few hours all night long. This morning I crawled out and peed. My leg hurt, but I could do it, and it isn't bleeding anymore."

"She stayed up all night?" Peter asked.

Devi nodded.

Tsering Wangmo made breakfast with *tsampa,* then fried potatoes and wild onions together. They were all ravenous and devoured everything quickly. Peter had lost three belt holes since the guerrillas took them, and now that he'd slept and eaten, he felt stiff and sore but surprisingly light. Devi's cheeks had lost their baby fat and hollowed out. Ramesh was, well, Ramesh—he was tough and matter-of-fact.

A little while later the old woman sat on her porch in the sun, meditating, while Peter and Ramesh washed the dishes. After a few minutes, though, Tsering Wangmo came back inside looking troubled, and spoke to Devi.

"Peter, you'd better listen to this," Devi said.

He put down the dishrag and leaned against the sink. Ramesh stopped what he was doing and sat on the floor.

"Tsering Wangmo says something may happen soon, and she wants us all to do exactly as she says," Devi said.

Peter and Ramesh exchanged a look. The old woman spoke for a little while, then Devi translated again. "She wants us to lie down perfectly still where we are, and to stay there with our eyes open, without moving," Devi said. "She says that no matter what happens, we are not to respond in any way. She wants you to say out loud that you will do as she says."

"Okay," said Peter, a little warily. Ramesh nodded and responded in Tibetan.

Tsering Wangmo gestured at the floor then, and they all lay down. Peter felt a little foolish, but at this point he was glad for any excuse to rest. Tsering Wangmo sat on her meditation cushion and took out her two-sided drum, her bell, and her *kangling,* a small horn made from a human femur. She began to play the drum and ring the bell while chanting a low-pitched song of some kind.

"She is doing *chöd,*" Devi explained quietly. "One offers one's body to pacify demons."

Demons, thought Peter. The whole thing was out of his realm, but then *he* was out of his realm.

Tsering Wangmo chanted and sang, and from time to time put down the bell and blew the *kangling,* which pealed into the room, piercing and high-pitched. Lying there, Peter felt a shudder go through him. He had the uncanny sense—the physical sensation, up and down his spine—that Tsering Wangmo was calling someone or some*thing,* and that it had heard her and was on its way.

A dull heaviness descended, and he seemed to fall half asleep, as if drugged. After a minute or so he couldn't move; it was like sleep paralysis, when the brain immobilizes the body with chemicals during dreaming. It seemed to him, in fact, that he *was* asleep, since he couldn't even move his eyes. His whole body developed a crawling sensation, as if insects were on him—*in* him—but he couldn't scratch or even blink. He wondered why he didn't feel afraid, but other than the itching, the sensation was like drifting in dreams during an afternoon nap, unable to move but strangely contented.

After a few minutes the mastiff began to bark. There was a rifle shot from outside, and the barking stopped. Peter heard boots on the porch, saw the light change as the door was pushed open, and still Tsering Wangmo sang her *chöd* practice. Three young men came into the room, apparently the last of the guerrillas who had tracked them there, and they began shouting at the old woman. Peter wanted to intercede. He realized that Tsering Wangmo's admonitions hadn't been necessary, though; he couldn't have moved or gotten up if he'd tried.

Tsering Wangmo ignored the men. Finally one of them went over to her and pulled the drum out of her hand, then the bell. He apparently knew some rudimentary Tibetan, and he shouted at her. She responded quietly. Peter's eyes stayed on the ceiling, and he could just barely see what was going on in his peripheral vision.

The men came over to them, one by one, and looked into their faces. Peter stared straight ahead. One man nudged him with his boot; his body felt slack, lifeless, and he didn't even flinch. When they looked at him, they seemed repulsed. He had the feeling from the tone of their conversation that they had a similar response to the others.

They shouted at the old woman again, indicating with their hands that they wanted food. She nodded toward the pot on the stove, where the potatoes were simmering. One of the men went to the pot and lifted the lid, then shouted, dropped it, and retreated to the far corner of the room. The lid clanged to the floor, then wobbled down flat and lay still. The other two guerrillas went to look into the pot, then backed warily away.

They were very angry and upset now, and appeared to have decided to leave. But on their way out, one of them turned back and leveled his rifle at Tsering Wangmo. He pulled the trigger, but the rifle did not fire. She picked up her bell and drum again, and began to play. The guerrilla pulled the trigger again, but the rifle just clicked. To test the gun, he aimed it at the ceiling, just over Peter's head. This time it fired and blew a hole out of the roof, and an azure patch of sky appeared. The guerrilla aimed the gun at Tsering Wangmo a third time and pulled the trigger. Once again, it did not fire. He screamed in frustration and turned to go, slamming the butt of the gun into the doorframe as he stalked out.

They all lay still for a few minutes more, until Tsering Wangmo finished singing and spoke to Devi.

"She says you are safe now," Devi said. "You may sit up."

The heavy paralysis dissipated, and soon Peter was able to move his fingers and toes. They all arose, sluggishly, and looked at one another, a little shell-shocked. He asked Devi what had happened.

The old woman chuckled as she spoke to Devi, as if three lunatics had just barged in shouting nonsense and there'd been nothing she could do about it. Devi said the men had apparently seen them as corpses. They were disgusted that she was keeping dead bodies in her house, all bloated with maggots and covered by flies. They found the stench unbearable, but at least they felt their job was done and they could finally go home. When they went to take the food from the stove, they found that the pot contained a live cobra, which reared up and puffed out its hood, and that's why they ran away.

"The business with the rifle you saw for yourself," Devi added drily. Tsering Wangmo clicked her tongue. "She says now, thanks to that stupid boy, she'll have to fix the roof."

Something suddenly occurred to the old woman, and she got to her feet and shuffled outside. Ramesh and Peter followed her, and Devi got up and limped to the door. The mastiff lay on its side on the ground, its tongue lolled out. It had been shot through the chest and lay in the dust, in a pool of sticky, drying blood.

Tsering Wangmo emitted a little cry of dismay and knelt by the dog, then put her hands on it. She probed the wound with her fingers but didn't find a bullet; apparently it had gone straight through. She bent down and sucked at the hole, turning to spit clotted blood into the dust until it came out rich and red. She spoke to Devi, who went back into the house and brought her needle and thread. Tsering Wangmo stitched up the wound, then she and Devi rolled the dog over and she sewed up the other side. Peter still felt woozy and sat down on the porch step. The old woman knelt there in the dirt for a long time, pressing on the wound with her hand and reciting her prayers. Devi stayed right by her, watching attentively. Peter didn't know why she'd bothered to stitch up the dog, since it was clearly too late for that.

But then, after about ten minutes, the mastiff's tail rose, just once, feebly, and thumped back down into the dust. Tsering Wangmo spoke gently to the dog. It opened its eyes about halfway, and the tail rose and thumped down again.

Peter, Ramesh, and Devi looked at one another. Devi began to weep; she helped the old woman up, bowed to her, and led her back inside. Tsering Wangmo said something to Peter as she passed; Devi smiled and said, "She says don't be too surprised; he's a tough old dog. She wonders if you'd get him some water so she can rest."

Peter nodded and took the dog's wooden bowl to the spring. The mastiff tried to lift its head, but it was still too weak, so Peter poured water into its mouth until it was strong enough to roll onto its stomach, raise its head, and lap some up on its own. Peter found it strange but vaguely pleasing to tend to the dog while Tsering Wangmo tended to Devi. The mastiff drained a couple of bowls, then lay down on its side in the sun, sighed, and went to sleep.

| | |

The next day they rested. Peter and Tsering Wangmo took turns changing Devi's dressing, and by late afternoon she was able to do it herself. The leg was still swollen, but the smell of putrefaction was gone. The skin around the wounds looked pink and good, and the holes had closed and begun to seal over.

"I've never seen a gunshot wound heal this fast," Peter said. In response, Devi just nodded toward Tsering Wangmo, who stood at the counter, humming to herself and chopping herbs.

| | |

The following morning, Peter and Ramesh patched the roof, then Peter cut a sapling and made Devi a primitive crutch. She still limped badly, though, and he wasn't sure she'd be able to make it down the mountain even with help. He knew that he and Ramesh wouldn't be able to carry her such a distance, in any case.

As he was mulling over what to do, the old woman told him to keep the shirt and offered them some *tsampa*, which they accepted gratefully. Peter told her he would find a way to send some money. Tsering Wangmo waved her hand dismissively and said she couldn't care less.

Devi sat on the front porch, drinking tea and watching. Peter went over and squatted down beside her.

"Are you strong enough for this?" he asked.

She surprised him by laughing. "We're thinking the same thing but for different reasons," she said. "My leg's no good yet, but that's not why I want to stay."

"What do you mean?"

Devi sipped her tea. "You've seen what this woman can do," she said. "I may never have a chance like this again."

"A chance for what?"

"Peter, think about it. You should know me by now. As long as she's willing to have me, I'll study with her."

"What about Alex?"

She looked briefly troubled. "I don't know," she admitted. "But it will be a couple of weeks before my leg is strong enough to walk down the mountain, and you can't wait. You've got to get back and figure out how to get her out of there."

Peter didn't know what to say, but he knew her well enough to doubt she'd change her mind. Ramesh spoke to her in Nepali and finally acceded to her wishes as well.

Peter hugged her and said goodbye. She and Tsering Wangmo sat on the porch as Peter and Ramesh headed down through the meadow. It was full of spring wildflowers just beginning to bloom.

"She always this way," Ramesh said. "Stubborn like goat." He looked back and waved at his sister one last time.

"That's why she and Alex got along so well," Peter said.

Late in the afternoon they came to the road and flagged down a truck. In Pokhara, Peter found a tour group of Americans at a small café. He used one of their cellphones to call the clinic and had them get Mina.

She came to the phone, and he said her name. There was a pause, then she began to cry.

TWENTY-SEVEN

She was waiting at 2:00 A.M. when the bus pulled in. Peter went straight into her arms, and they just stood together for a few moments. Sangita and Sonam had caught a ride to the station with Mina; Sangita rushed to her son and wrapped him in a hug so tight he cried out for her to take it easy. Everyone was in tears.

On the way home, Peter explained to Mina what had happened, while Ramesh, sitting in back with his parents, spoke rapidly in Tibetan, apparently bringing them up to date about his life and what had become of Devi. Sangita kept her arms around him and dabbed at her eyes the whole way.

Mina dropped them off and took Peter to his house. "What are you going to do about Alex?"

"I'll be at the embassy when it opens in a few hours, and we'll go from there." He was so tired he could barely stand.

"Have you eaten?"

"Just a little the past couple of days."

She parked and went inside with him.

"Your old man's not going to like this," he said.

"Too bad. Have a shower, and I'll get something ready."

When he came downstairs in his sweats twenty minutes later, he smiled, surprised that he was actually glad to see *dal-bhat*.

He ate until he thought he'd burst, then they left the dishes in the sink and she came upstairs with him. She put her arms around him and they kissed, but he gently pulled away.

"Look," he said. "I'm sorry, but I'm exhausted and I can't really think about anything but Alex right now. Could we just sleep awhile?"

They lay down together, and she put her arms around him. "I thought I'd lost you," she said quietly.

"Usha's all right?" he asked.

"She's fine. She's been worried, though."

He had something else he wanted to say, but his mind was blurring, he couldn't find the words, and then he was asleep.

| | |

He awakened three hours later, at 6:00, his heart pounding. Mina was still curled around him. He said her name.

She opened her eyes slowly, then started up. "Oh, shit," she said. "He'll be awake already. He is *not* going to be happy."

She kissed Peter, put on her shoes, and bolted.

He was at the gates of the American embassy at 8:00 when it opened. They steered him to an attaché who dealt with missing children and related emergencies. Alice Finley was a plump, imposing redhead in her forties who leveled a gaze at Peter that was at once sympathetic and skeptical. He got the feeling she had heard way too many tales of woe in her career.

There was a huge contour map of the country on her wall. "Show me where this village was," she said.

He went over and squinted at it. He marked the route with his finger, as well as he could figure, northwest from Pokhara to the Annapurna foothills. He didn't know the first village's name—or if it even *had* a name—but it didn't matter, because only a handful of the larger towns were marked. The stream they'd walked up could have been any of a dozen that branched out all through the mountains. He stared, then slowly traced a circle.

"Somewhere in here," he said.

She stood beside him, peering at the map. "That's roughly the size of Maine."

She called the RNA chopper squadron, but no one knew anything, because Colonel Pradhan, Mina's father, had made a private requisition and the pilot was, of course, dead. Pradhan himself had no idea where Krishna had been headed.

Finley hung up the phone, looking sour. "They were pretty unpleasant," she said. "They seem to feel that if you hadn't requested this favor, their friend Krishna would still be alive."

Peter called Franz.

"Siruyama, I think," Franz said. "I think that was the town's name, something like that."

Finley called the CIA station chief, who was downstairs and had satellite images. He emailed one that showed the location of a village with a similar name that appeared to be in about the right place. Peter traced their route upstream a few miles, but he had no idea where they'd left the river and crossed the ridge, or in which of several valleys they'd come to the town used by the guerrillas. What had seemed simple and straightforward on the ground looked convoluted and confusing from outer space.

The photo showed small villages all through the region. He made another circle with his finger.

"Now we've got it down to the size of Rhode Island," said Finley. "Rhode Island with twenty-five-thousand-foot mountains. I guess that's progress, sort of."

Peter called Sangita to see if he could reach Ramesh, but he'd gone out with his father and wouldn't return for a while.

Peter turned back to Finley. "There's got to be some way to get up there and get her out," he said. "Do you have someone who can fly me?"

Finley pressed the intercom button on her phone. "Karla, two coffees, if you please." She turned to Peter. "Maybe you should sit."

He had thought it would be straightforward: American citizen gets kidnapped, American embassy arranges for ransom, American commandos get the girl and bring her home. What the hell could be the problem?

Karla brought the coffee and left. Peter took a sip. He was trying to be nice but not too nice, the kind of person Finley would go out of her way to help because she liked him on the one hand but didn't want any trouble from him on the other.

"Okay," he said. "Let's hear it."

"First," Finley said, then stopped, choosing her words. "First, we can't fly you or anybody else in there."

"I just flew in. What are you talking about?"

She shifted her weight. "You flew in under the auspices of a relief organization outside of U.S. authority or control, on a helicopter provided by the RNA."

"So?"

"The compound was fortified with SAMs and various other ordnance, yes?"

"Yeah . . ."

"Look," said Finley. "The U.S. keeps no military aircraft in this country, and if we did we wouldn't use them for this."

"Why not?"

"Because if they too were shot down, we'd suddenly be on one side of a civil war."

He had a feeling of sickening descent, not unlike he'd felt in the helicopter itself. "You're not already?"

She shook her head. "We're doing our best to stay out of it, because Prachanda and his armies are strong enough now that soon they'll be able to force elections. We *want* them to force elections, in fact, because it will probably end the monarchy, and you know how we feel about monarchies."

"Monarchies that aren't Saudi Arabian and sitting on a ton of oil, you mean."

She eyed him a little disapprovingly. "Nevertheless," she said, "we want to bring them into the legislative process and end this disaster of a war."

"Why can't you contact Prachanda directly and get him involved?"

"Because first, he won't talk to us. Second, because despite everything I've told you, the State Department still considers him a terrorist. It would torpedo our leverage with the legitimate government."

"For Christ's sake, Alice."

She sighed. "Also, your daughter will probably turn into a PR bonanza for these guys, and releasing her would be admitting that she'd been captured instead of converted. So they'd lose both the human shield and the propaganda bonus."

Peter stared at her. "You can't be telling me there's nothing to be done."

She sighed. "I'm telling you there's nothing *we* can do. I already know what you're thinking, and we can't send in any sort of military personnel, for the same reason we can't send in aircraft."

He tried to keep his voice down, but he was frustrated and angrier by the second. "Alice, this is unbelievable."

"Look, I can call my best contacts in the RNA, and with any luck they'll meet with you this morning. It's their duchy; they've got to handle it."

"You have kids?" he asked.

"Don't start the 'You have kids?' thing with me, Peter, please. In fact I have a son and a daughter. They go to the international school here, and I know exactly how murderously crazed I'd be if a bunch of thugs with AKs overran the place and I found myself in your shoes. I think you're being a model of civility, frankly. But the situation would be exactly the same."

"For Christ's sake, we're the most powerful nation on earth—"

"We can't nuke them, Peter. We need a flyswatter, not an H-bomb, and the RNA has all the flyswatters."

He stood up. "Call them," he said. "While I'm standing here, I want to hear you do it."

"Of course."

She arranged for him to go later that morning.

"One thing," she said. "Bear in mind that she's probably safe."

He turned to face her. "She has dysentery, and they have no medicines or water filters there, so she's not going to be getting over it anytime soon. Every guy in the place was giving her the eye when we walked in, that lovely feral teenage-guy look that says, 'I might just decide to fuck you sometime and you won't be able to do shit about it.' So don't tell me she's safe, because she isn't safe. I brought her here to *make* her safe. Great how that worked out, huh?"

"All I'm saying is that they're going to want her to look good," Finley said. "No scabs, no bruises, no hollow, haunted eyes. They'll feed her and probably even find her something to wash her hair with. So yes, do what you have to do to get her out. But don't scream at the RNA and don't fall apart, because then you won't be any good to her. Okay?"

TWENTY-EIGHT

Peter borrowed a detailed topographical map of the area, went back to his house, and called Sangita again. Ramesh had come home, so she brought him over. Ramesh knew the name of the guerrillas' village, but it wasn't on the map. Nevertheless, by finding a couple of towns he knew, then triangulating, he was able to show Peter about where the compound should be. Peter folded the map and put it in his pocket.

When he arrived for his meeting with Colonel Sengupta, Peter found the man and his assistants standing in a room, watching television. The colonel eyed Peter coldly and gestured toward the set. Peter turned to look.

Adhiraj had moved swiftly. On the screen, set against a neutral backdrop of forest, was the image he'd been dreading. Alex was dressed in clean, pressed camouflage fatigues and a headband. A Kalashnikov sat on a table in front of her. She spoke briefly in Nepali, then repeated herself in English.

"This struggle is not about ideology, it's about income disparity," she said, and Peter realized where he'd heard those words.

He'd written her first speech for her the night he'd been pontificating on the way to the pizza parlor.

His daughter was unthreatening, convincing, and extremely telegenic. Peter was relieved that Finley had been right in one way, at least; Alex looked like she'd been fed and reasonably well cared for. Adhiraj had obviously figured out one way to get more attention in the United States.

"When you have ninety-five percent of the population living on less than three hundred dollars a year, and the other five percent rolling around in Bentleys, this is what you get," Alex continued, stopping briefly to adjust the microphone on the table in front of her. She rested her right hand on the stock of the rifle; then, tellingly, she pulled it away. It was her one misstep, but she quickly hit her stride again. "I've joined this cause not because I hate the king, and not because I love violence. I have joined because I love the Nepali people, and I hate what the royal family and its minions in the RNA are doing to them. This is a call to all Americans and all people of the international community, to see which side is in the right here and take a stand."

Jesus Christ, thought Peter.

"Turn it off," said Sengupta, and one of the others did. Sengupta turned to face Peter. "This is who you want us to rescue? A stupid girl who is killing our own soldiers?"

"She's not killing anyone."

"Words like this encourage the enemy, and the enemy kills us. We lost two hundred in raids last week. She might as well have pulled the trigger herself."

"She is a hostage doing what hostages do, which is *cooperate.*"

The colonel and his adjutants exchanged glances. "Come with me," he said. "Captain, join us." The two men escorted Peter down the hall to another room. They led him inside and shut the metal door.

The room held an old Steelcase table and several battered chairs. The only light was from a frosted-glass window at the end, which made it feel chilly even though it wasn't. Sengupta extended his hand toward a chair, and Peter sat.

"That was far more than cooperation," Sengupta said. "That was commitment, revolutionary fervor."

"With all due respect, Colonel, that was acting," said Peter. "If you'd seen her in drama club, you'd understand."

Sengupta exhaled in exasperation. "Where is the compound?"

Peter was about to pull out the map, but something in the way Sengupta had asked the question gave him pause. "What are you going to do when you find out?"

"These people are terrorists. It is now clear that your *daughter* is a terrorist."

"For God's sake, she's been there less than a week," Peter replied. "She's seventeen years old."

"Seventeen is young in your country but not here," Sengupta said. "She is probably older than half the guerrillas there. I ask again, where is this village?"

"So you can send in gunships and kill anything that moves? Is that your great plan?"

"Adhiraj is one of Prachanda's best operatives," he said. "We will take whatever action we deem appropriate."

Peter started for the door. "Then I'll get her out without your help."

"This is impossible."

"We'll see."

"You don't know the situation, Doctor."

It occurred to him that they might actually arrest him to find out what they wanted to know. He couldn't take the chance.

"What I don't know is where the compound *is*, Colonel!" he said. "There were three or four ridges, a couple of rivers, and rhododendrons so thick a goat trail was the only way through them. At the embassy we got it down to fifteen hundred square miles! I thought you'd be able to help with that, but thanks anyway."

| | |

By Peter's back porch, a dozen parrots were hanging upside down from the branches of the jacaranda, squawking at one another. They'd been eating fermented berries from the bush next door, and they were drunk. Peter watched them, exhausted but appreciating the lunacy of it.

Could he pray? he wondered. Was it just a matter of pride? He thought if there were a sort of trickster god, a drunken-parrot god, some sidelong, wisecrack aspect of God, to that god he could now conceivably pray. What such a supplication might bring he didn't know, and even answered prayers often seemed to come with a price. It didn't matter anymore what the price was, though. He sat still and took a long, slow breath and offered up his prayers as honestly as he could, for at this point there was nothing else to do. He wasn't sure if he had ever really prayed before, at least with any sincerity. It was humbling and scary, the feeling of relinquishing the reins.

When he had finished, he took another breath. He didn't feel much of anything. The parrots began a minor avian orgy, then all at once there was a green explosion of wing beats and they flew off together, their dozen thrumming hearts synchronized in air.

It was an old belief, of course, that if God wanted to talk to you, he might give you some sort of idea. But Peter sat there, trying to find his way through it all, bereft of inspiration.

He decided to go to bed. He didn't imagine there was a lot of time, but he would take some of it. He lay down. His heart thudded quietly. The room faded around him, and feeling as tiny and powerless as he ever had, finally he went to sleep.

When he awakened a couple of hours later, at sunset, he leaned on his elbow and looked out at the mountains, pink and beautiful in the evening light. Something had welled up as he slept, something that hadn't occurred to him before. He sat up, pulled on his pants, shoved his feet into his shoes, and called Mina.

| | |

An hour later he sat in his living room with Usha and Mina, who was translating for her.

"So her mother didn't know?" Peter asked.

Mina shook her head. "It turns out her mother thought they were selling her as a domestic slave to a rich family, which is still pretty odious," she said. "But the prostitution was her father's idea, because there was more money in it."

"Is there a way to get ahold of her mother?"

Mina spoke to Usha and told Peter that there was a phone in the village. "She's afraid, though, because she has a lot of relatives who will be angry if they learn the truth."

"Angry at her, or at her father?"

Mina asked her. "She says partly at her father but mainly at Bahadur. Their whole relationship is built on trust, and if he lied to her mother and her aunts it won't go down well."

"Get the number, will you? We're calling her mom tonight."

TWENTY-NINE

"Peter, my good friend," said Bahadur, his voice shaky. It was the next afternoon; the family had moved swiftly.

"Hello, Bahadur."

"You must drive to the address I give you and bring Usha. Please come right away."

An hour later Peter, Mina, and Usha pushed open the dented steel door of an abandoned warehouse in one of the city's old industrial districts. The concrete floor was filthy and littered with huge rusty gears and parts from old machines. The air smelled of axle grease. Sun shafts bored through holes in the roof, lighting up dust motes and patches of floor so that the room was as dappled as the shade under a tree.

At the far end stood a cluster of people. One of them broke away from the others and came toward them.

"Aama!" cried Usha, and threw her arms around her.

"*Chori,*" said her mother. "Usha *chori.*"

As Peter's eyes grew more used to the light he saw Bahadur tied out spread-eagled against the far wall. One man held a *khukuri* knife at his throat. The other had pulled down Bahadur's pants and appeared ready to geld him. Usha saw him and turned away. Peter and Mina walked over.

"Peter, my excellent American friend," said Bahadur, his face beaded with sweat.

"Who are they?"

"Parents, uncles, aunts," said Bahadur. He was pale. "It is a very close family from the hill country, if you follow my meaning."

Peter nodded. "Do any of them speak English?"

Bahadur shook his head. He explained the situation, and Peter did his best to pretend that it came as a complete surprise.

"So you'd like me to tell them that I bought her merely as a domestic."

"Immediately, if you don't mind."

"But that's not what you were selling her for. You know that."

Bahadur looked at him, stricken. "But Doctor . . ."

"Here's the deal," Peter said. "Mina will tell them I'm a doctor with a daughter of my own and that Usha is still a virgin."

"Of course, that is the truth," said Bahadur, with an ingratiating smile.

Peter went on. "After that, I'm going to buy them a couple of rooms at a hotel and pay the tab for their dinner. While they're there, you're going to do something for me, and if you fuck it up in any way whatsoever I'll take you back to them and tell them the truth, that you were trying to sell her as a whore."

"All right," said Bahadur. "Whatever you say. Just please . . ."

Peter nodded to Mina, and she spoke to the family. As she did, Peter watched the father, who stood a little apart from the others with his arms crossed, staring at the ground.

There were general sounds of relief, but then Usha's mother spoke up.

"She says she wants proof that Usha is still a virgin," Mina said. "She doesn't see why an American doctor should be different from any other man."

"If Usha doesn't mind, take them out to the car so she can

check for herself," Peter said, knowing that this is what it would likely take to allay their fears.

Usha nodded, and the women left. The men put their knives away and untied Bahadur, who quickly pulled up his pants. In a couple of minutes the women returned. Usha's mother spoke to them, and everyone seemed to relax. The men clapped Bahadur on the shoulder.

"Yes, yes," said Bahadur, with a big, shit-eating grin. "All a misunderstanding! No hard feelings!"

Mina told them about the hotel, which was presented as Peter's gift to the family in appreciation of their daughter. They gathered their things, smiling and talking excitedly, then departed.

| | |

Bahadur's house was commodious and elegantly furnished. He and Peter sat in the office, Bahadur watching nervously as Peter opened a database of names on Badahur's laptop.

"These are your clients in the army?" Peter asked.

"I can barely keep it up to date."

"I had no idea you were so organized, Bahadur."

"It is the only way to stay out of jail, I'm afraid."

Peter went to the S's, but Sengupta was not on the list. He then scrolled backward; he wasn't hoping for much, but when he got to the P's he nearly fell out of his chair.

"Pradhan?" he said, incredulous. "*Colonel* Pradhan? Mina's father?"

Bahadur cleared his throat uncomfortably. "An unhappy marriage, apparently. As so many are."

Peter closed the laptop and put it in his bag.

"You're keeping my computer?" Bahadur said.

"Just a little insurance, so you don't disappear, and so nothing happens to me. It will be safe with friends. Now let's go."

Bahadur paled. "Not Pradhan, Doctor, please."

"Usha's family is waiting at the hotel," Peter said. "It's your choice."

THIRTY

Pradhan kept an office in the old British headquarters building west of the Royal Palace. He was tall and slender, his hair and mustache the sleek gray of polished steel, his eyebrows dark over dry, penetrating eyes. Peter left Bahadur out of sight down the hallway and came into the office alone.

Pradhan reached into his desk and produced a pack of American cigarettes. "They are so much better than *bidis*," he said. "You don't mind?"

"It's your office, Colonel."

Pradhan lit up. He puffed a few times, then opened the window behind him. Traffic noise from below came into the room.

"What you are asking, I cannot do," he said. "I am retired, and because of that it is illegal and too risky. I am still in trouble over the helicopter pilot, and that was nothing compared to this."

"You want more money," Peter said. "I understand. I'll get it."

Pradhan came to the desk and put the cigarette in the ashtray. He extended his fingers and leaned forward on them, his face downward, the way a sprinter leans just before the gun.

"Money is not the issue," he said. "It is much more compli-cated than that."

"Name your terms, then. I'll meet them."

"Your daughter's television appearance would make it very hard to find men for such a job," he said. "It is a matter of honor."

"You think it's honorable to leave a seventeen-year-old girl out there?"

"You don't understand," said Pradhan. There was a picture of Mina next to the ashtray on the desk; he picked it up, regarded it absently, then put it down again.

Peter watched him and realized that in fact he had misunder-stood. "This isn't about my daughter, is it?" he said. "This is about *your* daughter."

Pradhan shrugged. "I have a good man for her," he said. "A Nepali man. Wealthy. I know you Americans don't give a damn about tradition, but we still do."

"Does Mina like him? Does she even know him?"

"That is not the point," said Pradhan, bristling. "My wife and I had an arranged marriage, and it has worked out very well."

"For you, maybe," said Peter. "I've heard a dissenting opinion, though." He got up, went to the hall, and brought in Bahadur.

Pradhan stiffened to attention. "What is this man doing here?"

"Hello, Colonel," said Bahadur sheepishly. "I am sorry for this, but as you may imagine, I have been put in a most unpleasant po-sition."

Pradhan glared at both of them, his eyes fearful and fierce, his mouth a tight rictus of loathing. Peter pulled over a chair and sat down.

"I have a lot of respect for your expertise in military matters, Colonel," he said. He opened up the map and spread it out on the desk. "Now explain to me exactly how you're going to get my daughter out of that village."

| | |

Once Pradhan became reconciled to his situation, he undertook the project with professional resolve. He told Peter that to do the job well and safely would take a few days. There were arrangements, logistics, things Peter knew nothing about. If he wanted his daughter alive, he must be patient. They agreed that Mina would know nothing of the blackmail, that she would be allowed to believe Pradhan had undertaken the project simply out of outrage at the rebels, and to help his daughter's friend.

For the first three days Peter paced his house. He had too much time to think. Had he done the right thing? Was there another, less risky way that he hadn't considered? He called Finley at the embassy, told her his plans, asked her what she thought.

"We haven't had this conversation, and I don't know anything about it," she replied. "And I wish you luck."

He called Mina and asked if he could trust her father to do it right.

"Look, he's a traditional military man," she said. "He's ultra-conservative and a real prick sometimes. But in this, yes—he's just the person you need."

That third sleepless night he lay there thinking about something that had once happened with Alex. Her sophomore year she had been making straight A's, but she also wanted to play basketball, and she wasn't very good at it yet. One evening Peter found her in back of their house shooting free throws, her lips pressed tight together the way they used to get when she was either determined about something or trying not to cry.

"Coach told me I can't shoot," she said. Her voice wavered a little. "He pulled me out of the lineup and gave my spot to Margaret Donnelly, who's like this fucking stork and can practically dunk without jumping."

Peter said he was sorry and asked her what she was doing.

"I'm not stopping until I can shoot thirty free throws in a row. If I miss one, I start over."

"He made you do this?"

She looked at him as if he were clueless. "*I* made me do this."

He decided to let her. When she finally came inside, four or five hours later, he figured she'd succeeded. Eventually she reclaimed her spot among the starters after Donnelly, who was way too thin for her own good, sprained her ACL, and an orthopedist suggested she build up some quads if she ever hoped to stabilize the knee.

It was later that year that Alex started cutting herself. Peter hadn't realized the connection at first, but after he got her into therapy, the shrink had pointed it out. Somewhere along the line she'd invented impossible standards for herself. It was partly hardwired and partly a reaction to Cheryl, the therapist suggested, an attempt to do whatever it took so she didn't end up like her mother.

Ironically, when it all started, it had been Cheryl who noticed that Alex was keeping her sleeves down all the time. She'd seen it before with people she knew who were heroin addicts.

Now, in the house in Kathmandu, the phone rang. Peter grabbed at it, his heart pounding. It was Mina. The clock read 2:00 A.M.

"Something's happened," she said, and he could tell it wasn't good. The adrenaline swirled up and his heart fluttered, then the dizziness came. He sat up on the edge of the bed, his lungs suddenly feeling so shallow he couldn't get air. "Tell me."

"They found Adhiraj's compound day before yesterday," Mina said. "They went in yesterday before dawn, but they hadn't allowed for the dogs. When they scouted the place they only saw a couple, but there turned out to be a whole pack that was let out just at night."

"His great Gurkha mercenaries couldn't account for a pack of *dogs*?"

"As soon as they were in the village the dogs attacked, and the guerrillas came out."

"Alex," Peter said, trying to get some air under her name. "What about Alex?"

"Listen, you'd better sit down."

"Tell me!"

"According to the men, she was fighting alongside the guerrillas."

It was so bizarre he wondered if he was dreaming it. "She doesn't even know how to fire a gun!"

"The three soldiers who got her out of there were crazy with rage. They swore she'd shot one of their men. On the way back, they stopped by the road and raped her."

He was on his feet then, shrieking. He would find them, her father included, he would kill them all.

"Peter—"

"Tell him!" he panted. "You tell him I'll cut his fucking balls off! Where's Alex?"

"She'll be here soon. I'll bring her over. Listen—"

"You told me I could trust him!" he said. "You said he was just the man for the job!"

"Peter—" she began, but he didn't want to hear her voice. He slammed the phone down and got dressed, then began walking circles around the upper hallway as the images played like film before his eyes. What they'd done to her and what he would do to them. He saw himself bashing their heads in with a crowbar. Shooting them, first up the ass, so they could suffer awhile, then in the mouth, to finish them. Beating Pradhan, then dousing him with gas and setting him afire.

None of that really seemed like enough, though. When he was done with them he would move on. He would go home and find Wayne Lee and his friends. He would track down all the rapists, the thugs, the molesters; he would find them all and empty clip after clip after clip, mow them down by the thousands, until the world was cleansed.

Mina was there a couple of hours later. When Alex saw Peter she ran to him, and he wrapped her in his arms. She was bony. He apologized to her, over and over, as she cried. Mina stood off to the side, her eyes downcast. Peter was so furious he could barely look at her.

Finally he thanked her, coolly, for bringing Alex, and took his daughter inside.

THIRTY-ONE

Peter made the next few days as easy for her as he could, but there were things they had to do, many of which were far from easy: get her checked out by a doctor at the CIWEC clinic, give a statement to the Nepali police (who seemed utterly uninterested in what she had to say), make plane reservations, pack, and generally manage the chaos of sudden departure. Sangita came and helped as much as she could. Alex was desperate for food and sleep, and she needed more Flagyl for whatever she'd picked up from the mountain streams. She would be distant and disengaged, then suddenly flare up in a fury, and she was deeply upset that she couldn't see Devi. Neither she nor her father wanted to discuss what had happened until they had more time, so they put on their armor and got through it.

Mina phoned. Peter was vaguely aware by now that what had happened was not her fault, that if anything he was far more to blame; but paradoxically this hot guilt only intensified his wrath—the way softer metals, when molten, alloy themselves into steel—and in this furnace of rage and shame he became all but incapable of talking to her. He asked her to call him in California a couple of weeks later, when they'd be settled and he would have had a chance to collect himself.

On the morning of their flight, Sangita came over before dawn to say goodbye. They hugged her, then she tied a small red cord around each of their necks.

"These from very great lama, for protection," she said.

Alex began to cry and put her arms around Sangita. "When you see Devi, tell her goodbye," she said. "Tell her I love her."

Sangita wept too. "I this doing, fair okay," she said. She held Alex tightly for a few moments, then let her go. The cab came down the block and pulled in at the curb. They loaded their bags. Peter kept enough rupees for the cab fare, then handed the rest of his money to Sangita. At first she refused, but he reminded her that he couldn't use rupees in America. She thanked him and tucked them into the pocket of her skirt.

As they drove away, Alex turned to wave. Sangita waved back briefly, then stood and watched them until they turned the corner and were gone. The last Peter saw of her, she was wiping the tears from her cheeks.

Alex fell asleep before the plane even left the gate, then slept off and on for ten hours. Peter dozed, read, and watched the clouds passing like great sea waves beneath them. He had come to feel alienated from America, but now he felt even more estranged from Nepal. It was as if their only home was on the plane, with each other, but that would end soon enough, and then they'd have to figure out something new.

They'd made arrangements to stay with Peter's sister, Connie, who lived in San Anselmo, across the bay from Berkeley in Marin County. She met them at SFO and drove them north across the Golden Gate Bridge. Alex didn't say much; she seemed content to look out the window at the ocean and the headlands, at this blue world that was familiar and newly exotic too.

Connie's house was cool and quiet, nestled on a narrow street that curved among oak-covered hills. Her fifteen-year-old son, Ben, hauled his stuff up to the finished attic so Alex could have his room. Peter had planned to sleep on the couch, but Alex wanted him with her, so that first evening he lay on the bed and held her.

"You can tell me whatever you want," he said, as she wept.

She just shook her head. "Not now."

"Is there anything I can do?"

"Try to make things normal, if you can. Normal is what I want."

"We're going for a lot of normal around here, don't worry."

After she dropped off, he stayed awhile to be sure she didn't wake up again. Peter felt as if he'd spent the past few days in a fast-moving car, a vehicle built of rage at both himself and the world. Now he'd blown through the windshield and could feel the ground rising up to meet him, and he knew the landing was going to hurt. His savage impulses—toward Adhiraj, toward Pradhan and his men, toward Mina and himself, all three sides of the lethal triangle that had joined in this catastrophe—had not abated much, but he was adjusting to his anger the way you adjust to a mean dog that lives in your house, a creature that you know is essentially wild, full of teeth and dark appetites. You keep the dog under control and pray that it doesn't learn the full extent of its power and tear you apart.

The next morning was Saturday, so Connie and Peter cooked a big breakfast—eggs, pancakes, sausages, everything Peter knew Alex liked. Alex remained withdrawn and quiet, though, and picked at her food. She sat next to Peter at the table, and every few minutes she touched his arm, as if she had to make sure he was really there.

Peter took her back to see her old shrink from her cutting days, Andy Edelstein. Alex wanted Peter to stay nearby, and she opened the door about every ten minutes to make sure he was still in the waiting room. It reminded him, of course, of when he *wasn't* there, and every time she shut the door and went back inside he felt as if a great fist had encircled his heart and begun to squeeze.

She was in there for three hours, after which she emerged, pale, with tearstains on her cheeks, her arms wrapped around herself. Edelstein briefly met Peter's eyes and gave him the slightest of nods.

At home she shadowed Peter, always staying within a few feet of him, though she rarely spoke. She didn't leave the house except to go to the doctor for follow-ups, or to see Edelstein. In both cases, Peter drove her and waited just outside the door of the room she was in. At least she wasn't pregnant, and the labwork showed that she hadn't gotten HIV.

| | |

Dear Lama Padma,

You have written about compassion and forgiveness, but I wonder how such things are even possible. As you may have heard by now, Alex was raped by three soldiers. The Tibetan nuns we met had undergone things even worse, and I still can't understand how they achieved any sort of equanimity about it. I wake up raging every morning, I'm furious all day, and I go to bed that way. I work straight through the nights sometimes, because at least when I'm exhausted I don't have any energy left over for anger, and then I can sleep a little, and if I sleep soundly enough I don't remember my dreams. I fantasize about revenge. I feel like I'm becoming some kind of savage animal and I'm powerless to stop it.

I know you have already told me things one should do in a situation like this. Meditate. Contemplate the terrible karma these men have made for themselves. Forgive. It all seems superhuman to me. But on the other hand I have no peace; I feel like I'm living in hell.

My fitful efforts at prayer have had very mixed results; I got my daughter back but not quite in one piece, as if there were a price for intercession. I don't know if I believe in prayer or not, now. Pray for us anyway, if you would. I get the feeling you're better at it than I am.

—Peter

| | |

One afternoon when Alex was asleep, Mina called Peter from Kathmandu.

"I never should have told you to trust him," she said. "I'm sorry. I really thought he could do it."

Peter stood in the living room, staring out the big bay window at the hills.

"So that's it? You're sorry, tough luck, hope it goes better next time?"

There was a pause. "Peter, you gave Bahadur's computer to the *Nepali Times.*"

"It was obvious the cops weren't going to do anything otherwise."

"Well, it worked. The whole story came out, and my father and the others are in jail."

"Good," said Peter. "When you talk to him again, tell him the day he or any of his men get out, I'll be waiting for them. I don't care if I spend the rest of my life in some shithole Nepali prison, I'll be there. Tell him that."

Mina's voice wavered. "Don't say things like that. Please."

"Why the fuck shouldn't I? I mean it. I'll do it."

"Peter, this is going to be hard enough for Alex. She's going to need you. You can't let it destroy you too."

"Nothing's destroying me."

"It will, if you go on like this," she said. "I've wanted to kill him too, I've been so angry. But if he was younger, if he'd been there himself, it never would have happened. They would have known about the dogs, no one would have died, Alex would be fine. His men weren't as good as he thought they were, and that's his fault. But he tried, and in fact he did get her out. He didn't do this to her."

"Oh, and I did? Is that what you're saying?"

"I didn't say it, Peter, you did."

These words, spoken simply and honestly, sucked the breath

right out of him. He knew, of course, that she was right. That without his idiocy, his pride, his foolish gullibility, none of this would have happened.

"Are you there?" Mina asked.

His voice was a reptilian croak, primitive and broken. "Yeah," he said. "I'm here."

There was another pause. "I don't want to stay in Nepal anymore," Mina said. "Our family has been wrecked."

"I did that," he said, as stupidly as a confessing child. "I did it on purpose."

"Yes, you did."

"Forgive me."

Mina began to cry. "You know I would never have done anything to hurt your daughter. Tell me you understand that."

He looked out the window. There were tears on his face too. He wiped at them with the back of his hand, but they kept coming.

"I understand," he said.

"I'll come there if you still want me to. I love you; I love you both."

He took a breath. "Give us some time, okay? We just need time."

He looked out the window; a hawk was riding a thermal high up over the oaks on the hill, its red tail fanned out and twisting to adjust to the breeze. Up still higher, twenty or thirty yards away, flew its mate. They rode opposite sides of the updraft, turning circles around each other at a distance, a dance of elegant, patient hunger.

"How's Usha?" Peter asked, at last.

"She's still staying with me," Mina said. "She really wants to come to the U.S. and be a doctor. She's so smart, Peter. You picked the right girl."

"Yeah, I'm good at that," he said, and heard her laugh a little through her tears. And then, almost without knowing the words were coming, he said, "The visa will be hard to get, you know."

She hesitated a moment, as if to be sure he meant by this what he seemed to mean. "Do you remember Alice Finley, at the American consulate?"

"The woman who couldn't do anything for me."

"I've spoken to her," said Mina. "She was so horrified by what happened to Alex that she said she'd make it happen, for me and Usha both, if we decide to come. She just needs a couple of weeks' notice."

"Okay. We'll let her know."

After they hung up, he decided to take a walk. He strolled along block after block of beautiful houses, tucked back into shade. When he got downtown, shiny, late-model BMWs and Lexuses and Mercedes filled the parking spaces and the crowded roads. The stores were full of expensive kitchen goods and linens and furniture. The restaurants had lunch entrées starting at fifteen dollars. Everyone was white or Asian American, well dressed, healthy-looking. There were no beggars, no panhandlers, no spent old people lying on the sidewalks, no shit in the streets. This had been home, and now Peter wasn't sure where home was. He passed a woman wearing diamond earrings that were probably worth more than most Nepalis would earn in a lifetime, and he was possessed by a sudden impulse to rip them right out of her earlobes.

He wondered who that other Peter was, the cardiologist who'd lived in a nice house in the Berkeley hills and driven a Land Rover. What did he like? What did he *want*? Mainly he seemed to have lived a life of desperate waiting—to get out of his marriage, to find some sort of meaning or direction. Cheryl had once said she'd rather *be* dead than live with the dead, and now he finally understood what she meant. He was as perplexed by his own identity as if he'd unearthed the yellowed diary of some ass from an earlier century who bled his patients with leeches, prescribed mercury for the clap, and felt very fine about himself indeed.

He remembered the evening in Kathmandu when he and Alex were out walking Wayne Lee and saw the plane flying in. Alex said she'd switched sides, that she used to think the plane was normal and now she could relate to the goat. It seemed that whichever place Peter inhabited, the other felt more like home, as if hereafter he would live always in exile.

When he thought of Alex, his eyes grew hot again. He stepped into an alley and walked to the end, where there was a dumpster. He leaned against the grimy wall across from it and lowered his head. The trash smelled of ether from rotting vegetables; that was a little better. The alley's walls rose up like canyons to a bright band of sky, but between the walls it was dark and cool. All it lacked to make him feel more comfortable was a pack of feral dogs.

Everything had been an emergency lately, and even though he'd worked enough ERs to know how to function in emergencies, he was not functioning well anymore. All these years of waiting and he would have to wait longer still; it was excruciating, like waiting for pain to stop and not knowing when or if it would.

After a few minutes a metal door by the dumpster swung open and a busboy brought out a bag of restaurant trash. The kid had pimples and long, pale arms. He looked at Peter and his eyes narrowed a little, in disgust or confusion or fear; then he put the bag in the dumpster and went back inside. Peter figured the next person to come through the door would be the manager, asking him what the hell he was doing, so he walked out of the alley and onto the street.

He found a park and sat down in the grass under an oak. He wanted to sleep, to just keep sleeping, but he knew sleep would be hard to come by for a while. A tabby cat was stalking the birds in the next tree. The cat wore a collar and a tiny bell, but it had learned to move so that the bell stayed quiet.

Peter didn't want to see the cat catch a bird, so he got up and left the park. On the way home, he came to a clot of traffic in the street, two cars together in the middle, others crawling out and around to pass. A fender bender. A couple of guys in their thirties had climbed out of the crumpled cars and were screaming at each other, raising their arms like enraged chimps. They looked demented. They had new cars, they had insurance, they had money, everything would be fixed. Peter couldn't figure out what the hell there was to yell about.

He walked up the hill to where the road ended. A cable was strung thigh-high between bent poles, and a trail began on the other side of it. He climbed over and followed the trail up to the ridge. From there, he could see the bay to the east, blue under a blue sky, two bright mirrors with a strip of land between. He sat down, but he was restless and soon got up again. He thought about calling Mina back, but he wasn't ready. Anyway, it was the middle of the night in Kathmandu. It hadn't been that long since her call, so apparently she wasn't sleeping either.

He walked back down the hill into town and found a store. He bought rice and lentils, thinking *dal-bhat* might somehow conjure a time when he and Alex were happier and felt more at ease in the world. When he got to the house, Alex was still snoring softly in her room.

Ben came home from school at about 4:30, ate a snack, and plopped down in front of the television to play video games. He sat there, mesmerized, clicking away with his thumbs while various engorged-looking creatures blew one another to bits on the screen in front of him. There were beautiful woods outside, and trails, and nothing in the streams that would kill you. No armed bandits roaming the hills to kidnap you or make you join them and carry a gun. Peter wanted to pick Ben up and throw him out the door. But it wasn't his house; Ben wasn't his son. Peter asked him to turn down the sound, then went into Alex's room and sat down to read, so he'd be there when she woke up.

He was making the *dal-bhat* when Connie came home from work. Alex came out and helped Ben set the table, but when dinner was served Ben took one bite of it and put down his fork.

"It tastes like dirt," he said. Connie apologized to Peter, but Alex smiled, which as far as he was concerned made the meal worth it.

Ben went off somewhere with friends after dinner. Peter sat with Alex for a while, but by 8:30 she had conked out again, so he joined Connie at the table. She got them a couple of beers.

"Your son is a lard-ass," Peter said. "He's going to have diabetes before he's thirty."

"You're welcome to step into the father-figure role anytime. Cody's trying, but he's two hours away."

"Cody? Whatever happened to Don?"

She sighed. "I got tired of feeling I had to dress like a hooker to make Don happy."

Peter smiled. "Did I miss this phase?"

"Jesus, you don't remember? I was always in some getup that made it look like my tits were about to leap out and launch themselves at Russia."

"That's quite an image. Sorry."

She glared. "Oh, you can laugh, it's funny now."

"You've always accommodated your men too much," said Peter.

"Like you, you mean?"

He looked down at his beer sheepishly. "I know I haven't been the easiest guy to have around. . . . "

"Forget it," she said. "Given the situation, you're practically a prince."

"That's a lie, but thanks."

"What are sisters for, if not to lie to you when you need it?"

Connie was forty, with frizzy hair and a comfortable, well-rounded figure. She still had a trace of the South in her speech, and Peter liked hearing it. In Jackson, where they'd grown up, their mother taught high school English. She'd become friends with Eudora Welty after their father had removed a precancerous mole from the writer's shoulder and they'd gotten to talking about writing and teaching and the importance of not ignoring melanoma. Miss Welty, as they called her, would on occasion read her work to their mother's class, though when she was older she gave it up, noting with her usual polite candor that most of the kids didn't actually seem to give a rat's behind—her term—about what she had to say.

Connie took a drink of beer and looked at Peter. "You going to call Cheryl?" she asked.

"If I tell her what happened she'll just scream at me, and the worst part is she'd be right to."

Connie spoke quietly. "Has anybody ever told you you're kind of a fuckup, bro?"

He rested his elbows on the table. "I appreciate your pointing that out, but you didn't really need to."

She looked out the window for a moment. "Do you ever wonder how much of our screwed-up lives had to do with Dad and Mama?"

"It's pretty obvious, isn't it?"

Their parents' lifelong war had had roots in both disposition and politics. Their father was a courtly conservative who cared deeply for his children and tended his patients with consideration and skill, but who frankly didn't give a damn about anyone he didn't know personally, which meant 99.9 percent of the world.

Their mother, by contrast, had a variety of causes going all the time, and was always expressing outraged sympathy for some endangered species, tribe, or wetland. She was sincere, her heart good, but these obsessions left her without much time or attention for her own kids. Her attitude seemed to be that there was plenty of *real* trouble in the world, and that whatever petty problems they had—say, eating on a given day—they'd best work out for themselves.

When things progressed from cold war to hot war, Connie and Peter would retreat upstairs and shut the door so they didn't have to listen to it. They couldn't imagine why their parents had married at all until they got into the family papers one day, compared Peter's birth certificate to the marriage license, and did the math.

"You're not completely unlike Dad," Connie said. "Thank God you're not a Republican, but you became a doctor, and you're kind in the way he was. You also suffer from the same sorts of anxieties."

"I didn't know he *had* anxieties."

Connie just stared. "When you dropped out of college and became a climbing bum he went on Xanax for months."

"Probably more because I'd dropped out than because I was climbing," he said. "Though I'm kind of touched, postmortemly, to hear it. You don't know how fucking hard it is to be a dad until you become one."

She smiled. "Anyway, I visited their graves last year."

"You didn't tell me that."

She nodded. "I think they're finally at peace with each other," she said. "All it took was dying."

THIRTY-TWO

Since Peter wasn't sleeping anyway, he started pulling a few night shifts in the ER at Marin General to help Connie with the rent. It was, if nothing else, perversely comforting to be reminded that there was plenty of suffering to go around.

Alex's eighteeth birthday came, so Connie baked a cake. They all ate some and sang "Happy Birthday" to Alex, who indulged them with reasonably good humor.

Afterward, Connie took Ben to a movie so Peter and Alex could have the house to themselves for an evening. They made popcorn and built a fire, even though it was late summer and still warm out. Alex climbed onto the couch, curled up, and leaned against him.

"You've become a cat," he said.

She made a sort of purring noise, her first attempt at a joke.

"See, this is normal," he went on. "Popcorn, fire, cat imitations."

"Extreme hyperglycemia from the cake," she added.

He put an arm around her shoulders. "Still don't want to talk?"

"It's not anything a father should hear," she said quietly. "I'm telling Edelstein. Let's leave it at that."

"Those guys are going to be in jail for a long time," Peter said.

"I hope somebody fucks them up the ass every day they're in there."

"If I could pay to make it happen, I would."

She sighed. "We're kind of vindictive, you know?"

"Are we?"

"Don't you think we are? Is this a family trait?"

"I think it's a *normal* trait, under the circumstances."

"We're melancholy in the same ways too, aren't we? I mean, before this."

He thought about it. "I guess maybe so," he said.

She started eating the popcorn; apparently there was nothing wrong with her digestion. "I should write Devi," she said, "but I don't know where to send it."

"Send it to Sangita; she'll know what to do. I should put in a note for Lama Padma too."

"If he's picking up our vibes these days he's probably having a heart attack," she said. "How is it with Mina? You guys barely talk."

"We're working on it," he said. "We just need time."

They sat quietly, watching the fire. "Speaking of forgiveness, sometime I want to see Mom," said Alex.

"Were we speaking of forgiveness?" he asked. "Is Edelstein planting crazy ideas in your head?"

"What's the alternative, seriously? Spend your life crazy with rage at everyone who's ever done something bad to you?"

"It's always worked for me."

"Yeah, but Dad, it *hasn't*," she said. "You see that, right?"

He looked at her, too stunned by this insight to speak for a few moments. "You're way too grown up for somebody your age," he growled, finally.

"For that I blame you." She took his hand and held it to her cheek. "Do we have anything else to eat?"

"There's a fridge full of steaks with your name on them," he said. "Want one?"

"Yeah."

He started the grill. She ended up eating two of them, with baked potatoes and a protein shake. Afterward, she noticed the weathered old basketball goal out over the garage, the hoop hanging down a little dejectedly in the front, the net half shredded.

"Is there a ball to go with that?" she asked.

He found it, flat, on one of the shelves in the garage. There was an old bike pump and a needle, so he filled it. It held the air. She bounced it on the cement, tentatively.

Her arms were still thin. She missed shot after shot, and Peter could tell she was getting pissed off. She finally sank one, and then another, and then after a couple more misses, a third.

"Edelstein tells me you're quite the hotshot these days," she said. "Saving lives left and right where lesser mortals fail, or something."

He leaned into the doorway, watching her. He thought, *I'm atoning the only way I know how.* What he said was that they'd offered him a spot at the hospital, but he wasn't sure if he wanted to take it.

"How come?" She dribbled, watching the ball rise to her hand and pushing it back to earth as if she'd never witnessed such a marvel. One, two, three, four, five, six, seven.

"I guess I feel a little disoriented, still," he said. "What do you think about it?"

She lifted the ball and shifted it over to her right hand, then cocked her arm and tried a hook shot. It hit the backboard, then bounced twice on the rim and fell through, just the way it had when she was wowing the nuns. She stepped forward to get it.

"I mean, it *is* Marin County," she said. "Is that not good enough? Should we maybe buy a map and a set of darts, and try again?"

| | |

After another few weeks, though, they were restless. The house was cramped, and both Connie and Ben were obviously feeling the strain. Things were going reasonably well with Edelstein, and Alex was seeing him only when she felt like it, every two or three weeks.

One day she tracked her mother down via Google. Cheryl had sold the Berkeley house and was living somewhere in the mountains up north, near Arcata.

"What are you going to do?" Peter asked.

"I want to see her but not really," Alex said. "I'm thinking of, like, getting closer but not actually going there yet. Is that totally weird?"

"Totally," he said. "Let's do it."

He went into San Rafael and bought a beat-up Subaru at a used-car lot. Then he signed up with a locum-tenens agency that placed temporary docs in the cash-starved, broken-down ERs of the North Coast. The next day they said goodbye to Connie and Ben, threw a couple of bags in the car, and headed out.

When Highway 1 left the valleys and crossed over to Garberville, and then to the sea, the coastal mountains bled all their color out and seemed to drift in shades of gray and green. A world of conifers on layer-cake ridges frosted by fog, a place they had no history. So what if this relief was illusory? Moving toward it satisfied some deep need for flight that itself held an ancient kind of promise.

"You okay?" he asked.

"This is good," Alex said. "This was the right thing to do."

"I'm glad you've got instincts, because I don't trust mine anymore." He recalled the last time he'd found himself in new territory, the morning he awakened in his hard bed in Kathmandu, and how he'd seen in his passport photo the face of a man who had begun to rely more on endurance than on enthusiasm as a way of living. Thinking about it now, he realized that endurance wasn't such a bad thing, if that was all you could count on. That half of the game, or more, was simply whether you could outlast whatever came up—the purification of karma, or the whims of the drunken-parrot god, who gave you what you wanted and only later exacted his price, with compound interest.

They stopped in Fields Landing for dinner. It was one of those old coastal towns that had experienced an influx of Bay Area retirees, and where the price of an average house had gone from fifty thousand dollars to ten times that in just a few years.

At Jimmy's they had bad Hawaiian music on the sound system and posterized photos of whales on the walls, with titles under them such as "Sea Trek" and "Twilight Tale." The waitress, Susie, was tall and slender and vaguely albino, a sort of human egret. But the place had the best clam chowder they'd ever tasted, five dollars for a huge bowl. Afterward they walked down to the beach before heading north. Long green whips of seaweed lay about on the sand. Alex picked one up and twirled it over her head, then tossed it out into the waves. Gulls shrieked and hovered, and from the surf emerged the black, whiskered head of a sea lion. It watched them for half a minute, then dove back underwater.

In Arcata, they found a motel with a couple of double beds. Peter rested awhile, then, after Alex went to sleep, he started his first shift. It came as a shock, working in an American ER, to remember that there were people who weren't just struggling to survive, who actually had the luxury of wanting to hurt themselves.

At about 2:00 A.M. he found himself stitching up the forearm of a Humboldt State student not much older than Alex. It was a nasty cut, a couple of inches long, deep and bloody, but fortunately her tendons were intact. Caroline was slender, with listless blond hair and big green eyes. She looked intelligent. Peter asked her what had happened.

She shrugged. "There's this sharp piece of siding by our front door that I keep asking my housemate to hammer in, but he never gets around to it. I was in a hurry, and I caught myself on it."

Peter numbed the wound, cleaned it, and stitched it up. She didn't remember when her last tetanus booster was, so when he tied off the stitches he asked her to roll up her sweatshirt sleeve so he could give her one.

"Couldn't you just do it down here, on the back of my wrist?" she asked.

This got his attention. "It's either your shoulder or your butt," he said. "You decide, but those are the choices."

She hesitated. "I don't much like people seeing my butt," she said.

"Then that leaves you one option."

Reluctantly, she rolled up her sleeve. Her arm was laced with scars. Peter counted seven, some old, a couple as fresh as the past few weeks, red and angry-looking. Two had been stitched before.

"Let's see the other arm," he said quietly.

She rolled up the other sleeve and watched his face while he turned over her arms for a better look.

"How long have you been doing this?"

"Doing what?"

He spoke as softly as he could. "You know what."

She looked toward the hallway, as if she might be thinking about bolting. Peter tightened his grip on her wrist just a little and cleared his throat.

Her shoulders sank, and she blinked back tears. "Eight or nine months," she said. "Since last fall."

"If I had to guess, I'd say X-Acto knife, the one with the curved blade. Am I right?"

She looked surprised, but she nodded. "How would you . . . ?"

"My daughter's preference, when she was fifteen," he said. "For some reason the pointy blade freaked her out, as did the right angle of a razor, but the curve didn't seem as bad to her."

The tears came. Peter handed her a box of Kleenex. "You know what happens next, right?"

She said she didn't, that he was the first doctor who'd noticed.

"They stitched you up and they didn't see the other scars?"

She smiled, a little wanly. "I tell them my family raises pedigreed cats. They actually believe it."

"Jesus," he said. "Just shows that a medical degree doesn't make you smart, huh?"

"Well, I always come to the ER; I figure they're really busy."

He could see why they needed docs up here. "Okay, what happens next is counseling," he said. "As in mandatory, arranged through the college. As in, if you don't show up, they boot you out of school." .

She nodded, watching him. He gave her the tetanus shot and put the empty syringe in the red sharps container.

"Why did your daughter do it?" she asked, rolling down her sleeves.

He hadn't anticipated the question, but he knew he should have. He didn't feel like bullshitting her with something vague, though. "She drove herself at everything," he said. "She told me sometimes it felt like there was so much pressure inside her she was going to explode. That was how she let it out."

Caroline nodded. "I think I understand that."

"I'll bet you do."

"Is she okay now?"

"She got over it," Peter said. "That's the thing: People can get over just about anything. Live long enough and you'll see. But you *do* have to live long enough."

He could see from her bone structure how she'd probably looked as a child, and he could see what she would look like as an old woman when the fat pads and facial muscles had collapsed and melted downward. This sort of vision had been happening occasionally since they returned from Nepal, with patients and even with people on the street. He could see their faces at all ages in an instant. It filled him with a vague sorrow he couldn't explain, perhaps partly because their lives seemed to accelerate from infancy to death right before his eyes, and he was beginning to understand that this wasn't actually far from the truth.

THIRTY-THREE

They decided to keep working their way north. Outside of Trinidad the road eased down a long, straight grade, and a wide bay opened up. Mountains and blue sky lay inland on the right, fog and gray on the left, as if the road were a boundary separating the kingdoms of hope and despair—both of them, Peter was beginning to understand, built on the same great lie. The passage between required navigational skill.

The highway flattened out at a series of freshwater lagoons. They passed the headquarters for the redwood parks; then, as they came into Orick, they saw a sign that read:

GASOLINE

SANDWICHES

Alex smiled. "I wonder if you can get unleaded on rye?"

Orick, population 650, elevation 26, was also the home of "Burl Art," and the road was lined on both sides by giant rough-hewn sculptures of grizzly bears, Indian faces, eagles, and indeterminate burly masses that might have been giant mushrooms, tiny

mushroom clouds, or disembodied brains with spinal cords at-
tached. Peter decided on the last option, which somehow made
him feel better about the town, as if it had melded chainsaws with
neurological research in some way that was better not to think
about too deeply. They passed an old red building with a tin roof
over a front porch and second-story windows looking out onto the
tin. A couple of blond girls in their teens were hanging out up
there, taking in the sun and watching the cars go by. As Peter and
Alex were passing, a log-truck driver blared his horn, and the girls
waved. Peter could see their futures the way he saw the future of
Caroline's face, and the whole panorama depressed him.

They made Crescent City by mid-afternoon. After the Alaskan
earthquake of 1964, the town had been flattened by a tsunami, the
primary reminder of which was now Tsunami Lanes, a bowling
alley. It was a village of tidy, if precarious, beachfront homes on
the west and worn-down blue-collar neighborhoods inland. They
parked on a bluff overlooking Pelican Bay. The fog had burned off,
and they got out and stood in the wind, facing the sea.

"It feels like the end of the world," Alex said.

"It is, in a way."

She smiled. "Visually, not apocalyptically."

He dredged up his best Mississippi accent. "Don't use them big
words, girl," he said. "Y'all make me feel dumb."

"Isn't hard, is it?"

"Way too easy, I reckon."

Pelican Bay was not only a bay; it was also the name of California's supermax prison, which they passed on their way back
into town, hunkered blocklike behind a stand of pines. The prison
was the county's biggest employer, but Peter had bought a tourist
map and the facility wasn't on it. It was a destination spot, for
sure, but not for people who'd be spending money here.

They drove by the hospital, a small, white, one-story building.
Humble but reasonably new.

A couple of blocks down, they passed two middle-aged men on
bicycles riding in opposite directions. One was lean and sun-

burned, with a scraggly beard; he had on torn jeans and a ball cap, and he pedaled a beat-up old Schwinn into the wind, on the wrong side of the street. Peter figured he'd lost his driver's license. The other guy was pink and clean shaven, packaged like salami in a bright jersey, bike shorts, and a white helmet. He rode a carbon-fiber Trek, and he was obviously out for exercise. Old poverty and new money passed each other without a look.

They checked in at the Travelodge, then showered and went to find some food. The evening fog had rolled in, chilling the air and dropping visibility to about a hundred feet. People seemed inward, guarded, and not particularly keen on strangers. He didn't know how often inmates got released from the prison, or how inclined they were to stick around afterward, but he figured a certain xeno-phobic insularity wasn't a totally unreasonable response to having this monolith of forcibly contained mayhem planted in the middle of your town.

"I don't like this place," Alex said.

"We'll blow on out tomorrow."

"Maybe it's time to go see her."

"Up to you. Call her while I'm on shift tonight, if you want to."

"Aren't you going to want to sleep?"

"Checkout's not till eleven. I'll get my usual four hours."

| | |

The hospital was quiet. Peter was handed over to an RN named Jane, who was in her thirties and had wild, curly blond hair, wolvish blue eyes, and a runner's build. She wasn't particularly cheerful, but she showed him around and seemed to know what she was doing. The place had tiled floors in the ER but was other-wise carpeted in an industrial red-and-blue pattern that would have looked at home in any airport.

They took a break for coffee, and Peter noticed the list on the bulletin board in the break room. There was something similar at almost every hospital where he'd worked.

"These your personal bests?" he asked.

She nodded.

"Lowest sodium and still awake: 116," he read. "Lowest potassium and still survived: 2.4. Highest serum calcium and still awake: 16.2. Highest blood alcohol and still conscious: 0.48." He turned to her. "You had somebody with a four-eighty who was *conscious?*"

"Hardy stock around here," she said. "The thing that kills me is these guys that come in after wrecking their cars, they're so plowed you can't tell where the alcohol leaves off and the concussion begins, and invariably they've only had two beers. It's the industry standard. So you give them a Breathalyzer and they're blowing 0.25, and the only thing you can figure is that they must have been the two hugest beers in the history of brewing."

Peter smiled. He liked that she'd said "hugest."

"What about your highest blood sugar in a diabetic patient?" he asked.

"Who survived? God, I don't know, about nine-fifty, I think."

"Twelve hundred here."

"Get out."

"As God is my witness."

They got called back to the ER; an older man had come in complaining of back pain.

Jane rolled her eyes. "We get a lot of gomers up here too, just to warn you," she said. Gomer, or "Get Out of My Emergency Room," usually meant narcotic-seekers who'd invent injuries so they could get shot up with opioids. They had a tendency to yell until you delivered, and once they got their fix, they vanished. Peter had seen his share in Berkeley.

This guy was in his sixties and didn't actually strike Peter as the type, though. He was reserved, a little cranky, and he claimed his only habit was a half-pack of cigarettes a day. Peter examined his back, but the pain didn't seem to have a locus anywhere. The man groaned the whole time, and his pulse was 166, so he probably wasn't faking the pain.

They checked his records, both at this hospital and throughout the state. He'd been in only once before, six years earlier, for a dislocated thumb. Peter had him roll over onto his back.

"Look at his legs; look at the veins," Peter said. "Don't they look a little blue?"

Jane examined them. "What are you thinking?"

"I don't think his circulation's too good down here. Do you have a CT tech on call?"

"Sure, why?"

"Because I'm thinking aneurysm, as in aorta, as in leaking."

Jane's eyebrows went up. "Please tell me you're kidding."

"I'm kidding," he said. "Except I'm not."

They called St. John's in Eureka, but the vascular surgeon was on vacation and they hadn't found a locum to cover for him. The next option was an airlift to Redding, but Jane said they wouldn't be able to get a helicopter in because of the fog.

Twenty minutes later they had the CT. The bulb was down low, between the hepatic and mesenteric arteries. It was a good eight centimeters, and it was definitely coming apart.

"You have a surgical nurse here?" Peter asked.

"That would be me."

"You any good?"

"As a matter of fact, I am. How about you?"

"I haven't done this since I was a resident, and the few I did were higher up. I'm going to need you."

"Fair enough. Thanks for scaring the shit out of me."

"Put a team together, whoever you can. You have a kit?"

"Sure."

They got the man prepped and moved to the OR. Jane turned out to be one of the best nurses Peter had ever worked with. He never had to ask for anything; it was in his hand as soon as he had the thought, and a few times *before* he had the thought, when he was still trying to figure out what to do next. The operation took hours, but the graft seemed to hold. The hospital had only two

ICU beds, so they moved the guy up to one of them, then Peter and Jane went outside to get some air. It was 4:00 A.M., and the town glowed like a spaceship, all streetlights and fog.

"Not a bad job for somebody who doesn't actually know what the hell he's doing," she said.

"At least I never claimed to. You should see me do an eyelid, though."

Their shift finished at 6:00, and she said there wasn't a decent breakfast place in town but that she'd cook for him if he was hungry.

He looked at her, unsure quite how she intended this invitation. "Sure," he said, though there was hesitation in his voice.

They stopped at the store and picked up eggs, milk, cinnamon rolls, frozen orange juice, fresh coffee, and a few other odds and ends. Just as they left the store, the sun came up. The light was diffused and distended by the fog, so it appeared as a great angry wound.

Jane lived in a little bungalow on the west side of town. Peter could just see the ocean in the distance, out her glass patio doors. She didn't want any help in the kitchen, so he wandered around the house. He picked up a photo of a baby from her bookcase. "Who's this?"

She looked up, then went back to breaking eggs. "That's Joshua."

"He's a cutie. Where is he?"

She just kept stirring, apparently concentrating hard on the bowl. "Josh didn't make it," she said.

Peter looked at her, then back at the picture, and set it down. "I may never learn when to shut up."

She brushed her hair away from her face with the back of her hand. "It's a natural question," she said. "He was born with a coarc just under his aortic arch. The peds locum missed it."

He appeared to be a healthy baby in the photo; his color was good, and he was smiling. "I might have missed it too," Peter said.

"That's the party line, but we both know better."

"Who was the father?"

She laughed, just once, the kind of plosive sound you'd make if someone knocked the wind out of you. "This young Brazilian anesthesiologist who was out to see the world, or more accurately to fuck the world," she said. "He was extremely charming, in a young-male-on-the-prowl kind of way. When I told him, he offered to stick around, but I said no."

"Brave of you."

"Sane of me. The brave part happens every morning when I wake up and think about my life and have to get out of bed anyway." Their eyes met for a moment, then she opened the fridge and started rummaging. "I guess you can come mix up the orange juice if you want."

There was a young-adult book on her shelf called *Nurse Jane Goes to Hawaii*. Peter picked it up and thumbed through it as he headed into the kitchen. She saw it and smiled—the first smile he'd seen from her that didn't seem shaded with some kind of disappointment or bitterness.

He held up the book. "And did you?"

"I did, in fact," she said. "That was a present. You can borrow it if you like; it's compelling reading if you're twelve."

Peter mixed the juice while she took two plates out of the cupboard and started loading them with food. They had scrambled eggs, hash browns, sausage, rolls, juice, and coffee, and it was all very good, in extremis like that, after the long night.

She asked if he had any kids.

"A daughter," he said. He explained the situation.

"Well, jeez, you should have brought her. There's plenty of food."

"I try to let her sleep these days. She'll call me when she wakes up."

"You want to take the extra?"

"That would be great."

For ten or fifteen minutes, then, they picked at their food and talked about unrelated things, politics and weather and crazy patients they'd had. She was easy to be around, and it was a relief not to have to discuss anything overwhelmingly urgent or important. Peter came to understand, without her having to say anything, that the invitation had just been about breakfast, nothing more. He was a little relieved. About a quarter to seven Alex called, sounding groggy, and he told her he'd be there in a few minutes.

He helped Jane do the dishes, then she took his face in her hands and kissed him, not all that passionately but *nicely*. He picked up Alex's breakfast, then got his coat and his keys, and went out into the morning light, feeling blessed by this small kindness, and tender, and grateful for it.

THIRTY-FOUR

Alex, at age five, sat cross-legged on the living room floor, having mastered the stereo remote so she could listen over and over to a Joni Mitchell song, "Cherokee Louise," with which she'd become obsessed. The song contained such innocent themes as child molestation and a runaway girl in a subway tunnel. Alex didn't notice these things because she didn't understand them yet. What snagged her attention was this lyric:

> *Tuesday after school, we put our pennies on the rails*
> *and when the train went by*
> *—Cherokee Louise!—*
> *We were jumping 'round like fools, going "Look, no*
>   *heads or tails,"*
> *going, "Look, my lucky prize!"*
> *—Cherokee Louise!*

Alex didn't completely get what putting pennies on the rails meant, either, but she was captivated by the notion that doing so could erase the heads and tails, and she wanted to know how. So Peter explained to her about the softness of copper, the weight of trains, et cetera, and her eyes grew wide.

Soon she tired of the song and stopped listening to it. But three months later, when Peter asked what she wanted for her birthday, she answered matter-of-factly, "A penny that's been run over by a train."

He said he hoped she was kidding.

"Amanda's present cost thirty-five dollars," she answered, referring to a friend of hers and content to let the economics speak for themselves.

The next day Peter waited by the siding. The freight had three big engines up front, and he felt its deep, trembling thunder just before the sun-bright light swung into view down the tracks. He'd already put the penny in place, and he was actually pretty excited about the whole thing.

The train passed, the dinging stopped, and the gate went up. An old green Chevy pickup joinked across from the other side and disappeared up the road. Then there was just Peter and the blackbirds but no penny. He wandered up and down the tracks, but he couldn't find it. There wouldn't be another train for at least an hour, and he had to pick Alex up at daycare before that.

Some Hispanic guys were breaking rocks at a construction site on the way home, so he stopped and, feeling like an idiot, asked to borrow a sledge. The kid handed it to him with a grin, glad to take a break. He sat down to watch as Peter took the next-shiniest penny from his pocket and laid it on a cinder block.

He put his legs into it and shattered the block on the first blow, but the penny emerged largely unscathed. An older fellow came over and suggested a piece of nearby granite, so the three of them strolled over to see if his luck would improve. It was like being at a county fair, trying to win your sweetheart a stuffed bear. The shock from the stone traveled right up the sledge's shaft and into his hands, and although it hurt like hell, it had almost no effect on the penny. Peter handed back the sledge regretfully and went to get his daughter.

After dinner, Cheryl distracted Alex while Peter discreetly pocketed more pennies, a flashlight, and a tube of Krazy Glue. A half hour later, shortly after sunset, he'd just finished gluing down the pennies when a cop pulled in behind his car and turned on his flashers. He got out and asked Peter the predictable questions.

"You glued them down?" he said. "What if you'd derailed the train?"

Peter laughed at this, then realized too late that the cop was serious and was now displeased that his concerns were being ridiculed. Twenty minutes later Peter called Cheryl from the station and asked her to come down and bail him out. She showed up with Alex in tow.

"Look, honey," she said. "Dad's a criminal." Then, as Alex gazed, clearly impressed, Cheryl pulled out a camera and took Peter's picture with the scowling cop. They couldn't explain to Alex why he was there, of course, because it would ruin the surprise. So Cheryl told her it was because he'd left too small a tip at a restaurant.

"Don't ever do that," Cheryl said, sounding extremely serious. "When you're older, you'll learn how to figure percentages." Alex looked at her gravely and nodded with pretend comprehension.

Three hours later, breaking the terms of his bail before it was even technically the next day, Peter was back at the tracks with a hammer and a chisel. The 8:18 had flattened the pennies pretty well, as it turned out. They were slightly oval now instead of circular, and although Peter could still distinguish heads from tails, he figured it was a good enough job for a six-year-old.

When she opened the package the next morning, she turned the coins over and over in her hands, inspecting them as if she'd been trained to identify counterfeit. She looked at Peter, then at the pennies, then at Peter again. She opened her arms, then he picked her up and she said "Thanks," softly, in his ear, with her sweet breath.

Before that moment, she had always considered anything made of metal to be immutable. Peter realized what he'd really given her was a firsthand understanding that this was not true, not of copper or of anything. With the right forces, any face could be erased.

THIRTY-FIVE

They found Cheryl at a scarred-up kitchen table in a moldy trailer, twirling her hair around her finger. She looked fifteen or twenty years older than she was. Her hair had gone gray and strawlike, and what teeth she had left were rotten.

"Mom," said Alex, both longing and horror on her face. Cheryl got up and gave her a hug, but she was emaciated and tottering. She sat down again and lit a cigarette.

"Well," she said. "Home from the wars, huh?"

Alex was fighting back tears, but for Peter this wasn't a completely unexpected trajectory. He'd held out some small hope, for Alex's sake, that Cheryl might have finally gotten her life together, but it didn't take an ace diagnostician to see that she'd been heavily into booze and meth, and was eating mainly on whim.

Alex looked around apprehensively. "Wayne Lee isn't here, is he?"

"He got offed last spring," Cheryl said, not quite matter-of-fact but also not with the emotional heft you'd expect from someone reporting the demise of her lover.

"He's *dead*?"

"Somebody sweetened his gas tank and his engine seized. Pulled a big ender on 101. They were picking up the pieces for a quarter-mile."

She took a drag from the cigarette. Peter didn't want to, but he couldn't help it, he felt sorry for her. He sat down at the table. "You find out why?" he asked.

"Well, he was Wayne Lee," said Cheryl. She reached for the Kleenex box, but it was empty. "This was outside a bar. Probably came on to the wrong guy's girl."

She opened her mouth and pulled one of the loose teeth out of her lower jaw, studied it absently, then put it back in. Alex looked at Peter, alarm in her eyes.

"Mom, is there anything we can do for you?"

Cheryl launched into a rambling monologue of apology, blame-lessness, and persecution, the gist of which was that Wayne Lee had taken all the money and gotten her hooked on various drugs. One day they'd had a fight and he'd roughed her up, so she moved out here to the trailer. She finished the story with a vague digres-sion about how rude the local Hoopa Indians were and that this trailer really wasn't her kind of place, but it was all she could af-ford, because her lawyer had screwed up the divorce settlement. She spent a minute or two cursing the lawyer and then cursing Peter, as if she'd forgotten he was sitting right there. Then she just trailed off and sat staring, tracing patterns with her finger in the tabletop dust.

"Anything else you want to say to your daughter before we go?" Peter asked.

Cheryl looked at him, and then at Alex. She shrugged. "I don't want you to think I'm a bad person," she said. "I always loved you in my own way."

Alex wiped her eyes. "You need any money, Mom?"

"I'm all right," she said. She took her daughter's hand briefly, then let it go.

Alex got up and looked in the fridge. There were two bottles of Miller, a tin of sardines, and three eggs. In the cabinets were Cheerios, saltines, chocolate-chip cookies, a jar of peanut butter, and enough mouse droppings to start a fertilizer plant.

"Dad?" she said.

Peter stood and opened his wallet. It had been futile in Nepal, it would be futile here, but he did it anyway. Four twenties, a ten, three ones. He put it all on the table. Cheryl reached out and took it, then shoved one of the dollar bills back at him.

"What's wrong?" he asked.

"The ten and the three," she said. "It's thirteen; it isn't lucky."

Peter took the dollar and put it in his pocket. "You're right," he said. "Sorry."

"Anyway, I appreciate it," she said. Her voice echoed a little in the tinny trailer. "I know you think I don't, but I do."

"We know, Mom."

"I'm not a bad person," Cheryl went on. Her hands were against her forehead; she wasn't even looking at them. It was as if they'd already left, or she had. "I loved both of you in my own way. In my own way, I always did."

| | |

Peter drove them east, up 299 and into the mountains.

"You think there's anything we can do for her?" Alex asked.

"I only had one house to sell."

She made an exasperated noise. "You know what I mean."

"There's nothing I can do if she doesn't want it herself, Alex."

"You're lacquering the cat," she said. It was an expression she'd coined a year or two previously, which meant slapping a thin intellectual gloss on a clawed, fanged, unruly thing. "You make it sound like there are no emotions involved."

"There are too many emotions involved, is closer to the problem," he said.

"Just because you're done with her, it doesn't mean I have to be, does it?"

"No, but I think it might be a good idea if you took care of yourself for a while."

She looked pensively out of the window. "Where are we going, anyway?"

"Weaverville."

"Why?"

He explained that one advantage of the disintegrating American healthcare system was that small rural hospitals were folding up left and right, so he was able to get good deals on used medical equipment. He'd promised to send Franz a crate with an autoclave, a ventilator, a case of IV saline, and whatever else he could pick up.

They drove through a series of beautiful canyons on the Trinity River, then crossed Oregon Mountain pass. Weaverville was a pretty little town supported largely by a lumber mill, framed to the north by the peaks of the Trinity Alps.

"What happened to the hospital?" Alex asked.

"I read that the locals voted down a bond measure to keep it open," Peter said.

She looked at him, incredulous. "So these people will be dying because they wouldn't part with, like, a buck a week for a *hospital*?"

"Frontier mentality up here, I guess."

"Talk about survival of the fittest," she said. "A self-culling herd."

Peter was delighted to find that there was, indeed, an autoclave, along with two plastic crates of ER supplies, a hundred sheets of X-ray film that wouldn't expire for another year, and sundry other supplies.

They stopped for lunch at Miller's Drive-in, where Alex had three burgers and a shake. They headed south out of town toward Hayfork, where they picked up Highway 36 back toward the coast. Peter thought it might do Alex good to see some of this country, which was pristine and stunning. She put her feet up on the dash, let her seat back, and opened her window. The cool air smelled of conifer forest and dust.

Peter was thinking about all his fuckups, and what exactly was required of someone before he could be said to have put things right.

After they'd been driving for fifteen or twenty minutes, he turned to his daughter. "There's something I want to ask you," he said. "You don't have to answer, but someday I might like to know."

She sounded a little sleepy. "Mmm?"

"Mina said you shot one of the men who came to get you."

That woke her pretty well. She sat up and put her feet on the floor, but she didn't reply.

"Alex?"

She set her elbow on the armrest and ran her fingers through her hair nervously. "I might have," she said.

"You don't know?"

"It's a long story," she said. "Edelstein's heard it."

He watched a doe and her yearling cross the road ahead of them to the west. "You don't have to tell me if you don't want to," he said.

She rubbed her forehead. "We didn't know who they were," she said. "All of a sudden, in the middle of the night, these guys in fatigues were running through the place, shooting the dogs and whoever came out. They killed two of the others right in front of me before I got back inside."

"You had friends there?"

"Not exactly," she said. "I thought they'd killed you, but then we heard you'd gotten away, and the last guys who went after you never came back."

"They didn't?"

She shook her head. "We never found out what happened to them. They may have just snuck back to their families."

Peter thought of the boys, and of Tsering Wangmo, and smiled.

"So you didn't even know if I was dead?"

"I figured you must be, or you would have come back for me," she said. "Anyway, I thought the kids in the camp might be all I had left. So they weren't really my friends, but they weren't exactly enemies either."

He was trying to figure out if he actually did want an answer to the question. "But you really shot somebody?"

"We were scared shitless and we couldn't *see,*" she said. "There were just the fires and these blinding flashlights, and it was chaos. I ran back inside, grabbed one of the rifles, and hid behind some crates. I was shaking, I was so afraid, and then this guy kicked in the door and three of them came inside. I don't know if I fired; if I did, I don't remember. But one of them somehow ended up on the ground, and then the other two grabbed me and pulled the gun out of my hands, and they were screaming at me and really angry."

"Jesus."

"Believe me, I was totally freaked and basically just cried for hours. But later, when they took me off the road and did what they did . . ."

He wasn't sure he wanted to hear what came next, but he said, "Go on."

She was sobbing. "After that, to tell the truth, I pretty much wished I'd killed them all."

He was quiet. "Nobody's judging you," he said. "I just wanted to know."

They drove on. The road passed across mountainsides and wound through verdant meadows and tall stands of fir and pine. Some of the hillsides were dotted with huge old oaks. After a while Alex sat back and seemed to calm down some.

"Do you blame yourself for what happened to me?" she asked.

He hadn't expected the question, but he nodded.

"Don't," she said. "You did the best you could. I know that, and you should too."

It was such a grown-up thing to say. Tears welled in his eyes and rolled down his cheeks. They felt scalding. He couldn't forgive himself, but she could forgive him.

"Thank you," he whispered.

She realized he was crying and put her hand on his shoulder, and then they were both in tears. He steered the car around a wide bend in the road, and a beautiful valley opened before them. Alex wiped at her cheeks and smiled. "We're quite a pair," she said.

It seemed crazy that you could raise someone from birth and still be mystified by who they really were inside. But it had been true of his father and him, and it was true of him and Alex. Was anyone capable of anything, as Sangita had once implied about the Chinese soldiers? What could you do except take people as they were and do your best to love whatever they brought with them?

What struck him then was how hard it was to love it all, but also how easy it was. The notion of Alex with a rifle, or other things he might have thought would shock him, when it came down to it, didn't end up shocking him very much at all. Things he didn't understand, and at the same time understood completely. He thought again of Tsering Wangmo, how he couldn't comprehend what she'd done but had to acknowledge she'd done it, that she apparently altered whatever he took to be reality solely by the force of her chanting or even by her mind. The world was everything he thought it was and nothing he thought it was. Messiness and misery coexisted with perfection—were, paradoxically, *part of* perfection—and there was no way to reconcile these things except to accept them and live with them the way old lovers lived together, with understanding and humor, and with mercy.

He was sick of his own insufferable cleverness, too, which now struck him as a kind of golden idol, the antithesis of genuine wisdom. He wanted to be rid of it, but he wasn't sure what to replace it with, for he still felt a long way from any sort of transcendent knowledge. Maybe it wasn't necessary to replace it at all. One thing he felt increasingly convinced of, though, was that emotions were more than just the means by which DNA drove his behavior. They were, at least in the best case, how he understood in his heart what he was unable to comprehend with his mind, and they deepened his

264 | CARY GRONER

intelligence in ways that were no less real for being difficult to artic-
ulate. He wondered what Lama Padma would think about all this.

Alex watched the mountains. "It's beautiful up here. Even if we
don't buy hospital stuff, we should just come out sometimes."

He was glad she suggested it. "Well, how's your schedule?" he
asked. "Should I call your secretary?"

"Yeah," she said. "I'm worried about Edelstein, though."

"Why?"

"He practically falls apart if he doesn't see me."

"Is that right?"

She nodded. "Oh, yeah. Sooner or later I guess we'll just have
to wean him, don't you think?"

| | |

A week later they were surprised to get a letter from Devi.

Dear Alex & Peter,

I've been so upset since I heard what happened. Please
keep me informed. When I learn about something like that I
think maybe my mother was right after all, that no one can
really be trusted. I've been thinking of that nun, Ani Dawa,
because now I understand what she was feeling when she
wanted to kill those Chinese soldiers.

I am at Lama Padma's for a couple of weeks to receive
teachings, though, so of course I must give up any such notions of revenge. He is very strict about this kind of thing—
not just acting but thinking. I hope your minds are more at
peace and less unruly than mine.

When they got to this, Peter and Alex just looked at each other
and smiled.

The letter continued:

You should know that Lama Padma is quite ill, and we
aren't sure how long he will live. I guess Peter's concerns

about heart failure were right. He was distressed to hear what happened to Alex, and he is praying for her, as you requested. He says that if he does not have an opportunity to see you both again, he very much appreciates meeting you, and that you wrote to him.

As for your last letter, he asked me to tell you that it is perfectly natural for you to be angry, but he hopes you will not cling to these emotions, thinking they will somehow give you the power you did not have when you needed it. They do not, and you will become their prisoner if you believe otherwise.

Soon I will return to Tsering Wangmo's. I may stay there for some time. Ramesh came to visit and brought the goat. Tsering Wangmo is delighted to have her, and Wayne Lee is thriving there. She and the dog often sleep together for warmth, and they seem to have become friends.

Tsering Wangmo says I should plan to stay as long as she lives, and maybe even after she dies. So in fifty years you may find me still there, all wrinkly, as her replacement! But for now, she and Lama Padma think it is time I went into solitary retreat, in a small cave up behind her house, possibly for three years or more. Tsering Wangmo has agreed to bring me mail from time to time, though, and to take mine out, so I won't be out of touch with you.

I miss you and think of you all the time. I don't know when I'll see you again, but I love you both. I am so glad to hear you have found your way home.

—Devi

Alex cried for her Devi, lost and found, and for Lama Padma.

"I wish he'd let me operate," Peter said. "He'd have a few good years left."

Alex brushed her tears away. "It's not who he is, you know? That's the trouble with these people. They ignore all our terrific advice, and then they miss the chance to be as unbelievably happy as we are."

THIRTY-SIX

Peter accepted the night position at Marin General and bought an old clapboard house near the water in Sausalito. It wasn't fancy but it was big, and they were going to be needing room.

In late September, almost a year to the day after they had flown into Kathmandu, Peter and Alex drove down to SFO to meet Mina and Usha. Mina walked down the ramp from the boarding gates and right into Peter's arms, then Usha joined her, and finally Alex glommed on, and they all just stood there in a scrum, breathing one another in.

The next day, after Alex and Usha took off to see a movie, Peter and Mina went for a walk in the hills.

"I'd forgotten how much I like it here," she said.

"We'll get you back up to speed," he said. "Most days I'm free."

They sat in the shade under an oak. "Usha really does want to study medicine, you know," Mina said. "She's already into biology."

"Well," he said. "A chip off the old block."

"We have to figure out how to get her visa extended."

"That's easy. We'll just explain to the INS that I paid good money for her."

She laughed. "I checked it out a little," she said. "It seems like it's important to have a stable couple."

He considered this. "Any chance we could impersonate one?"

"We'll have to practice," she said. She kissed him on the cheek. "Sure you want to keep the night shift?"

| | |

Two months later, Alex and Usha loaded the car with potatoes and beans and pie, while Mina and Peter packed in the soda and the wine.

"Explain this holiday?" Usha asked as they set out. Alex launched into an elaborate description of the origins of Thanksgiving in the English-Nepali patois that the girls had developed to communicate with each other.

"So these Indians gave food, and you killed them?" Usha said. "I do not understand."

"No, you understand," said Alex brightly. "China's got nothing on us."

They drove north and west toward Mendocino, following Connie's scrawled map. After a couple of hours, Peter came to the turnoff, and the gravel drive took them up a little rise to a clearing. The house, two stories of blue clapboard, was built in a broad, open field of mown grass, with acres of apple orchard to the west. A stand of pine began where the orchard ended, and beyond the pines the Pacific glinted in the afternoon sun.

They carried the food to the sliding back patio doors, where Connie let them in and introduced everyone to Cody. He was a rangy fellow in his fifties, with a ponytail and an amiable grin.

Ben and the girls quickly bolted for the woods.

"Was that my nephew, headed to the great outdoors?" Peter said, incredulous.

"This is new," Connie said. "This is just his second time here, but he loves it. Until now the only parts of his body he developed were his thumbs, for PlayStation."

Cody got them drinks, and they stood around talking, getting to know one another. He'd developed software for Adobe before retiring the previous year; he and Connie had met online. They'd been going out for only two or three months, but from their easy affection it looked to Peter like it was going well.

Ten or fifteen minutes later the kids came out of the tall grass onto the field. Ben held something green in his hand. They walked up the stairs to the deck.

"Look what I found," Ben said, grinning and holding up his prize. It was a leaf from a healthy-looking marijuana plant. "There's about a quarter-acre of this shit out there."

"Language," said Connie.

"This *stuff*," said Ben. "This totally sinsemilla-type serious dope *stuff*, Mom."

She rolled her eyes and took it from him. The kids, smirking, trotted into the house. Peter and Connie looked at Cody, who smiled and shrugged with the closest thing to a Nepali shrug Peter had seen in months. "It's my neighbor Ed's land," he explained. "He mainly grows apples and pears, but he finally bowed to economic reality and set aside a little plot for this."

"And it's safe?" Peter asked.

"A few years ago the cops realized that if they kowtowed to the DEA, the local economy would tank," Cody said. "So they bust the meth labs and take their tithing of the dope revenues, and everyone is happy."

Connie, irritated, said she hoped the field wasn't booby-trapped.

"Not really Ed's style," said Cody. "But sorry, I guess I should have told them to stay on this side of the fence."

Peter was glad to see him apologize; he'd come to understand this as a good sign, an indicator of strength rather than weakness, and he hoped it boded well for the two of them.

Connie, evidently mollified, put a hand on Cody's arm. "Kids are going to roam," she said. "I guess you can't shelter them from everything."

Peter wondered, in fact, if you could shelter them from *any-thing*.

"Ed shares, at least," Cody said, smiling. "Let me know if you guys want some later."

"Maybe if the kids aren't around," Connie said.

Peter shook his head, though, feeling like a square but not minding all that much. "I need all the brain cells I can get at this point," he said. "If I want to kill off a few I prefer a good cabernet, though I've learned it's best to drink it at sea level."

Cody smiled. "Well, we're almost at sea level, and we've definitely got cabernet." He put a hand on Peter's shoulder and turned to go inside. Peter's eyes met Connie's. Cody seemed nice enough, but Peter felt protective of his sister, and he was unsure about so many things now. If the kind of awakening Lama Padma had described meant that everything you were used to relying on crumbled under your feet, he figured he was on his way. It wasn't comfortable, particularly if it meant giving up the intoxicating acuity of his own capacity for judging others, but he suspected it was necessary. If Connie was happy with Cody, that would be good enough for him.

A few minutes later, as the kids set the table and laid out the food, Connie cornered Mina and Peter in the pantry. "So when's the date?" she asked, her voice hushed with mischief.

Mina looked at Peter. "I thought this was a secret."

Peter peered at his sister suspiciously. "I did too," he said.

"For God's sake, I know my own bro," said Connie. "He's been looking way too happy."

Mina smiled. "Next month," she said. "Then we can finish the paperwork for Usha."

"You going to have one of your own?"

"Jesus, Con," said Peter. "Give us a second or two, will you?"

Connie put up her hands. "Sorry, sorry, don't even consider having any fun on my account, God forbid."

Cody called to them from the dining room. "We're all set," he said. "Let's rumble."

At the table, Usha looked astounded at all the food.

Alex turned to her. "The rule is," she said, "you have to eat till it hurts. Otherwise you've failed."

"*Alex,*" said Peter.

"True story," said Ben. "You've got to totally want to hurl."

"*Ben,*" said Connie.

Cody asked Usha if she'd like to say grace, but Usha didn't understand. Mina explained, briefly, in Nepali. Usha then interlaced her fingers and said a few words.

"She said thank you Peter and Mina for saving her life and giving her books and food," said Alex. "She's sorry to hear about the Indians, though."

Peter, holding Mina's hand on one side and Alex's on the other, sent his own thanks out to the universe.

After dinner Cody cleared the table and piled the dishes in the sink while Peter, Connie, and Mina adjourned to the deck and watched the kids play Frisbee in the field. Usha was new to the game but got the hang of it quickly. Ben was getting tall, leggy, and fast, but he still couldn't catch Alex.

"My niece is looking good," said Connie. "How'd you manage that?"

"Tough stock," Peter replied. "You should know."

The clouds were turning purple overhead. Cody came out with another bottle of wine and opened it. "How can they eat so much and run around like that?" he asked.

"It's called metabolism," Connie said. "Remember metabolism?"

He smiled. "Vaguely."

"They're beautiful, aren't they?" said Mina. "Look at them go."

"Ben could turn out to be a sprinter," said Cody.

"He's too wiry," Connie said. "I'm thinking cross-country."

To sit with a full belly on a cool fall evening, talking about the children, felt to Peter like brilliant, extravagant luxury. But they *were* beautiful. They moved like young cats, fluid and graceful and capable of startling acceleration, and then they'd get their legs tangled up and fall over one another, laughing.

One of Usha's throws got away from her and headed toward

the house. Peter got up and caught it, then went down the stairs and threw it back to her. She grabbed it, trotted a few steps, and threw it to Ben, who leaped in the air and turned, trying to catch it behind his back. He missed, and it hit him in the head. He staggered around, pretending to be hurt, and Usha laughed.

Peter looked over his shoulder at Mina, who was looking at him. He knew that look, of yearning and of love and of lust, and it sent jangles of energy right down through him and into the ground, as if a slender finger of lightning had slipped from the sky and found him waiting for its charge.

Connie noticed and fanned herself with her hand. "Getting warm out here," she said. Mina dipped her fingers in her drink and flicked the water at her, and Connie ducked, grinning.

The sun dipped behind a low scrim of pink cloud, and a soft, warm radiance fell upon everything so evenly that the world seemed to glow. It was like the light at Lama Padma's, a light that held secrets, and Peter felt his heart fill with love for these children.

Ben threw a long one about halfway between Alex and Peter, and they both ran for it. The Frisbee caught a little gust and sailed far out over the grass, and Alex outran him. At the last second, just as it was about to get past her, she leaped up high and caught it in midair, then fell and rolled and came to her feet with it in her hand. They applauded, and she took a little bow.

She nudged Peter with her shoulder as she trotted by. "Better get in shape, old man, I'm leaving you in the dust." She skipped away from him toward the others, laughing, her hair flying.

And he thought, Okay, kid. Leave me in the dust.

Run.

ACKNOWLEDGMENTS

I'm greatly indebted to my agent, Barbara Braun, for seeing the potential in this book and urging Cindy Spiegel at Spiegel & Grau to give it a read. Cindy has been a wonderful editor, and her suggestions have vastly improved the novel.

Many friends helped bring the manuscript along from my original, vague ideas about it. Jane Dwyer and Marilyn Montgomery, both nurses who took their children to Kathmandu when they went there to work in health clinics, provided many excellent stories about their sojourns. Sandy Shum, Paloma Lopez, Peter Moulton, and Marilyn Cohen generously consented to lengthy interviews about their time in Nepal and gave me extremely helpful information. I was also inspired by sources that included Barbara Scot's *Violet Shyness of Their Eyes,* Tulku Urgyen Rinpoche's *Blazing Splendor,* and the *Traveler's Tales Guide to Nepal,* including Broughton Coburn's hilarious first-person account of having a leech ensconced in his nose.

My brother Cam and his daughter Christine talked to me at length about the pleasures and pains of fathers and daughters traveling together in foreign countries. My brother Chris provided sound information and juicy stories about life in the trenches of medical practice.

At the University of Arizona, my instructors Jason Brown and Bob Houston gave me important insights into the manuscript that helped lift it from its early abyss. My kind and tireless mentor, Elizabeth Evans, guided me further with excellent suggestions as I sought to address a variety of difficult issues.

My parents always encouraged me to follow whatever path I considered important, no matter how nuts it seemed to them, and for this I will always be grateful. My wife, Patti, has been amazingly supportive and patient; she's a great soul and, as added benefits, smart as hell and totally beautiful.

The descriptions here of atrocities committed by Chinese soldiers are based on documented accounts and include stories related to me personally by Tibetans I have known. I have a profound debt to all those courageous enough to speak about their ordeals.

Finally, what modest knowledge I have of Buddhism I credit entirely to my extraordinary teachers of many years, the late Chagdud Tulku Rinpoche and his Dzogchen lineage holder, Lama Drimed Norbu. I owe them far more than I can put into words.

ABOUT THE AUTHOR

CARY GRONER worked for more than two decades as a journalist, then earned his MFA in fiction writing from the University of Arizona in 2009. His short stories have won numerous awards and have appeared in publications that include *Glimmer Train, American Fiction, Mississippi Review, Southern California Review,* and *Tampa Review.* He lives in the San Francisco Bay Area. *Exiles* is his first novel.

www.carygroner.com

ABOUT THE TYPE

This book was set in Sabon, a typeface designed by the well-known German typographer Jan Tschichold (1902–74). Sabon's design is based upon the original letter forms of Claude Garamond and was created specifically to be used for three sources: foundry type for hand composition, Linotype, and Monotype. Tschichold named his typeface for the famous Frankfurt typefounder Jacques Sabon, who died in 1580.